W9-AAY-525

PRAISE FOR

★ "Myracle is running on all cylinders here, exercising an agile teenage drama, a Stephen King–like yarn of high-school horror, a cautionary tale of '60s race relations, and some affecting social commentary." —*Booklist*, starred review

★ "Socio-historical details revitalize classic horror conventions in this suspenseful thriller." —*Kirkus*, starred review

"Part horror, part social commentary, this novel is simultaneously creepy and smart." —*VOYA*

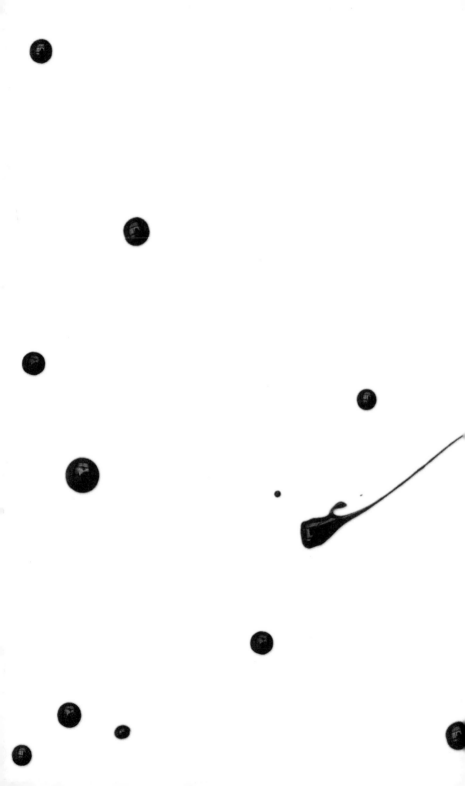

ALSO BY
LAUREN MYRACLE

Luv Ya Bunches: *A Flower Power Book*

Violet in Bloom: *A Flower Power Book*

Rhymes with *Witches*

ttyl

ttfn

l8r, g8r

bff: *a girlfriend book u write 2gether*

Eleven

Twelve

Thirteen

Peace, Love, and Baby Ducks

Let It Snow: Three Holiday Romances
(with John Green and Maureen Johnson)

How to Be Bad
(with E. Lockhart and Sarah Mylnowski)

LAUREN MYRACLE

BLISS

AMULET BOOKS
NEW YORK

PUBLISHER'S NOTE: This is a work of fiction. Names, characters, places, and incidents are either the product of the author's imagination or are used fictitiously, and any resemblance to actual persons, living or dead, business establishments, events, or locales is entirely coincidental.

The Library of Congress has cataloged the hardcover edition of this book as follows:

Myracle, Lauren, 1969–
Bliss / by Lauren Myracle.
p. cm.
Summary: Having grown up in a California commune, Bliss sees her aloof grandmother's Atlanta world as a foreign country, but she is determined to be nice as a freshman at an elite high school, which makes her the perfect target for a girl obsessed with the occult.
ISBN 978-0-8109-7071-7 (Harry N. Abrams : alk. paper)
[1. Interpersonal relations—Fiction. 2. High schools—Fiction. 3. Schools—Fiction. 4. Occultism—Fiction. 5. Grandmothers—Fiction. 6. Atlanta (Ga.)—History—20th century—Fiction.] I. Title.

PZ7.M9955Bli 2008
[Fic]—dc22
2007050036

Paperback ISBN 978-0-8109-4072-7

Text copyright © 2008 Lauren Myracle
Book design by Maria T. Middleton

Page 73: From the song "Little Boxes." Words and music by Malvina Reynolds. Copyright © 1962 Schroder Music Co. (ASCAP) Renewed 1990. Used by permission. All rights reserved.

Page 209: "Happiness Is a Warm Gun." © 1968 Sony/ATV Tunes LLC. All rights administered by Sony/ATV Music Publishing, 8 Music Square West, Nashville, TN 37203. All rights reserved. Used by permission.

Page 275: "Easy Rider." Lyrics originally copyright © 1924 Gertrude "Ma" Rainey.

Originally published in hardcover 2008 by Amulet Books, an imprint of Harry N. Abrams, Inc. Paperback edition published in 2010. All rights reserved. No portion of this book may be reproduced, stored in a retrieval system, or transmitted in any form or by any means, mechanical, electronic, photocopying, recording, or otherwise, without written permission from the publisher. Amulet Books and Amulet Paperbacks are registered trademarks of Harry N. Abrams, Inc.

Printed and bound in U.S.A.
10 9 8 7 6 5 4 3 2 1

Amulet Books are available at special discounts when purchased in quantity for premiums and promotions as well as fundraising or educational use. Special editions can also be created to specification. For details, contact specialmarkets@abramsbooks.com or the address below.

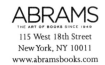

ABRAMS
THE ART OF BOOKS SINCE 1949
115 West 18th Street
New York, NY 10011
www.abramsbooks.com

With deep and abiding love,
I blame this one entirely on my mother.

FROM *THE ANDY GRIFFITH SHOW*

Welcome to Mayberry, the friendly town

—sign at Mayberry city limits

randmother won't tolerate occultism, even of the nose-twitching sort made so adorable by Samantha Stevens, so I'm not allowed to watch *Bewitched*. Jeannie from *I Dream of Jeannie* is indecent in her filmy pants and sparkly halter, so I'm not allowed to watch that, either. *Mod Squad*? Miniskirts. Scandalous. Those ultramodern miniskirt girls purse Grandmother's lips up almost as much as boys with long hair and girls who neither shave nor wear appropriate undergarments. Almost, but not quite, because when it comes to the destruction of traditional values, hippies trump witches and mod girls, hands down.

Hippies use marijuana.

Hippies don't bathe.

Hippies cohabitate in flimsy tents and eat goat cheese. The girls don't wear bras, and their unfettered breasts bounce shamelessly beneath tank tops reading MAKE LOVE, NOT WAR. They have sexual relations indiscriminately, and they burden their offspring with ridiculous names. And—the most dire offense of all—they deposit said offspring in the imposing Southern mansions of their even more imposing Southern parents, shirking the responsibility of raising their children themselves.

To clarify: I'm the offspring. My name is Bliss. Mom and Dad fled to Canada to avoid supporting President Nixon's version of American patriotism, and they abandoned me here, in Atlanta, with a well-coiffed grandmother I barely know. My grandfather is dead.

This is a situation neither Grandmother nor I would have chosen, but Grandmother is nothing if not morally upright, which made it impossible for her to turn me away. She's also uptight, and it seems that often the two go together. Mom hugged me hard after dropping me off, whispering that I should stay true to myself no matter what anyone said. By "anyone," I assume she meant Grandmother, whose sole remark to Mom was, "Well, Genevieve, I didn't think you could fall any further. Once again, you've proven me wrong." Then she turned to me, her mouth pruning into a frown. "Pigeon Carrier's Disease?! Dr. Montgomery will be aghast."

The penicillin made my pee stink, but it got rid of the fever and most of the scaliness. Even more remarkable, I'm no longer coughing. My clean breaths fill me with joy and guilt in equal measure.

Something else I feel guilty about: I like my daily hot showers, and I like Grandmother's expensive toiletries. The soap from the commune never lathered. It was lumpish and gray, and it itched my scalp. Grandmother has lavender shampoo to match her lavender soap. My hair is as soft as angels' wings.

I like TV too. Grandmother's TV is a brand-new Zenith Giant-Screen, with a Space Command "600" Remote Control. I can change channels from the sofa. Truly! I stretch out on the chintz cushions—*no feet on the coffee table, please*—and with a push of my thumb, *The Andy Griffith Show* flickers into resolution. *Andy Griffith* is one of the few shows Grandmother tolerates, and of the others on her approved list—*My Three Sons, Green Acres, Petticoat Junction*—it's my clear-and-away favorite. Plus, it's in reruns already, so I can watch it every day.

I love Sheriff Taylor in his crisp uniform, and sometimes (how embarrassing) I think about him as I fall asleep in my four-poster bed with freshly laundered sheets and down pillow. He's got a kind smile, he's a great dad to Opie, and he teases gray-bunned Aunt Bee, but never in a mean-spirited way. Plus, he's nice to Barney, the bumbling deputy sheriff who causes more problems than he solves.

If I were still on the commune, I wouldn't be watching *Andy Griffith*. I'd be digging a new latrine or helping Flying V pick herbs or looking after Daisy and Clementine, the twins. We weren't lazy on the commune, despite what Grandmother thinks. I'm lazy here. Grandmother's maid, a black woman named Rosie who's at least as old as Grandmother, whispers past me, picking up crumbs before I realize I've dropped them. She folds my underwear. She collects the hairballs from the shower drain and makes them disappear. Quite a lot of my hair seems to be falling out, which I attribute to my new regimen of washing, conditioning, and brushing.

If Flying V could see me, she'd shake her head. "Letting an old auntie wait on you? That ain't the Bliss I know."

Well, she's right. I feel newly born, dropped like a baby into this slippery world of giant-screen TVs and lavender soap and feather pillows. Last week Grandmother hosted a "sip and see" to introduce me to her friends from the Ladies Auxiliary, and because I was nervous, I crossed and recrossed my legs in the school-issued knee-length cotton skirt Grandmother had given me to replace my gypsy skirt with the bells. Grandmother glared, and I didn't know why. After everyone left, she informed me that young ladies are to cross their legs at the ankles only. To do otherwise suggests wantonness.

I also made the mistake of mentioning Daisy and Clementine during the sip and see. Daisy and Clementine will have a new baby brother or sister next month, not that I'll be there to meet him or her. But everyone likes babies, so when one of the ladies showed off a bonnet she was knitting for her soon-to-be-born granddaughter, I beamed and said, "Oh, groovy! My friend Flying V—well, really, it's Virginia—she's pregnant too."

Everyone fell silent, and my smile faltered. Grandmother later told me that you're not supposed to say "pregnant"; you're supposed to say "expecting" or "in the family way." Um, okay. I don't get it . . . but okay.

There are so many things I don't get, that I'm afraid even daily doses of *Andy Griffith* won't bring me up to speed. School starts in a week, and I'm petrified. Grandmother has enrolled me in Crestview Academy, the most prestigious private school in the South. It used to be a convent, and when Grandmother showed me the brochure, I imagined nuns in black habits patrolling the vast grounds. The imposing buildings are constructed from stone; the lawns are green and dotted with stone benches. It's quite stately looking, which, despite my apprehension, appeals to my imagination. There's not a latrine in sight.

The school shifted from Catholicism when it lost the nuns, but Grandmother assures me that Crestview students follow a Christian code of conduct. They also follow a Christian code of attire—though when I said, "Neat-o! Tunics and sandals!" Grandmother didn't crack a smile. Crestview boys, I gathered from the brochure, wear khakis and collared shirts. Girls can wear either a blue or gray skirt, a white blouse with a Peter Pan collar, and brown penny loafers. Grandmother bought me two skirts in each color, three blouses, and a blue cardigan for chilly weather. Also, five pairs of white knee-highs, five pairs of nude hose, and the penny loafers.

I'll be a freshman, Grandmother informed me, and I could sense her amazement that I tested into my appropriate age-based grade level despite the fact that I've never been formally schooled.

"Well . . . I did read on the commune," I told her. "Quite a lot, actually."

"How?" Grandmother asked.

"What do you mean, how?" I said. I didn't want to be rude, but surely she didn't want a description of how I moved my eyes from line to line.

She made an impatient sound. "The books, where did you get the books? You were squatting like animals in the wild."

I felt a surge of shame. "The bookmobile came every week," I said as levelly as I could. "It was government funded." I was never an animal squatting in the wild, but she had just made me feel like one.

So beginning next week, I'll be in a homeroom with twelve other fourteen-year-olds. There are three other ninth-grade homerooms in addition to mine, which means fifty-two freshmen, give or take. Grandmother informed me that unlike myself, they all attended a freshman orientation last spring.

"They will know all about the school, while you will know nothing," she said. Her tone implied that she held me personally accountable for my ignorance. "You'll be a babe in the woods."

I refrained from pointing out the irony of her remark.

There are approximately fifty sophomores, fifty juniors, and fifty seniors at Crestview as well, bringing the total number of students to around two hundred.

That's a lot of teenagers.

I haven't had a lot of experience with teenagers.

Last year a sixteen-year-old guy lived on the commune for about a month, but his parents decided to follow the Dead, and that was that. Daisy and Clementine shared a tent with me, but they're four-and-a-half. I did meet other kids at festivals and concerts—I'm not a total freak—and yes, I've even kissed a boy. Once. His name was Peter, and he had B.O. Then again, I probably did too.

So while I'm terrified of starting at Crestview next week, I'm also twisty-turvy, stomach-flopping excited. Going to Crestview equals being around people my own age, and being around people my own age equals (maybe? hopefully?) making friends.

Sheriff Taylor has Barney. Aunt Bee has Clara. Opie has Johnny Paul Jason, which is an awfully big name for an awfully small boy. But even Opie has a best friend.

I would like a best friend. I'd like that very much.

On the day I left the commune, Flying V pulled me to the edge of the fire pit. She'd had one of her visions, and her expression was dogged.

"You know I ain't happy 'bout you leaving," she said, "but ain't nothing either one of us can do about it."

"Don't worry, I'll be fine," I said, trying to sound more confident than I felt.

"'Course you will. It ain't you I'm worried about."

"You're not?" Perversely, I now wanted her to be worried about me. Why wasn't she worried about me?

"Bliss, baby, you got a light inside you as bright as they come," Flying V said. "You don't always have the best of *sense*, but you do got light. It'll burn within you even in the darkest of times."

I rolled my eyes. I was being shipped off to the land of indoor plumbing, not the ninth circle of hell.

"But you listen to Flying V now," she said. She clasped my hands, lacing her brown fingers through my much paler ones. "There's change coming your way like you ain't never imagined. New sights, new smells—new people, too. Two people in particular." She squeezed. "That's what I seen."

"Yeah?"

"Two girls, just your age. Your lives are intertwined."

My lips went loose, twitching into a smile I couldn't control. Here Flying V was, acting all agitated, but this was fine news. Not just one dear friend in my future, but two?

Flying V frowned, reading something in my face she didn't like. "Hold on, baby. I can tell you're spinning plans, imagining the three of y'all whispering and giggling and telling secrets. But this ain't no magic friendship ·spell I seen."

"I know!" I protested. She made it sound so childish: a magic friendship spell. I knew friendship had to be nurtured. I knew it wouldn't happen magically.

"There's trouble in that mix, and girls your age . . ." She shook her head. "They can be downright cruel. Downright *bloodthirsty*, baby. I think it's best you stay clear."

"And, what? Be *alone?*" I said. "I think I can handle a few spats and hurt feelings, V. I *am* a girl myself."

She snorted. "Yeah, uh-huh. A girl who can't tell a snowberry from a nightshade berry."

I pulled my hands free and turned away. I appreciated Flying V's mothering, especially since my flesh-and-blood mother did so little of it, but even I wasn't such a dumb pudding that I couldn't hold my own with girls my age. And of course I could tell the difference between a snowberry and a nightshade berry. Snowberries are white; nightshade berries are bright red. Snowberries are harmless; nightshade berries are deadly.

"Maybe I've never had a lot of friends," I admitted, my voice breaking. "But I haven't exactly had a lot of opportunities, either." I swallowed. "I think—I mean, I hope—that I'd be a really *good* friend."

"Oh, baby," Flying V said. She took me by my shoulders and turned me back toward her. "You got me *all* wrong. Anybody would be blessed to call you a friend. Absolutely blessed." Her eyes were the deepest brown, full of concern. "I want you to be careful, that's all."

I still didn't get what I was supposed to be careful *of,* but I was ready for the conversation to be over.

"I will," I said, hearing the petulance in my voice.

Flying V sighed, and I sensed she wished she'd kept her vision to herself. Right then, I wished she had too. But now I'm glad she didn't. An unseen world shimmers beneath our

seen world, and for Flying V to share a glimpse of it . . .
well, I like it when the universe reminds us how intricate
our world is.

I miss Mom and Dad, but their absence is nothing new.
Even when we lived on the commune, they were always
hitching to San Fran or Seattle or wherever. Sometimes they
let me tag along, but more often they didn't.

As for Grandmother, yes, she's one huge frown. But I'm
her granddaughter. She'll come around.

Occasionally, I have visions too. Mine don't come as
frequently at Flying V's, nor, I suspect, do they pulse with
the same degree of clarity. Flying V was helping me with
that. She said I had "the gift"—as, indeed, most people
do, though they often don't realize it—but that I needed
guidance in order to interpret what my gift revealed. Our
training sessions were cut off, of course, but I'm not too
terribly worried. I think I'm clear-sighted enough to divine
the general sense of my visions, even if I miss the more
subtle particulars.

At any rate, on my first night in Atlanta I had a strange
and telling dream. In it, I walked along a footpath on
Crestview's sprawling campus. It was the footpath pictured
in the brochure, only more heavily wooded, with dappled
shadows making spots of light and dark. The sweet tang of
lemons inexplicably filled the air. I felt as if I were exactly
where I was supposed to be.

But as I ambled along, the shadows shifted and became

mouths, hungering for me. I tried to run, but couldn't. The lemony scent grew cloying and veiled me in a misty shroud.

Then, out of nowhere, swooped a dove. I knew it was a dove and not an odious pigeon because it was snow-white, and because it was unafflicted with parasites. Also, its coo was soft and beguiling, nothing like the ugly chup-chup of a pigeon. The dove alit on my shoulder, its wings a whisper on my cheek. The mist around me cleared.

My sight may not be as clear as Flying V's, yet I'm not completely unversed in life's mysteries. Yes, starting school will be hard, possibly even scary. But my dream dove was a sign, just as solid and real as Grandmother's bone china tea set. Doves are incapable of malice toward any creature, and as long as I remember that, as long as I never stoop to spite or meanness, I'll surely be able to navigate the occasional catfight between friends.

After all, fourteen-year-old girls *are* just fourteen-year-old girls. They may bicker, they may hold silly grudges, but they certainly don't thirst for blood.

Cats are considered deities all the world wide. Ancient Greeks linked cats to the moon goddess, Diana. Freyja, goddess of the night, is always accompanied by feline companions. The goddess Bast has the face of a cat, and in Egypt, corpses of cats have been found in countless tombs. They are placed there to usher their dead owners into new life.

According to Agnes, Liliana was fond of cats. Liliana, who died by her own hand so long ago. Would the magical essence of a cat bring her back?

Notes:
* Regular, when placed in closet with dead snake, objected strongly.
* Snake remained inert.

FROM THE BEVERLY HILLS POLICE LOG,
BEVERLY HILLS, CA

"I'm the devil. I'm here to do
the devil's business."

—Charles "Tex" Watson, member of the Manson Family execution team randmother had hoped to take me shopping today. She wanted to buy me some "play" clothes (does she think I'm five?), but instead she retired to her bedroom with a migraine. Something awful happened—not here in Atlanta, but in California—and Grandmother deems it one more horror to blame on the lawless, shiftless hippies.

Grandmother has Rosie burn the newspaper before I can read the article, but I glimpse the headline: FIVE SLAIN IN BLOODY CULT-STYLE MURDER. It's terrible that five people were murdered—terrible!—but I don't understand why Grandmother would read about such a brutal crime and automatically think *hippies*. Hippies aren't about hate. Hippies are about love. Does she think that just because hippies reject society, they're going to fan out and slay those who don't?

Her daughter—my mother—is one of those "shiftless hippies." Mom taught me to be kind to spiders, and she insisted the mice had just as much right to our food as we did. When Layla slashed her chest on a piece of exposed wire,

Mom used a shirt to bind her up. My shirt, actually. The one with the embroidered peace sign.

Dad called Layla a "rat with wings" and said Mom should let nature take its course. Mom refused to talk to him for two days, and he had to coax her from her sulk with a Hershey's bar he'd stashed in the bottom of his rucksack.

"Where did you get this?" she demanded, scowling as if he'd been holding out on her.

"Remember that roofing job I did?" he said. "She paid me in chocolate, and I saved it for my lady." He broke off a bite of candy and placed it in her mouth. She tried to stay grouchy, but ended up closing her eyes and making an *mmmm* of pleasure.

Layla's gash eventually healed, and I reclaimed my shirt from the filthy coop. I shouldn't have bothered. The bloodstains never came out.

"Without a front, flanks, or rear,
we fought a formless war against
a formless enemy who evaporated like
the morning jungle mists, only to
materialize in some unexpected place."

—Marine platoon commander Philip Caputo

wo more people were murdered in California last night. This time I get to the paper before Grandmother, and I learn that the victims— Leno and Rosemary LaBianca—were tied up and stabbed to death in their own house. The article provides details about the other slayings as well. I find out that the people killed the night before were having a dinner party at the house of Roman Polanski, who's apparently a pretty well-known movie director. Only Mr. Polanski wasn't there; it was just his wife and four friends. His wife's name was Sharon Tate. She was eight-and-a-half months pregnant.

When I hear Grandmother coming downstairs, I quickly refold the paper and place it on the kitchen table. She reads it and goes pale.

"Have mercy," she says faintly. "What is this world coming to?"

"What happened?" I ask, since supposedly I don't know.

She gives a bare-bones account of the crime, and I give her a cup of tea. She takes a shaky sip and tells me we must install a gate at the end of the driveway.

"Maybe we should get a dog," I say. "Maybe a German shepherd." A German shepherd probably isn't needed to protect us from a killer in California, but I've always wanted a pet I could actually play with. And German shepherds just sound so loyal.

"Those deviants, they stabbed that poor woman forty-one times," Grandmother says. She puts down her cup. "Oh, Bliss, how could people be so heartless?"

Without thinking, I rise and embrace her. She stiffens, and I feel how frail she is beneath her blouse. I am young and strong, and the last of the scaly patches on my skin have flaked off, thanks to daily scrubbings with my all-natural loofah.

"Those murderers are far, far away," I tell her. "We're safe here."

"Yes, of course," Grandmother says. She pulls away. "Thank you, Bliss. You're a good girl."

"Mom's a good girl too," I say without thinking. Maybe I'm afraid that by "deviant," Grandmother once again means "long-haired hippie freak"?

"I mean, she's a good *person*," I go on. "She's not a girl, she's a grown-up, obviously . . . but—"

"Oh, Bliss," Grandmother says.

"She is!"

Grandmother's mask slides back into place.

"Sometimes good girls go astray," she says, and she goes to check on Rosie, who's polishing the silver.

FROM *THE ANDY GRIFFITH SHOW*

"Can I go outside and play, Paw?"

—Opie Taylor

O n the Tuesday after Labor Day, Grandmother drops me off at Crestview with an air kiss and an admonition to be good.

"I will, I will," I say, climbing out of her Cadillac. I'm all stirred up, as Flying V would say: antsy and excited and fluttery with nerves. The campus is intimidatingly grand, the buildings constructed from cold, gray stone.

bones, says a voice in my head. *tombs.*

I stop dead in my tracks, because it's not my voice that whispered these thoughts. And whoever's voice it is, it's not a nice voice.

I look up at the tallest of the buildings, which sits and watches from the middle of campus. HAMILTON HALL reads the carved inscription above the entrance. Lush, green vines of ivy snake up the stone blocks, as if they might wrap around you and never let you go. There are windows built into the stone façade, but they're ungenerous and cramped. I imagine long-ago girls staring blankly from behind them.

trapped, murmurs that chilly voice.

"Stop it," I say out loud. I blink. The day is sunny,

and there isn't a shadow in sight. Students stroll down the footpaths, chatting happily, and I remind myself that although I do on occasion perceive things from a realm beyond the physical, I would be foolish to assign dire meaning to such perceptions without further cause. Sorrow lingers, while joy takes to the air like a bird in flight. The dark wisps I'm registering could be a hundred years old or more.

Plus, while I myself am quick to smile and glad to laugh, I do appreciate a good ghost story. I love the gothic novels that tell of innocent girls lured deeper and deeper into remote and unfamiliar settings, and I could easily be giving myself a delicious shiver on purpose.

Yet when I cross past Hamilton Hall on the way to my homeroom, my pace slows, and it unnerves me, because I'm not dragging my feet intentionally. Hamilton Hall is *not* delicious. Hamilton Hall is the old convent's forbidding Mother Superior, grimly surveying her charges, and the fear I feel is genuine.

blood, says the voice with a terrible urgency. *blood!*

With a jerk of will, I quicken my pace.

My homeroom is up the hill from Hamilton Hall, in the Woodward Building. Like Hamilton Hall, the narrow corridors and high ceilings of the Woodward Building call to mind processions of solemn novices, but the walls are plastered with cheerful hand-lettered posters, urging us to embody Crestview's "Can-Do Attitude."

With willful concentration, I shake off the creepiness of the blood voice. I'm here at school not to seek ghosts, but friends. Fresh-faced, cleanly scrubbed friends like the kids who live in Mayberry. Kids who drink malteds. Kids who say "Gee, Paw" and whistle as they walk.

My homeroom consists of thirteen girls, as the boys have their own homerooms. Everyone obviously knows each other. I overhear snippets of talk about the California murders, but the girls are primarily gossiping about their summer vacations. There's lots of giggling and twittering and checking of lipstick in cute round mirrors that they snap shut and put in their purses. They remind me of busy sparrows.

I don't have a pocket mirror, and I don't have a purse. I'm not wearing lipstick, although that's another thing Grandmother wants to go shopping for. "A girl needs some color on her face," she said, looking me over this morning. "And for heaven's sake, Bliss, can't you do something with that hair?"

I took her advice and plaited it into a thick braid, and I'm glad. None of the other girls have their hair loose. Headbands, barrettes, and elastic ponytail holders are the restraints of choice. I study my classmates curiously, though I try not to be obvious. The girls from Flying V's vision—are they among this flock of chattering birds?

Our homeroom teacher claps to call us to attention, and girls fly to their desks. I've been hovering, not wanting to be the only one sitting down, but suddenly I'm the only one standing up. I quickly take my seat, and the legs of my chair make a farting sound as they scoot against the floor. My face heats up.

"I'm Mrs. Elliot," our teacher says. "Welcome to the ninth grade." She wears a navy dress and, I suspect, a girdle. She's not nearly as pretty as Miss Crump, Opie's teacher on *Andy Griffith*, but she has a kind face. I can imagine her with a lovely book, reading by the fire with a cup of cocoa by her side.

"Most of you know each other from junior high," Mrs. Elliot says, "and of course I had the privilege of spending time with you during your orientation session last spring." Her smile is one of tolerant amusement, and the girls giggle. I glean from this that the freshman orientation was a giddy affair.

"Today we have a new student joining us, however," she goes on. Everyone's heads swivel my way. "Girls, please help me welcome Bliss Int—" She breaks off and frowns at the attendance chart.

Oh no.

"Bliss Inthemorningdew?"

My face grows several degrees hotter. "Um, yes." Grandmother enrolled me under her last name, Gilliland, but apparently the school acquired my old social work records. Bliss in the Morning Dew, that's my legal name. Mom and Dad just crammed all the words together to make it fit.

The girls share delighted glances. Several of them titter.

"Well. Bliss," Mrs. Elliot says, "I've assigned a peer mentor to help you get settled so your first day doesn't feel too overwhelming." She directs her attention to a plump girl with blond hair held back with a pink headband. "Thelma, will you please escort Bliss to Mrs. Morgenstern's homeroom when the bell rings? Sarah Lynn Lancaster will be waiting."

"Of course, Mrs. Elliot," Thelma says. She grins at me, and it's a friendly grin, I think, even if the girls near her are openly giggling. Is Thelma the girl I'm destined to meet?

Mrs. Elliot goes over the school guidelines, and I try to take it all in. But I'm not accustomed to so many rules. A bathroom pass? What's a bathroom pass? And all the fuss over the Honor Code, which makes my classmates grow solemn. It seems unlikely that any of these girls would be less than honorable; how funny the school feels the need for a written code.

A bell rings, and I jump. The girls rise as one, and I realize we're moving on to the next part of the day. First period, that's what it's called. On my schedule card, I see that I've got English.

"Ready?" Thelma asks, appearing by my side.

"Yeah, sure," I say. In my haste to get up, I knock over my books. I squat to gather them. "Oh, man, I'm such a clod."

She waits patiently. I stand, and she links her arm through mine.

"You are so lucky to get paired up with Sarah Lynn," she

says as we navigate the crowded hall. "She is just . . . well, she's just absolutely choice, that's what."

"Um . . . what?" I'm having trouble concentrating, because there are so many sights and sounds and smells to take in. And boys, they've joined the mix. One guy brushes against me, and I catch a whiff of pine. His deodorant, maybe? It's intoxicating.

I vow to throw away the crystal Mom gave me to combat the smell of perspiration. I'll stop by King's and buy a deodorant called Secret, which keeps you cool, calm, and protected. I've seen commercials for it.

"*And* she's beautiful, *and* she's loaded," Thelma says. "The whole package, you know?"

"Of what?"

"What do you mean, of what?" The look she gives me makes me feel as if I'm missing some key component of ninth-grade girlness, which I doubtlessly am.

"Oh," she adds, "and she's pretty much my best friend." She comes to an abrupt stop in front of room 212, and I bump into her. She gives me that look again. "Ow. You *are* a clod, aren't you?"

"Sorry," I say.

She steps away to give herself space. "Anyway, this is Mrs. Morgenstern's homeroom . . . and, oh, there's Sarah Lynn!" She waves, and all of a sudden, Thelma is *on*. Like, electric lightbulb on, way more lively than she was with me. "Sarah Lynn! Sarah Lynn! Hi!"

The girl who comes over has honey-colored hair and great posture. Her eyes skim over me, but I don't think she really sees me. She doesn't give Thelma an especially warm welcome either—and by that I mean no welcome at all. She scans the hall as if she's looking for someone. Someone who isn't us.

Thelma doesn't clue in. "Sarah Lynn, this is Bliss, the new girl," she says importantly. "Bliss, this is Sarah Lynn."

"Hi," I say. Sarah Lynn reminds me of someone. Who is it she reminds me of?

"Thelma, could you do me a huge favor and take over?" Sarah Lynn asks. Her voice is sweet, but she still hasn't made eye contact with me. She's hardly made eye contact with Thelma, but instead keeps looking down the hall. "I know you'd be great at it, and I've got, um . . . I'm just . . . *wow*. So busy, you know?"

"Sure," Thelma says. She stands up taller. "And I hear you, 'cause oh my gosh, I'm so busy too. But yeah, absolutely!"

"Hi," I say again. I give a sweeping wave. "Hellooo."

"Oh!" Sarah Lynn says, turning to me with a confused expression. "*Hi.* Right. Did I not say that?"

I smile and shake my head.

"Very nice to meet you," she says, and in my head, I roll my eyes. She didn't even catch my name, I just know it. And I've figured out who she reminds me of.

"Okay, gotta split," she says. "Thank you, Thelma—so much!"

She dashes off, and I watch her blend in with the crowd.

Despite her golden hair, she blends easily. The only person who doesn't blend is a tall black guy a few yards ahead of her, just now stepping out of his own homeroom. It occurs to me that he's the only black person I've seen.

"So . . . looks like I'm your student mentor," Thelma says, pulling back my attention. "Groovy. I know pretty much *everything* about Crestview, so don't worry."

She seems to mean it, which I appreciate, because Sarah Lynn made me feel like a big fat zero.

"What grade is she in?" I ask.

"Who, Sarah Lynn? Ours, not that you'd know it. She mainly hangs out with upperclassmen."

I almost say, *I thought she was your best friend.* But I don't.

"Ah," I say. "Well, I should get to class, huh?" I check my schedule card and see that my destination is two rooms down. I start to go, but Thelma grabs my arm.

"Wait," she says. "Is your last name honestly what Mrs. Elliot said it was?"

It takes me a moment to patch together what she's asking. I'm still recovering from being snubbed, and also from the intrusive memory of Ms. Sturgess, the person Sarah Lynn reminded me of. Ms. Sturgess was a social worker in California who made me feel as small as Sarah Lynn did.

Then my brain clicks into gear: homeroom, the giggles, Bliss in the Morning Dew.

"Um, yeah?" I say.

"But that's not a real last name."

"Actually, it is."

Her expression tells me that's not enough, so I say, "My parents are kind of . . . hippies." I hear the way it comes out, and I feel a twinge of guilt. Why did I say "kind of"? And why did I say "my parents," as if they were hippies, but not me?

"Oh, wow," Thelma says, eyes wide. "For real? My dad says it was hippies who killed those people in California."

"I don't think so," I say.

"That one lady? Sharon Tate? She was expecting her first child. Isn't that awful? She only had one month to go, but now—" She makes a throat-slitting movement with her hand.

I don't know what I'm supposed to say to that. Apparently nothing, since Thelma is already moving on.

"So do you, like, have lots of dads?" she asks.

"I'm sorry, what?"

"You know—free love and all that. Does your mom wear a bra?"

I blink. Mom doesn't wear a bra; she burned them all with a bunch of friends as an ironic poke at the "bra-burning ceremonies" invented by the press. Mom's bras were gray and stretched out, so burning them was no great loss. But I'm reluctant to share this with Thelma—especially since I'm finally processing her "lots of dads" remark. She thinks my mom sleeps around. I can't decide if I'm more astounded or offended.

"I just have one dad, and my mom wears a bra," I say.

Thelma's face falls. Then she shrugs. "Okay, well, have fun in English. I'll swing by to walk you to your next class." She grins. "Oh, and like Mrs. Elliot said—welcome to Crestview!"

LIVE FEED FROM THE *APOLLO 11*
MOON LANDING, JULY 1969

"That's one small step for man,
one giant leap for mankind."

—Mission commander Neil Armstrong

y lunchtime my head is spinning, but it's exhilarating. Everyone is *so* nice—well, other than Sarah Lynn—and it just goes to show that you don't have to live on a commune in order to love your brothers and sisters. It can happen at a prep school just as easily, with everyone dressed in matching uniforms, even!

Thelma meets me as promised at the cafeteria. Once we have our trays, she leads me to a table in the middle of the room.

"This is where you get your big lesson, okay?" she says. She's realized how clueless I am about pretty much everything, and she's taken to explaining the hidden rules of high school life, which she either knows intuitively or absorbed during freshman orientation. I'm grateful, although I'm not a hundred percent sure she's the expert she makes herself out to be. Still, she sure as heck knows more than I do.

"Girls, this is Bliss," Thelma says to our table companions. "Sarah Lynn asked me to take over her duties as student mentor, and of course I said yes."

Two curious faces gaze at me. One girl has red hair and a

heart-shaped face; the other has brown hair and really pretty brown eyes.

Thelma puts her hand on my forearm. "Bliss is a *hippie*. Tell them your last name, Bliss."

I sigh and say, "In the Morning Dew."

The brown-haired girl wrinkles her forehead.

"That's her last name!" Thelma says. "In the Morning Dew!"

I smile with closed lips at their astonished squeals. But it's just a name. Geez.

"Can you change it when you turn eighteen?" the girl with the red hair asks.

"Um . . ." I've never thought about it, to tell the truth.

"*I* think it's far-out," the brown-haired girl says.

"You do?" Thelma says. She tilts her head, and I get the sense that Thelma is the sort of girl whose opinion changes depending on what others think.

"It's tons better than Roach, that's for sure," the brown-haired girl says.

"Is that your last name?" I ask her.

She nods. "Jolene Roach. Isn't that lovely?"

Thelma giggles. "I would die if my last name was Roach. I would seriously die."

"Shut up," Jolene says.

"Roaches are vile, but we let Jolene hang out with us anyway," the redhead says, hugging her friend. "For the record, I'm DeeDee."

"DeeDee's daddy used to work at the paper mill, but then he made it big in property development," Thelma says, as if this has relevance to the conversation. "Now, down to business. You eat. I'll talk."

"Yes, ma'am," I say. I obediently take a bite of my fried chicken, which is out of this world. I'm not missing Mom's unleavened bread one bit.

Thelma directs my attention to the entrance of the cafeteria.

"That's Lacy," she says of a slender girl talking to a broad-shouldered guy in a letter jacket. "She got her ears pierced over the summer. Her mother made her take the earrings out, but if you look closely you can see the holes."

I look closely. I see no holes.

"And that's Burt, her boyfriend. So dreamy. He's the captain of the football team, of course."

The black boy I saw earlier strolls in—alone, I notice—and Thelma gets animated. "Ooh, look, there's Lawrence. He's here on scholarship. Everybody absolutely adores him."

DeeDee jumps in, saying, "Other colored kids? At public schools? My cousin says you have to do whatever they say. Like if they say, 'Give me your lunch money,' you give them your lunch money, no questions asked."

"They're rough," Jolene agrees softly. "Even the girls."

"Especially the girls!" DeeDee says. "My parents sent me here just so I wouldn't have to go to Northside, now that the coloreds are being bused in. Did you know all the Northside girls have ulcers?"

"They do?" I say. "Why?"

"Because they're so scared. Of the colored girls. *And* they have bladder infections because they're too afraid to use the school bathrooms."

I glance from DeeDee to Jolene to Thelma.

"They do," Thelma confirms. "Dr. Roberts told my mom, when she took me for my annual check-up. He said he sees so many public-school girls with ulcers and bladder infections, and it's too bad the integrationists didn't think of *that* before they stirred things up."

"People are happier with their own kind," DeeDee says. "It's just a fact of life, and I mean that for coloreds and whites." She lifts her drumstick and tears off a bite. "If you were colored, would you want to be in a class full of whites? I don't think so."

"But . . ." I'm confused. I look at the front of the cafeteria, where Lawrence waits in line. His skin is darker than anybody's I've ever seen. "What about Lawrence?"

They regard me blankly.

"He's different," Thelma finally says.

"How?"

She looks at the other girls as if to say, *Isn't she too funny?*

"For starters, his parents are educated," she says. "His dad even went to college, and you just don't see that a lot."

"Hold on, I don't think that's—"

41

"*And* he's clean, *and* he dresses nice, *and* he's not lazy," Thelma continues.

"He's as close to being white as a Negro can be, even though he's just about as dark as they come," DeeDee says. She claps her hand to her mouth. "Oh my gosh, can you imagine if my father heard me say that?"

"Usually the light-skinneds *are* more intelligent," Thelma agrees. "I guess Lawrence is the exception."

Jolene, who's watching my face, pulls her eyebrows together. She's the only one who realizes I'm struggling with this, I think.

"My daddy says most Negroes are fine folks," she says hesitantly.

"As long as they stay in their place," finishes DeeDee.

Jolene nods. "Segregation's better for everyone. That's why I go here too."

I want to like these girls, but I can't comprehend them. Are their brains made of wool?

"Lawrence is black," I say.

"It's nicer to say 'our colored friend,'" Thelma says.

"Yes, but that means Crestview *is* integrated," I say. I don't want to be confrontational, but good heavens. If a black boy goes to a white school, then the school isn't segregated.

Thelma, DeeDee, and Jolene look puzzled. Then comprehension dawns on Thelma's face. She giggles.

"What?" I say.

She falls back into teacher mode, only I sense I've been demoted from clueless to downright dim-witted. "Okay, see, the board of trustees always planned on Crestview being white-only," she says. "That's the whole reason Crestview was founded. After the public schools went mixed?"

"After they were *forced* to go mixed," DeeDee puts in.

"But then one of the board members—"

"Who gives heaps of money and who works with Thelma's dad," says DeeDee.

"—decided it would be smarter to go on and let a few select Negroes in, just 'cause of all the outside agitators coming to Atlanta and working people up. They didn't want Crestview to be a target, so they handpicked Lawrence, and we all think they made a real good choice."

"So . . . he's your token black person," I say.

"Exactly," she says, and there's not one ounce of embarrassment. She doesn't realize there's any call for embarrassment.

"Are there more?" I ask.

"More what?" DeeDee says.

"Token black people."

"I heard that last year there was one other, a girl, but kids kept tripping her and dumping her lunch tray. She didn't last long." DeeDee frowns. "She had that awful name. What was it?"

Thelma titters. "I think it was Floydzella."

"Eeuh," DeeDee says, shuddering.

43

My stomach is tight, and if I don't say something, I'll hate myself. Only, I don't want to draw lines between me and these other girls on the very first day.

But if I don't stand up for what's right, what kind of person am I?

I clear my throat. "Before I moved, the person I was closest to—other than my mom and dad—well, she was black." My heart thumps. "Her name's, um, Virginia. Her two little girls are the cutest things. They shared a tent with me."

"You slept in a tent?" Jolene says.

"With *colored* girls?" DeeDee says.

"What was their hair like?" Thelma asks. "Did you touch it?"

I look at her, baffled. "Um, I braided it sometimes, sure."

"In cornrows?"

"Sometimes."

Their eyes widen.

"Hope you washed your hands," DeeDee says.

"DeeDee, that's not nice," Jolene says. I'm figuring out that DeeDee's the catty one, Jolene's the nice one, and Thelma's the boss lady, so to speak. Or at least, she wants to be. But all of them, even Jolene, are making me feel awfully uncomfortable.

"Oh my gosh," DeeDee says. "What if you did it to us one day! Put our hair in cornrows!"

"*DeeDee*," Jolene says.

"Dr. Evans would flip," Thelma says. "Oh my gosh, it would be the biggest scandal."

"Well, almost the biggest scandal," DeeDee asserts. "Have you told her about the girl who died here?"

I think of the blood voice. My drumstick's halfway to my mouth, but I lower it. "Someone died? Here on campus?"

"She didn't just die," Jolene says, making a cringing face as if apologizing for what she's about to say. "She killed herself."

"She threw herself out of a window," Thelma says, and her tone holds no apology whatsoever. "There was a lot of blood—or so the story goes."

"Was it in Hamilton Hall?" I ask with a sense of foreboding.

"How'd you know?" Jolene says.

"It's not like it's a secret," DeeDee says to her. "It's pretty much common knowledge."

I put my chicken on my plate and push the plate away. "Who was she? Why did she jump out the window?"

"No one knows," Thelma says. "Just that obviously she wasn't right in the mind, because she decided it would be a really super idea to fling herself headfirst out of a third-story window."

I wince.

"Some people say you can see the bloodstains," Jolene says. "Um, I never have."

"Nor me," says DeeDee.

"Me neither," says Thelma. "If a girl really did kill herself, it was a really long time ago, back when the school was full of nuns. So maybe the blood wore off. But it's probably just a ghost story anyway."

"I don't know," I say slowly. Can I tell these girls about the voice I heard, or will it simply brand me as more of a weirdo?

"What?" Jolene says. "You're thinking something, I can tell."

I look at her kind brown eyes and decide to risk it. She's not the type of girl just to turn on someone for being a little different. "Well, this morning as I was—"

"Oh, oh, oh!" Thelma says, squeezing my arm. "There's Sarah Lynn. Look!"

Jolene and DeeDee grow as animated as Thelma, and any interest in the girl who died evaporates into thin air. They're far more fascinated by the girl entering the cafeteria. Their reaction makes something go sour inside me, and that sourness edges out my own thoughts of the dead girl.

"Sarah Lynn, hi!" Thelma calls.

Sarah Lynn turns, and so do the two girls with her. Sarah Lynn smiles and lifts her hand, but there's something fake about it, like she's going through the motions.

Thelma beams. "Isn't she perfect? She's *perfect*."

I keep my opinion to myself, because I've had a one-minute encounter with her, and that's it. Less than one minute. Thirty seconds. But in those thirty seconds, no,

Sarah Lynn didn't strike me as perfect. The way she was too distracted to say hello? The way she passed me off on Thelma? I'd call that self-absorbed at best, stuck-up at worst.

Ms. Sturgess, the government social worker assigned to me to make sure I didn't slip through the cracks, was young and pretty too. I had an appointment scheduled with her, an "appointment I couldn't miss," according to the authorities, and Mom sent me into the city with a friend who was heading to a craft fair. I was excited, leaving the commune to meet this important woman who wanted to talk to me. I wore my best dress.

But Ms. Sturgess met with me for a grand total of five minutes before closing my file and pasting on a smile.

"Beth, would you mind terribly if we cut this short?" she said. "I can tell you're doing *just fine*, and I would *really* love to pop over and visit my grandfather before my next case." She arranged her delicate features into an expression of worry. "He's getting along in age, and he's beginning to struggle. You know how it is."

"Uh, sure," I said. "No problem. But it's Bliss, not Beth."

"Mmm," she said, nodding as if I'd said something deep. "Well, thank you for understanding. And don't hesitate to call if you need *anything*, anything at all."

I left her office thinking how nice it was that a busy career woman like Ms. Sturgess would still find time for her grandfather. Then I turned on my heel and doubled back, realizing

I'd left my paperback copy of *Jane Eyre* in Ms. Sturgess's waiting room. I'd just discovered the existence of the madwoman in the attic, and I was eager to read more.

I knocked lightly on the door; no one responded. I slipped in, recovered my book, and was on my way out when I heard Ms. Sturgess in her inner office. She was laughing gaily and seemed to be talking on the phone.

"That sounds lovely, Gail," she said. "I can be there in ten minutes. Let's go wild and order Pink Ladies, shall we?"

I clutched my book. Gail wasn't Ms. Sturgess's grandfather, and Ms. Sturgess's grandfather surely didn't drink Pink Ladies. After a pause, Ms. Sturgess laughed again.

"Oh, I did, yes," she said. "But I sent her away. A nice kid, I'm sure, but why bother with a full assessment? We both know she's going to end up making goat cheese and popping out babies with the first long-haired freak who comes along."

There was more laughter. I hurried away with flaming cheeks.

I know that Sarah Lynn isn't Ms. Sturgess, and if she turns out to be as great as everyone seems to think she is, then terrific. But I'm not ready to join her fan club.

Thelma props her chin on her palm. Still gazing at Sarah Lynn, she says, "She's going to be a Snow Princess, I just know it."

"Thelma, the Winter Dance isn't for months," DeeDee says.

"So?" Thelma says. "Sarah Lynn's a shoo-in. She's nice and smart and not at all full of herself, even though she has every right to be."

"Um, neat," I say, as a response seems required.

"But don't worry. She's not a square, even though last year she entered the junior high science fair."

"She was the only girl who did," Jolene says.

Thelma pulls her eyes from Sarah Lynn and gets to work on her mashed potatoes. "On the weekends, she volunteers at Good Mews."

"Good News? What's that?"

"Good *Mews*," Thelma repeats. "It's a cat rescue center. I signed up to volunteer there too."

"You did not," DeeDee says.

"Well, I'm going to."

"She's been saying that for months," DeeDee tells me. "She wants to be like Sarah Lynn, only without actually having to clean out cages."

"I don't like cat poo," Thelma says.

"Who does?" Jolene says, giggling.

DeeDee brings the conversation back to Sarah Lynn. "Her parents have a mansion on Habersham Road that's straight out of *Southern Living*, I'm not kidding. Her daddy's filthy rich."

"He owns a gentleman's country club," Jolene says.

"Wow," I say.

"And like I said, she's not the slightest bit conceited," Thelma says. "Everybody absolutely *adores* her."

"Just like Lawrence?" I ask.

"What?" she says, taken off guard.

"Do they adore her just like they adore Lawrence?"

She regards me as if I'm certifiable. "Not 'they.' *We*. And noooo, because she's *not* Lawrence. She's Sarah Lynn." She keeps looking at me, and I notice a dot of potato on the side of her mouth. "What a nutty thing to say. Why would you even say that?"

"Because . . . because you said, earlier . . ." I falter, looking from face to face. Does none of them get the irony here?

Thelma regards me earnestly. "I would do *anything* to be Sarah Lynn," she says. "Any of us would."

"True," Jolene says wistfully.

I study Sarah Lynn, who's now sitting at a table across the room with a tray of food magically in front of her. She is different from the other girls, I admit it. Not different like me, but different like . . . well, like a porcelain bird placed high on a shelf. A beautiful, fragile creature who's been given everything she's ever wanted and, because of this, is untouched by the coarser aspects of life. I wouldn't be surprised to find she's never been touched at all, to be frank.

She holds herself with such reserve. She smiles, but her smile doesn't reach her eyes, even in the company of the girls she's chosen to eat with. Why?

I have no clue, and I really don't want to spend my time wondering about it. But my brain pushes at the question anyway.

Why are people aloof?

Because they don't want to let others in.

Why don't they want to let others in?

Well, sometimes because they're shy, and sometimes because they're convinced of their own superiority.

But those aren't the only reasons. Sometimes it's because they have something to hide.

Cats have excellent night vision. Their eyes gleam as if lit from within. Medieval alchemists identified this inner flame as "the fire of life," and numerous attempts have been made to harness its power.

Regular, when placed in a room of utter black, expressed initial discontent, but ceased protesting after eighteen hours. Displayed disorientation when released.

Regular's measure of dry kibble halved so that I might perceive how caloric intake influences intensity of life force.

Fluid intake likewise reduced.

FROM A TV COMMERCIAL FOR TRIX, THE CORN CEREAL
WITH THE NATURAL TASTE OF FRUIT

"Silly rabbit! Trix are for kids!"

I dream about the commune more and more infrequently. I haven't heard from Mom and Dad, but I don't expect to. I miss Daisy and Clementine and Flying V, and it's weird to think that their lives are spinning on without me, just as mine is spinning along without them.

I do hope Flying V found a way to get Clementine some penicillin. Her forehead was so hot the day we left.

I also hope (forgive me) that the pigeons have died, so they can no longer spread the infection.

Today marks the second full week I've been at Crestview, and I have to laugh at how different it is from what I expected. On *Andy Griffith*, everyone is decent and honest, and there are always wholesome lessons to be learned, such as don't throw rocks at birds, or don't underestimate a child, as a child can teach a grown-up quite a lot.

At Crestview, it's not that people aren't decent and honest, necessarily, but being decent and honest seems less important than wearing someone's class pin or gossiping about who got caught smoking in the girls' bathroom. Also, at Crestview nobody calls kids "young'uns" or says "Well, that's a fine howdy-do."

I'm okay with that. Life in Mayberry sure seems perfect, but life at Crestview is a lot more interesting.

I wish I could tell Flying V about Crestview, and I wish I could let her know that her worries were unfounded. Thelma and Jolene and DeeDee, they're good girls. They can be small-minded at times, but their spats are short-lived and infrequent, tending to revolve around hairstyles or fashion. It's Thelma and DeeDee who bicker the most, so I suppose Thelma and DeeDee are the two girls Flying V saw in her vision.

Or not. I like Jolene better than either of them, so maybe there are three girls I'm destined to be involved with? Or maybe Flying V was wrong altogether. Her premonitions have surely been wrong before, though I can't call up an example.

I do think I'd *feel* a little more while in the company of the girl—or girls—whose lives are meant to entwine with mine. Sometimes Thelma and the others just seem . . . silly. But I suppose any friendship requires time to deepen and take root.

As far as Crestview itself goes, I still get creepy vibes at unexpected moments, especially when I'm alone. It's as if someone, or something, is trying to figure me out. I'm pretty sure it's the spirit of the dead girl Thelma told me about, and I'm pretty sure something terrible did indeed happen to her long ago. That tends to be why spirits stick around, to right old wrongs and all of that.

The thing is, the energy I sense from the dead girl is "wrong" itself. Off-kilter, like a rotting jack-o'lantern with a slipping-down smile. Like maybe she *was* crazy.

I never did tell the girls of my experience, and I don't plan to. I'm sorry for the dead girl, but I want nothing to do with her, and by staying clear of Hamilton Hall, I'm mostly able to ignore her.

What's harder to ignore are certain right-out-in-the-open vibrations given off by my classmates and teachers. Not about everything; just about some things. Like race. It's confusing to me that visible wickedness—because that's what racism is, wickedness—is in some ways harder to fight than whiffs of blood and ancient bones. I'd think it would be the opposite.

I'm grappling with this during my cultural studies class today, because Mr. Harris is pacing back and forth at the front of the room, talking about this very issue. He wants us to think about what we, the new generation, can do to restore the South's reputation as a bastion of grace and gentility. As an example of what needs to change, he brings up the case of Ruby Bridges, one of the first black students to attend an integrated Southern school. He reminds us of the protest that occurred that first day: how a mob of angry whites gathered to hurl insults, flaunt Rebel flags, and wave white sheets.

"Now was that any way to treat that little Nigra girl?" Mr. Harris says in his thick drawl. "She had to be escorted by a U.S. marshal. Think on that a minute: *A U.S. marshal had to protect the safety of a six-year-old.*" He shakes his head. "Do y'all see what a mistake it was, forcing integration on folks that just weren't ready?"

I'm so floored by his words that I have to put down my pencil. Mr. Harris is my *teacher*—a college-educated man—and here he is telling a room full of white students that, yes, it's wrong to terrorize a black child, but the situation could have been avoided altogether if "the little Nigra girl" had stayed where she belonged.

Jolene's in Mr. Harris's class with me, and afterward, I ask her about the white sheets. I'm pretty sure I know what they meant, but I'm not positive.

"The Ku Klux Klan," Jolene responds without hesitation. She walks to the end of the hall and goes out the door, stepping into the sunshine. "You know what that is, right?"

"Of course," I say. My next class is in the Woodward Building, which we just left, but I stay with her so we can keep talking. "Only I wasn't sure the Klan still existed."

She laughs. "Are you kidding?"

"Not here in Atlanta, though. Right?"

She laughs again. "Um, *yeah.* They meet at Stone Mountain." When I frown, she says, "Stone Mountain? Largest granite outcropping in the whole United States? What, you've never heard of it?"

I haven't, so she explains that Stone Mountain is thirty minutes outside of the city, and that stoneworkers are hard at work carving a Confederate memorial into the rock. As we cross the quad, she tells me that the end result will be a ninety-foot-tall bas-relief of Stonewall Jackson, Robert E. Lee, and Jefferson Davis.

"The Klan has their Labor Day picnics there," she tells me. "Hoods, robes, the works. They burn crosses, too, but not till the night."

"That's awful," I say. "It's . . . *sick*."

"I know," she says, but not with any degree of passion. It's the tone someone might use in response to being reminded that it was leftover day in the cafeteria or that there was a history quiz that afternoon.

"But . . . ," I say. "I mean . . ."

We've reached Hamilton Hall, the very building I've gone to such pains to avoid. Jolene pauses on the steps. "What?"

I can't find the words to say what I want to say, probably because I don't know what I want to say. I feel like I'm in some spooky mirror world where all the rules of right and wrong are reversed, and no one except me seems to notice. Also, being this close to Hamilton Hall is making my head hurt, as if someone is pushing on my brain.

"Is your father in the Klan?" I ask queasily. It feels crazy to even voice such a question.

"My daddy? In the Klan?" Jolene's appalled, and it makes me feel better—like *yes*, it is a crazy question. "My daddy has opinions, sure, but Bliss, Klansmen are bad news. They hurt people."

"They lynch people," I say.

"My daddy would never lynch anyone," she says.

Students stream past us through the main door, chatting and laughing. Jolene joins the flow of traffic, and after a moment's hesitation, I follow her. *It's just a building*, I tell myself. *And if within this building there's a dead girl, well, she's just a dead girl.*

"There is Klan presence at Crestview, though," Jolene says in the hall.

A chill trembles through me. "Where?"

"What do you mean, where?"

"The Klan. At Crestview. Do they meet in one certain place?" As I say this, a thought sighs through my mind like a rattling breath: you are *the* key. It's the dead girl's voice. The blood voice. It makes my own blood seem to thin out.

"Bliss, what are you talking about?" Jolene says as she enters the stairwell and starts up.

I trail her. My body doesn't like mounting these stairs. The dead girl plunged from the third story, that's what they say. I don't want to go up and up. I don't want to go closer.

come, says the blood voice. be with me.

"Ohhh," Jolene says. "They don't meet *here*, silly. Not in this building."

It's an effort to focus on Jolene. "But you said—"

She giggles. "No, you goof, they don't meet anywhere on campus. Good heavens! I just meant that certain fathers of certain students . . ." We exit the stairwell on the second floor, and she breaks off, as if remembering there are people around us. Her voice, when she next speaks, is stilted. "That's just what I've heard. I don't know anything."

My body feels so strange. So airy. I need to leave this place before I no longer want to. "Okay," I say. "I better go to class—and it's back that way, so I better run."

Jolene frowns, perhaps puzzled as to why I've come all this way with her. "See you at lunch?"

"Yeah." I force a smile because I don't want her to see how upset I am. Flying V used to tell me I felt things too strongly . . . but shouldn't we feel things strongly, especially when those things are wrong?

When I double back to the stairwell, it's empty. Everyone's gone to class . . . or rather, everyone but me. My footsteps echo in the chilly passageway. So does the blood voice: *be with me . . . i've been waiting.*

My heart beats faster, and I can't . . . I can't feel my head exactly right. Or my lungs, they're so floaty . . .

I can't hear my footsteps. Is my tread so light that I no longer make sound, or has my flesh taken on new form?

my flesh . . . my bones . . . my blood . . .

Out, I need out. I need air and sunlight and noise. I hasten down the last few steps, but as I round the bend, I see someone in the shadowed recess. I freeze. It's a boy—a boy possessing a broad back, strong shoulders, and a muscled black neck that extends above the collar of his Crestview shirt. *Lawrence.*

I process this in a flash, just as I see, in the next flash, that Lawrence isn't alone. He's murmuring to a girl with honey-colored hair. He leans in, and his lips brush hers.

I suppose I suck in my breath or make some other noise, because they jerk apart. Lawrence steps protectively in front of the girl, but it's too late. I've seen her and she's seen me.

"I said *don't*," Sarah Lynn says sharply, and her voice breaks through my fog and brings me back hard. She shoves him. He's bewildered. My skin is tingling, but I'm no longer disoriented, and this I know: They were kissing. It was mutual. Then I stumbled on them, and suddenly he's a plaything to push away.

Sarah Lynn strides out of the stairwell. Lawrence watches her go. The door slushes shut behind her, and he turns to me with a tightened jaw. I want to tell him *No, no, you've got it all wrong. I don't care if you kiss a white girl. I don't care if you love a white girl. I just wish you'd chosen a white girl worthy of your love.*

Lawrence's Adam's apple jerks up and down, and I realize that in addition to whatever else he's feeling, he's scared. He's in love with the darling of the school, Sarah Lynn Lancaster, and he's afraid I'll expose his secret. I give a tiny shake of my head, wanting him to know he has nothing to fear, not from me.

not from me, echoes the blood voice, fainter than before. *come back to me, you are the—*

I hurry past Lawrence and flee this cursed building.

This afternoon I chanced upon three fledgling cardinals. Their nest, through misfortune and a long stick, had been dislodged from a tree, and the birds were weak and sorry orphans. I left two, but scooped the smallest into my hands and brought it to my room, a trifle for Regular to amuse herself with. With her pupils dilated and her ears half back, she traps the thing, then releases it, then traps it again and bats it about, all the while emitting the strangest feral chirruping sound. It amuses me, observing the pleasure she derives from playing with her food.

Tomorrow, as I am selfless in my service to the weak, I shall carry out as usual my charitable duties. While doing so, I will make a point of visiting Agnes. I will urge her to talk of Liliana, and as Agnes requires little

persuading on this matter, I am certain she
will oblige.

esley Hall is the prettiest of all the buildings on campus. You enter through the foyer, with its black-and-white marble floor. It's like a giant chessboard, only so shiny you can see yourself in it. On both sides of the foyer are railed marble staircases that spiral to the second floor. That's where the actual classrooms are. If you bypass the twin staircases and choose instead to cross the gleaming foyer, you reach two ornate wooden doors that lead to the loveliest chapel I've ever seen.

Unlike the rest of the building—and I find this strange, but nice—the chapel itself is simple and unassuming. Its wooden pews are the color of caramel, and stained-glass windows cast rosy shafts of light through the room. Motes of dust glitter in the air like memories. I'm glad that the nuns, back in the olden days, had this place to worship in.

According to Thelma, Wesley Chapel is no longer used—she was surprised I'd even peeked inside. But I found it beautiful. Sacred.

My music appreciation class is on the second floor, in a low-ceilinged room that has no charm whatsoever. For fifty minutes we listen to Bach, and then the bell rings, and all at once everyone's pushing back their chairs and chattering. I collect my books and head toward the door with the others.

I'm moving with the throng down the marble stairs, humming and wondering what it would be like to be a butterfly, when I hear a cry. My eyes fly to the opposite staircase, where I see a girl tumbling down the bottom five or six stairs. It's an ungraceful fall, full of thuds and limbs and books, and it seems to go on and on. She lands in a heap, her skirt in disarray. Her underwear is exposed.

She lies there, stunned, and everyone stares. I stare too. I stop short, though I made no conscious decision to do so, and I think, *That poor girl, is she okay?* And also, *Pull your skirt down! At least sit up and fix your skirt!*

It's shameful that that's what I think about—her sad, exposed underwear—when she could be brain damaged, for all I know. She could have broken a limb! But everyone else must be thinking about her underwear too, because they've started to snicker. The girl who fell is a snicker-at sort of person—I don't know her, but she's scrawny and frizz-haired and obviously clumsy—but that's no excuse. Not a single person helps her. Everyone just laughs.

I force my way through the students in front of me, accidentally elbowing someone in the process.

"Hey!" she says indignantly.

I get halfway down the stairs, but by then—finally!—

someone else is striding to the girl. She's a big girl, this Good Samaritan, and when she squats beside the fallen girl, there's an audible *ooomph*. The snickers grow downright gleeful, and the big girl looks up and glares.

Good for you, I think, rooting for the sole Crestview student decent enough to reach out to another. *You show 'em.* In solidarity, I glare at the girls to my right. One of them pulls a face, as if I'm the one being juvenile.

The big girl leans over and speaks quietly to the girl on the floor. The girl seems too addled to be comforted. Her eyes are big, and I think of a mutt Mom once brought to the commune—all fur and mange, its expression glazed.

The big girl leans in to whisper something else. This time she must hit the right note, because at last the girl on the floor pushes herself up. She takes in the double staircases of laughing students. Her face turns scarlet. She scrambles to her feet, tugging at her skirt, and runs straight out of the building, neither gathering her books nor thanking her benefactor.

With the show over, the crowd disperses.

"Too bad it wasn't Sandy who fell instead of Gayla," a slender girl says as she pushes down the stairs in front of me. It's the girl who made a face at me moments earlier.

Her friend titters. "Are you kidding? If Sandy had taken a fall like that, she'd have brought the whole place down."

"True," the slender girl says. "I take it back."

I'm filled with distaste for both of them, and I think what

a small difference there is between scrawny and slender, fallen and proud.

"Did you see Gayla's panties?" the friend says.

"Didn't everybody?"

"Imagine if it had been Sandy—and everyone had to see *that!*"

The slender girl shoves her friend's shoulder. "Marla, ew!" She shoves her again, because apparently once wasn't enough. "Seriously—*ewww!*"

I want to shove them both. Instead, I tell myself they're pathetic individuals who aren't worth my time. The Good Samaritan, whose name I now know to be Sandy, has more class in her pinky finger than they do in their whole bodies.

Someone rams into me. "Watch it," he says.

"Oh, sorry," I say.

I pick up Gayla's books and deliver them to the front office, and the secretary tells me what I nice young woman I am. Then I go meet Thelma and Jolene on the quad. The three of us have fourth period free, so we usually study together, or pretend to.

Today, we don't even pretend. I tell them about Gayla's fall, and their eyes widen.

"Her skirt flew all the way up?" Thelma asks. Her shock is threaded through with excitement. "People saw her *underpants?*"

I nod.

"Poor Gayla!" Jolene says.

"I know."

That Jolene would care, and not just for the thrill of the scandal, makes me feel better.

"So what happened then?" Thelma wants to know. "Did she just lie there for all the world to see?"

"No, a girl named Sandy helped her," I say. "And then people laughed at Sandy, which made me so mad. She's helping someone in need, and everyone makes fun of her for it? Why would they do that?"

Neither Thelma nor Jolene answers. Instead, they share a look.

"What?" I say.

Thelma sighs. "They made fun of her because she's Sandy, that's why."

That's no answer; in fact, it just makes me madder.

"You mean because she's plain?" I say. "Because she's . . . large? Is that what you're saying?"

Jolene fidgets. "That, and she's just . . ."

"Sandy," Thelma fills in. "She's just Sandy, and let's just say"—she smiles brightly—"well. Let's just say nothing, okay?"

Later, Jolene tries to temper Thelma's nonexplanation. She lets Thelma get ahead as we walk to our next classes and says, "About Sandy . . ."

"Yeah?"

"It's not because she's unattractive. She can't help that. She's just . . . strange, that's all."

"Ohhh," I say. "Well, thanks for clearing that up." I speed up, ready to leave the subject behind.

"Wait," Jolene says. She grabs my arm. "You know how some people just . . . rub you the wrong way?"

I shrug her off. "No," I say, although actually I do. Only the girls who rub me the wrong way are girls who judge others, not girls who go out of their way to help others.

"And she has B.O.," she says uncomfortably. She blushes. "Sandy, I mean. Someone left a stick of deodorant on her desk, it was so bad."

"That's cruel," I say.

"Is it?" Jolene says. "Wouldn't it be worse not to tell her?"

"Did someone tell her? Or did whoever it was just leave out the deodorant?"

Jolene drops her eyes and hugs her books to her chest. "Anyway, she's queer, that's all. She doesn't have any friends."

I'm disappointed. Doesn't Jolene see that Sandy's lack of friends is even more reason to be nice to her?

At the same time, I'm glad I've started wearing my Secret. I'm glad I bought it on my own, saving everyone the trouble of alerting me to my own stench.

"And they all have pretty children,
And the children go to school,
And the children go to summer camp,
And then to the university,
Where they are put in boxes
And they come out all the same."

—Malvina Reynolds

There's a boy at Crestview who makes my lips curve into a smile whenever I see him. I don't mean to smile; it just happens. Giddily. Happily. Uncontrollably.

I don't know the boy's name, but he's beautiful, with disheveled brown hair that grazes his collar. Were it any longer, Dr. Evans would have to write him up for violation of the dress code.

He carries around a paperback copy of On the Road, which has a coffee stain on its cover. He slouches. The back of his neck is both strong and vulnerable, and I would touch it if I could. If he were asleep, for example. If I were an angel, visiting him in the night.

Only he's the angel, with his dark, soulful eyes. He always looks sad, even when he's talking with his friends and his lips quirk into his sardonic smile.

I spot my angel-boy after lunch one day. I don't tell Thelma or DeeDee or Jolene. But my heart beats faster, and I miss whatever it is that Jolene is saying to me.

"Hmm?" I say, pulling my eyes from the boy. It's warm,

we're on the quad, and Thelma has slipped her hand under her shirt to scratch her belly.

"I said *sing* it for us," she repeats.

"Sing what?"

She groans, and DeeDee giggles.

"The song you were telling us about? About people living perfect little lives in perfect little boxes."

"Oh. 'Little Boxes,'" I say. The boy is coming our way. He's walking up the sidewalk, and his head is bobbing as if maybe he's singing a song of his own, silently to himself.

"Yeah, that one," Thelma says. She and the others think it's so funny that I know all these folk songs. I think it's funny that they don't.

My angel-boy is close now, as in five-feet-away close. There's no way I'm going to burst into song in front of him. But then the contrary part of me says, *You're going to let a boy keep you from singing out loud? Sing, sister! Sing!*

So I do, and my angel-boy turns his head.

"Bliss!" Thelma squeals. She tackles me and claps her hand over my mouth. "Oh my gosh, will you hush?!"

It's another "don't cross your legs above the ankles" moment, even though Thelma is the one who egged me on.

But my angel-boy smiles, and my heart takes flight. I smile back, and something passes between us. Something fizzy and fine.

He laughs and continues along his way.

Thelma swats me. "Bliss!"

I watch my boy stroll up the hill. I appreciate the play of muscle beneath his khakis.

"She's smitten," Jolene says affectionately.

"I am," I agree.

"Well, don't be," Thelma says. "That's Mitchell Truman, and he's a junior. Juniors don't date freshmen."

"That's his last name, 'Truman'?" I say. How perfect—*true man.*

"Unless the freshman's Sarah Lynn Lancaster," DeeDee says. "Any junior in school would date her. Any senior, even."

"Only she doesn't date," Thelma says pompously, since she's pretty much Sarah Lynn's best friend. A best friend who does little more than worship her from afar, but who am I to judge? From what I've seen, that's about as close as Sarah Lynn likes anyone to get.

I think of her stolen kiss with Lawrence, and how she pushed him away when I appeared on the scene. "What do you mean, she doesn't date?" I ask.

Thelma rolls her eyes. "She doesn't *date*, that's what I mean."

"Her daddy's scary strict," Jolene says. "He told her he'll send her to a convent if he ever even catches her holding some boy's hand."

I frown, trying to absorb this. I've grown comfortable enough with my assessment of Sarah Lynn as shallow and privileged that I resist adjusting my opinion.

"Bliss, not everyone's parents believe in free sex," Thelma

says, and there's a meanness to her comment that isn't a loving tease. She's punishing me for something, though I don't know what.

And then I do. It's because Mitchell smiled at me even though I'm a freshman.

I regard her. Not coldly, not as a challenge, but without an ounce of apology, either. I hold her gaze until she's the one who backs down.

"I have an itch," Jolene says, angling her spine toward me. "Will you scratch it?"

"Sure," I say. I push her brown ponytail to the side and scratch her shoulder.

"Omigosh, thank you." She wiggles. "A little lower? Little more to the left? Oh, that feels so good."

I keep what I know about Sarah Lynn and Lawrence to myself. I also remind myself that even if Sarah Lynn does have a scary strict father, that doesn't release her from the responsibility of treating others with respect. Abuse of power is wrong, no matter the context, no matter the history.

What is "power," anyway? Power is an ego trip. Power is a way to raise yourself up by lowering others, and I want nothing of it.

"Now, here at the Rock we have two rules. Memorize them until you can say them in your sleep. Rule number one: Obey all rules. Rule number two: No writing on the walls."

—Deputy Sheriff Barney Fife

he next day I take a new route to French in hopes of running into Mitchell. With my sleuthing skills—and a winning way with the secretary, who thinks I'm such a nice young woman—I've gotten my hands on his schedule. He has calculus this period, and his classroom is in Hamilton Hall. My stomach sank when I saw that. But love conquers all, right?

I am amazed to find that it does. Not that what Mitchell and I have is love; what we have is a shared smile and nothing more. (Yet.) But it turns out that I am indeed willing to face Hamilton Hall for the sake of Mitchell. Or maybe I'm unwilling to let a dead girl keep me from entering a building that dozens of students stroll into every day.

death is not forever, says the blood voice the moment I enter the building. I turn and promptly leave. And then scold myself, regain my composure, and head back in.

This time, there is no voice to deter me.

The first floor of Hamilton Hall is all hustle and bustle, and I hold myself tall. I can do this. Mitchell's schedule card says CALCULUS, HAMILTON HALL 313, and though I'm momentarily confused—I thought his class was here on level one?—I'm not about to turn back now.

I push through to the stairwell, which is far less crowded than the hall. I don't like the stairwell. But I lift and lower my feet—left, then right, then left—and I climb toward the second story.

ah, yes . . .

I stop. I listen, my senses on high alert. But I hear nothing but the chatter of the two girls behind me, so I continue.

The girls veer off at the second floor, and I find I'm alone, just as I was the day I chanced upon Lawrence and Sarah Lynn. Why is no one else heading to the third floor? The stairwell is cold, and my satchel bumps against my side.

As I step into the third-floor hallway, I register the absolute lack of life. There was no one on the last flight of stairs; there's no one in this third-floor hall. But why? The tardy bell hasn't rung yet, has it?

I press my fingers to my temples. My thoughts . . . they're not as clear as I'd like them to be.

yes, oh yes, a special place . . .

Maybe only special classes are held here, special classes for special people. I walk down the hall as if in a dream, and other dreamlike details filter in: the murky light, the unadorned walls, the musty air. To my left is a small room with a high, narrow window. Doorways to other rooms are visible ahead. This must be where the convent's initiates were housed, fourteen-year-old girls fresh from their families' farms. I imagine them chatting, praying, attending to their studies. This bleak hall must once have been full of life.

yet i am alone, my companions long gone . . .

I continue down the hall. Mitchell's not here, and I suppose I should turn back, but something in the shadows entices me to take one step farther, then another, then another. The tickle of lemons fills my nostrils, and the tingling of my skin tells me I'm stepping into the vast unseen-ness that overlays our world. It makes me feel special, that I, rather than Thelma and the others—

you are special, you hold the key

—hold the key to entering this realm.

Wait. Key? I've never thought of my gift as a key. Indeed, Flying V schooled me most sternly *not* to think of it as a key or a tool or something to "use" for gain.

It's the blood voice. I try to dislodge it. Surely I'm stronger than a shapeless, shadowy whisper.

I'll go a little farther, that's all.

At the end of the hall is a gray metal door, clearly a product of renovation. It's the sort of door that opens by pressing a metal bar, and it takes several firm shoves before the release finally clicks. I use my shoulder to push open the door, and I slip through. It bangs shut behind me.

The corridor I've entered is dark and cool, like a burial chamber. Along the hall are timber doors fit into stone, each door intricately carved with religious icons. Crosses, chalices, supplicants kneeling in prayer. The carvings are in the style of "fear me or I will smite you"— lots of thorns and anguished expressions.

I imagine the ossified gloom behind these doors, and it is almost enough to puncture the altered state I seem to be in. If I were a young girl training to be a nun, I wouldn't want Tortured Jesus carved onto my door. I'd want Friendly Jesus, the one with bunnies and little children.

Or maybe it's just the thought of being trapped *behind* one of these doors that presses in on me. Even on the commune, I didn't do well in enclosed spaces. Especially the pigeon coop. Especially in the pit of night.

It could be night here in this desolate corridor. In the outside world, the sun itself could have been snuffed out, leaving me alone save for dread spirits behind closed doors. I wish I'd never thought of entombment—what if there *are* spirits in these forgotten chambers? What if they've been waiting all this time for someone to stumble blindly down the hall?

And yet I don't turn back.

good girl special girl my girl

There are numbers on the doors, and if I strain my eyes, I can make them out. 308, 310, 312. On the opposite side of the hall are the odd-numbered rooms. Room 313 is directly ahead of me, carved with the image of a dove carrying a laurel branch.

I swallow.

open the door, that's a good girl, such a good girl

Below a dark keyhole is an iron latch, and I watch my hand rise toward it. I marvel at its movement, for I'm not controlling it. Am I?

I rattle the latch, but it holds firm. My hand drifts down, and I trace the carving of the dove. Then the fragile laurel branch. Then back to the dove, which is no larger than an egg. My fingers flutter over the delicate ridges of its wings. There's the slightest gap at the tip of one wing, a fracture in the wood. My thumbnail catches on the grain. I pull at it, and the dove moves. I wiggle the dove as I'd wiggle a loose tooth, and slowly, millimeter by millimeter, it begins to come out.

I'm pretty sure my mouth drops open, because I'm breathing differently. I can feel air moving over my lower lip.

The dove is like an incredibly well-made puzzle piece. I'm in love with the smoothness of its edges. I'm in love with the satisfying *sluice* it makes when at last it flies free.

I draw in my breath. In the space behind the dove is a key. A real key. A physical key.

you are the real key you are flesh and blood

I lift the key from its hiding spot. It's rusty and old and brings to mind clanking metal jail cells. I hesitate—

go on

—then insert it into the lock. I twist it, but it sticks. I rattle it.

84

HARDER, YOU NINNY, YOU FOOLISH—

Wh-what? I'm jerked out of my trance, only when I try to step back, I can't. My hand is glued to the key, and the key is glued to the lock. I can't withdraw it. Panic slicks me with sweat.

The smell of my own fear drowns out the hypnotic scent of citrus, and with a mighty effort I pull the key from the lock. From the dusty recesses comes a rage-filled *NOOOOOO!* I turn and run down the dark corridor, shoving both the key and the small wooden dove deep into my satchel. But when I reach the heavy metal door, I can't get it open. It's dark, so dark, and no one knows I'm up here! I could be trapped here forever!

Finally the latch releases, and I flee, my satchel thwacking the flesh below my ribs. Down the hall, down the deserted stairwell, out the door onto a neatly tended stone pathway. But this isn't where I came in, is it? I don't remember these bushes. And the stone path that leads to the newly constructed gymnasium, where we girls wear our green-and-white gym clothes . . . well, there it is in front of me. Only, that means I'm on the south side of the building, when I know I entered from the north.

I squint. Is that blood on the flagstones?

I blink again, and it's gone. Lightheaded, I lean against the wall of the building—then flinch away just as quick. I stumble across the trail and sink to the grass.

Breathe, I tell myself. *Slow down. Calm yourself.*

Trembling, I fish Mitchell's schedule card from my satchel. It's printed on Crestview letterhead, and the heavy cardstock reassures me.

Period four, it says halfway down. *Calculus. Hamilton Hall, Room 103.*

There's a rushing in my head, and I have the prickling sensation of danger barely averted. I fold the schedule in half, draw my thumbnail along the crease, and stuff it in my bag. The key and the wooden dove knock against my hand, and I reflexively yank my hand back out.

I stand up unsteadily, because I need to get to class. I need to be around others who are made of flesh and blood.

FROM *THE ANDY GRIFFITH SHOW*

"The luckiest thing a man can have
is friendship."

—Sheriff Andy Taylor

fter French—in which Madame Guittard scolds me for being tardy—I head for lunch. When I enter the cafeteria, I do a quick scan, but there is no Mitchell. No Thelma, either. Also no Jolene or DeeDee. I must still be recovering from my haunted hall scare, because my response is stomach-plunging dismay. Where *are* they?

I take in the scrum of students—minus my friends—and I think, *What if they're gone forever, their souls stolen by some unseen force?* And then: *Who will I sit with if not Thelma and the others?*

"Good, there you are," Thelma says breathlessly, rushing up behind me.

"Thelma!" I say. I give her a spontaneous hug.

"What was that for?" she asks when I release her.

"Just glad to see you, that's all. Hey—have you ever been to the third floor of Hamilton Hall?" I think of showing her the key I found.

"No, of course not," she says. She looks at me strangely and doesn't ask why. "Listen, we have a Booster Club meeting today—me and the girls—so we won't be eating in the cafeteria. I just wanted to let you know, okay?"

"Oh. Okay. Um, what's the Booster Club?"

"Just the funnest school club, that's all. We do bake sales and car washes and stuff to earn money for school events, like the Winter Dance. It's going to be far-out!"

Far-out? A dance? That I'll have to see to believe. Giggles and gossip and girl-talk sound pretty good right now, though.

"Can I come?" I ask.

She shifts. "Well . . . it's just that today is voting day."

I wait.

"New members can't vote," she explains. "And you're not even a new member. I mean, you haven't paid dues or signed the pledge or anything."

"There's a pledge to be in the Booster Club?"

"Lookit, I've got to go. The girls are waiting."

The relief I felt starts to slip away. "But who will I sit with?"

"Whoever you want," she says impatiently. "I'm not your babysitter, you know."

She hurries off, and my gaze drifts to the congested cafeteria. So many teeming bodies. So many beating hearts. Well, that's what I wanted, isn't it?

Someone walks past me, snagging my gaze. It's Sandy, the Good Samaritan who helped Gayla that day. I watch as she navigates the crowd. Her socks refuse to stay up, and her blouse is too tight, straining over the full breasts that come with being chubby. She wears a shiny yellow headband. Her face is free of makeup.

I follow Sandy hesitantly to the food line, because I've been wanting to meet her since that day with Gayla. Now's the perfect chance. I don't care that she's not pretty or popular. I certainly don't care that she's not a rah-rah Booster girl, too busy planning the Winter Dance to think about anything else. The Winter Dance may very well be great fun, but it's hardly going to change anyone's life.

A lady in a hairnet plunks a slice of meat loaf on my plate along with a serving of green beans, and I trail Sandy into the dining area. She drops into a seat at a vacant table, and the way she does it—without even scanning the other tables—tells me she's accustomed to eating alone.

My heart pounds as I approach her. "Can I sit here?"

Her head jerks up. "What?"

"I said, can I sit here?"

Her eyes narrow. "Why?"

"What do you mean, why?"

She makes an impatient sound, as if she and I both know that there are girls at Crestview who get the stamp of approval and girls who don't. Sandy falls into the second category—and yes, I suppose that distinction hasn't escaped me. I've been at Crestview more than a month now, and by standing here, I know I'm crossing an invisible line.

Yet on the commune, I was taught to open my heart to everyone.

"I just want someone to sit with," I say. "Is that a problem?"

Sandy's expression is mulish. Seconds tick by, and I feel stupid. I turn to leave.

"Wait," she says—or at least, I think that's what she says. Her voice is low.

She nudges the chair next to her with her foot, pushing it out so there's room for someone to slide in. "Suit yourself, New Girl. It's your funeral."

"Death is the greatest form of love."

—Charles Manson

unch with Sandy is different from lunch with Thelma and the others. The two of us eye each other, and chew, and eye each other some more. She's the silent sort, I decide, but I'm okay with that. I'm okay with simply being meat-loaf-eating companions. Meat loaf is essentially unthreatening, and the blood voice retreats farther away with every scrape of fork against plate.

When I join Sandy again the next day, she doesn't protest—and this time we *do* talk. It starts when I tell her, jokingly, that there must be something wrong with me since I've been ditched by not one, but two, peer mentors. Thelma's eating in the Booster Club room again, and I suppose I'm a little miffed.

"First Sarah Lynn, then Thelma," I say, sighing as if it's *so* tragic. "I'm beginning to wonder if I stink or something."

Immediately, I regret my words, remembering what Jolene told me about Sandy and the deodorant. But Sandy exhibits no discomfort—and anyway, she *doesn't* stink. Not from across the table, at least.

"Sarah Lynn?" she says. "Sarah Lynn Lancaster?"

"She was assigned to show me around, but she passed me off," I say. "Alas."

"Sarah Lynn is your peer mentor," Sandy repeats. It's a little annoying. Is Sarah Lynn so fabulous that even Sandy can't help but fixate on her?

"No, Thelma is," I say. "Not that I need one anymore. But when I first got here, I was, you know, fresh off the boat. Only the boat was really a commune."

"You lived on a commune?" Sandy says, her eyebrows arching.

Here we go, I think, but at the same time, I'm aware that I brought it up. She didn't ask; I told. And it wasn't to get her off the subject of Sarah Lynn as much as it was to test Sandy's reaction—kind of. I didn't know I wanted to until now, but I do. Is Sandy a Sarah Lynn worshipper who—because she's different—will never get the chance to taste Sarah Lynn's power? Or is Sandy her own person and proud of it, open to the idea that we all have gifts to offer?

I take a bite of pizza. "Yep, lived on a commune. Slept in a tent, wore hand-me-downs and skirts with bells. And my last name, just in case you were wondering"—I chew and swallow and say quite matter-of-factly—"is In the Morning Dew."

Sandy's normally cautious expression loosens. She laughs with relish. "You're kidding me."

"Nope." I rip off another healthy bite of pizza. "Bliss in the Morning Dew, that's me."

"What a gas. I love it."

"Do you?" I ask.

"What was it like on the commune?" She wants to know.

She leans forward and puts her chin in her hands. "Did you have run-ins with the law? Were you ever in any protests? Could anybody be whoever she wanted to be?"

I study her, this moon-faced girl with intelligent eyes.

"You really want to know, don't you?" I say.

"Are you kidding? You lived on a commune. You were willing to challenge the existing social order."

"Well, not *me* specifically."

"Of course I want to know," she asserts. "I want to know everything."

Something lightens in my chest, because it's nice to be around someone who is interested in that part of me. Except . . . what if Sandy's enthrallment stems from prurient fascination, as Thelma's did? What if all she's after is the cheap thrill of mythical bra-burnings?

"Why?" I say.

"Why do I want to hear about your life on the commune? Because it's far-out. Because living there had to be better than being stuck here at Crestview. Because I want to change the social order too."

"Ah," I say. A smile twitches at my lips.

"'*Ah*' is right," she says brashly. Who would have thought that beneath her bland exterior, Sandy was a smart-aleck? "It's all part of my plan for world domination, you see."

I let loose my grin, liking this girl who has not only strong opinions but a sense of humor too.

It was in the form of a giant cat that the Egyptian goddess Bast brought her lover back from the dead. With her massive head, she inhaled Osiris's expended life force. Then she exhaled, her mouth to his, and so restored his vitality.

Regular, when she leaps upon my chest at night, brings her face to mine and sniffs. I know it's my breath she's interested in.

Note: disposed of bird carcass, saved the bones. Perhaps I shall bring them to Agnes, who likes such things. She calls them "little offerings."

FROM *THE ANDY GRIFFITH SHOW*

"Oh, flibbertigibbet!"

—Aunt Bee

n Saturday, Grandmother goes to her Ladies Auxiliary meeting. They're planning their spring flower show.

I watch TV for a while, then grow bored and turn it off. I listen to the ticking of the grandfather clock, and I think about how with each tick, another second of my life is gone. Tick, tick, tick. I lean back against the sofa cushion and stare at the ceiling. That lasts for a minute or two, and then with a tug of my neck muscles, I pull my head forward and look at my toes.

"Hello, toes," I say. They're good toes. I like that they're long and slender and not the slightest bit stubby. I wiggle them, ten unstubby waves that say, "And hello to you, Human Host!"

Except they're toes. I'm talking to my toes. Maybe I'm not bored . . . maybe I'm lonely? I slip on my sandals and go find Rosie, who's wiping the iron railing of the front staircase. She's kneeling on the wooden stairs, her rag swooping up and over the ornate curlicues.

"Hi, Rosie," I say.

She lifts her head, but doesn't stop working. "Afternoon, Miss Bliss."

"I wish you wouldn't call me that," I say, meaning the "Miss" part. It sounds so dumb, *Miss Bliss*. Plus, Rosie's in her seventies. I should be calling *her* "Miss"—or if not "Miss" then "Missus" or "Ma'am."

Is Rosie married? I realize I don't know.

"Would you, um, like some help?" I ask. I hate seeing her there, puffing with exertion. Her knees must be killing her.

"Oh, no thank you, Miss Bliss," Rosie says.

I shift. Why is Rosie cleaning the banister, anyway? Did Grandmother tell her to? Did she say, "Today I'd like you to dust the banister?"

"Do you have a family, Rosie?" I ask.

"Yes, Miss Bliss."

"Do you have kids?"

"Yes, Miss Bliss."

I wait. She offers nothing.

"Girls?" I say. "Boys?"

"That's right, Miss Bliss," Rosie says. Her breathing is labored, and I realize I'm making her talk *and* work, when she'd much rather simply work.

"Are you sure you don't want any help?" I ask. "I'd be happy to. Really."

"No thank you, Miss Bliss. You go on, now. Go on and play."

Play. Right.

I leave the house and wander outside. Terrence, the gardener, is weeding the flowerbeds, and I watch him for a moment or two. I consider offering to get him a glass of water, but I don't. There's a plastic thermos right there beside him, beads of condensation making their slow way down its side.

I go back indoors and return to the den, where I flop onto the sofa and kick off my shoes. I grab the remote, ready for the weekend to be over.

"She's as pretty as a peach. Why, the boys ought to be buzzing around her like flies 'round a spoonful of honey."

—Aunt Bee

A t school, when Sandy laughs, I feel a hum of pleasure. Her laugh is low and deep; it sounds like a man's laugh, actually. But it feels good to draw it out of her. So good, in fact, that sometimes I say things I shouldn't, just for that satisfaction.

I fear such a moment is fast approaching. I *could* exercise restraint, but I don't. Instead, I giggle.

"What?" Sandy says. She and I are sprawled on the grass, out in the middle of the quad. We're not supposed to be. It's unladylike and against the rules. But I like to feel the earth beneath me, and I like the sense of belonging that comes from being with a fellow rebel, no matter how small the insurrection.

Also, sitting way out here keeps Hamilton Hall out of my line of vision, which is the way I like it.

"Nothing," I say.

"What?!"

"Well . . ." I jerk my chin at the path in front of us. Thelma and DeeDee are heading to class, and Thelma is giving me the evil eye. She's been put out with me for the last week. Even though I make sure to give her and Sandy equal time—I've worked out a lunch schedule, for example, where I alternate which of them I eat with—Thelma can't comprehend why I choose to spend any time at all with Sandy, not when I could be spending time with her.

I've realized that Sandy is the other girl from Flying V's vision, of course. Not Jolene, after all. I'm fond of Jolene, but Sandy pulls more out of me.

"She calls her bottom her 'ham hock,'" I confide.

"Who, Thelma?"

"Uh-huh." I'm being wicked, and I know it. Worse, I'm being thoughtless, as I remember too late that Sandy's own ham hock is twice the size as Thelma's. Three times the size.

But Thelma's skirt is twitching up the hill as if with its own self-righteous disapproval, and I can't help it. I giggle again. Sandy's laugh rolls out, gravelly with pleasure—and Thelma stiffens. Then she resumes her indignant march, her skirt twitching even more huffily.

"What a prig," Sandy says, leaning back on her hands.

"Ah, she's not so bad," I say. I realize that making fun of someone and then turning around and saying, "Ah, she's not so bad" is pretty feeble. Also, I'm a fool to set the two against each other, given Flying V's long-ago warning about a dangerous triangle. But being around Sandy brings out the devil in me, I'm afraid.

I spot Mitchell walking along behind Thelma and DeeDee, his brow furrowed as he squints at his book. He's so cute, walking and reading at the same time. He could walk right into a tree—*bam!*—and I'd find him equally adorable.

Sandy follows my gaze to see what's making me smile. "Oh, God," she says. "Tell me it isn't so."

"It isn't so," I say to oblige her. I sigh happily. "Only, it is."

"You're keen on Mitchell Truman?" she says.

I nod, and Sandy shakes her head as if I'm pathetic. Then her gaze shifts. Her mouth flattens, and I wonder who in this parade of humanity we're to be treated to next.

"Why, look," she says in a monotone as I glance over my shoulder. "It's your peer mentor."

Sure enough, it's Sarah Lynn Lancaster. Sandy has mentioned Sarah Lynn to me more than once, invariably calling her my "peer mentor" when she knows she's not. I think Sandy just likes bringing up Sarah Lynn. I think that despite her rebel leanings, she can't resist Sarah Lynn's prom-queen appeal. Or Snow Princess appeal, Thelma would say, since that's the Crestview way.

I'm not immune to Sarah Lynn's lure either, much as it vexes me. She's simply one of those people who's hard to look away from. Yesterday, I spotted Sarah Lynn with Lawrence in the Woodward Building. The two of them were chatting with some other kids, and other than the fact that Lawrence was the sole black person in a sea of white, there was nothing out of the ordinary about the scene.

But I paused. I watched. And I was rewarded by the sight of Lawrence shifting his weight so that his body bumped hers. She shot him a warning with her blue eyes, yet she didn't step away. He returned her stare for a long moment, and the intimacy of their exchange gave me goose bumps, even as shrouded and suppressed as it was. Their bond was there for all the world to see, if only anyone was paying attention.

"My *ex*–peer mentor," I say as Sarah Lynn strolls up the footpath. "Ex, ex, ex, remember?" Sarah Lynn is flanked by her constant companions, Heather and Melissa, and she doesn't look like a girl who toys with the hearts of others for fun. Then again, who would guess that under Sandy's doughy exterior lies a freethinker hungry for change?

I admire the way the sun glints on Sarah Lynn's hair. "She *is* beautiful," I admit. "Whatever else she is, she's lovely on the outside, isn't she?"

I half-hope Sandy will disagree with me, but she says nothing. When I turn to her, I see that she's pulling and pulling at a strand of her own hair, which is thin and drab compared to Sarah Lynn's.

"What's wrong?" I ask. I search her face, remembering the way everyone laughed at her when she helped poor Gayla. "Has Sarah Lynn—has she been mean to you?"

"Yes. No. I don't know," Sandy says. Her voice is strained, and I realize that Sandy is afraid of these girls.

Melissa spots us. She stops and says something that makes Heather laugh. Sarah Lynn frowns and puts her hand on Melissa's arm, but Melissa shakes her off and strides toward us. Heather jogs to catch up. Sandy's breath quickens, and I smell the tang of her sweat.

It brings back the sense memory of my own fear-drenched sweat that day in Hamilton Hall.

vapid ninnies, lock them up

I don't know what's going on—or why the blood voice is suddenly intruding. Or why that word "ninny" makes my stomach tense. But my fur rises like that of a cat protecting her young.

"Don't worry, I'm not going anywhere," I say. "I'm staying right here."

lock them up and hide the key
take what's theirs to give to me

A breeze makes me hug my torso. Tree branches in the distance sway, revealing flashes of Hamilton Hall's vacant third story. Its windows are eyes. I think of the key in the bottom of my satchel. I've kept it with me since I found it—a niggling pressure compels me to—but I'm loath to touch it or the dove again.

Heather and Melissa plant themselves in front of us. Melissa puts her hands on her hips.

"You're not supposed to sit on the grass," she states. "It's against the code."

I flash my winningest smile, while in my head I think, *Put your money where your mouth is, private-school-girl-who's-never-started-a-fire-in-her-life.* "Hi, there. I'm Bliss. I know I've seen you around, but I can't remember your name. What is it again?"

She blinks. "Um . . . Melissa?"

"Right, Melissa." I turn to Heather, still smiling. "And you are . . ."

Heather is equally thrown. This isn't going according to plan, I suppose.

"I'm Heather," she says.

"Nice to meet you, Heather." I pat the grass. "Come. Sit. Chat."

Melissa and Heather share a glance.

"Did Sarah Lynn send you?" Sandy demands.

Heather straightens her spine. "If Dr. Evans saw you, he'd write you up."

"Bluh, bluh, bluh, bluh," Sandy says, mocking Heather's intonation.

"Sandy!" I say. I stifle a shocked giggle.

"God," Melissa says. "Do you have to be so different?"

"Bluh. Bluh bluh bluh bluh bluh bluh bluh-bluh?"

Now I can't help it. I cover my mouth and laugh. Sandy's bluh-bluhs are childish and uncalled-for, but I do admire her defiance.

Then Sandy spits, and a glob of saliva lands just in front of Heather, who jumps back. She cries out in disgust, and I stop laughing. Spitting at someone—no. That's not right, even if that someone is a self-righteous pill.

"Girls . . . we're going to be late!" Sarah Lynn calls anxiously from the footpath.

"Freak," Heather says to Sandy.

Sandy juts out her tongue and blows, so that what comes out sounds like a fart. Blood rushes to my face, and I attempt to stammer out an apology. This situation has gotten out of control, and fast.

Heather cuts me off. "And you?" she says. "Thelma's no prize, but anyone's better than her." She juts her chin at Sandy.

Together she and Melissa flounce off.

I'm speechless. Sandy is sullen, but her cheeks are red and splotchy.

"What was that about?" I finally manage.

Sandy clamps shut her lips. She rips blades of grass from the lawn and tears them up.

"Look," I say. "I realize you must feel threatened by them or whatever—"

"Who says I feel threatened?" she says. "I couldn't care less what those clones think!"

"Okaaaay," I say. "And that's why you stuck out your tongue like a two-year-old and made a raspberry?"

Sandy moans and starts beating her forehead with her fists. Tufts of grass cling to her hair. Others fall free.

"Sandy, stop."

She moans and beats.

"*Stop!*" I say. I grab her wrists, and I hold tight when she resists. Finally, her hands fall to her lap. I wait until I'm sure the fight's gone out of her before I let go.

"Sandy, what's going on?" I demand.

"It doesn't matter," she mutters.

"Um, I think it does."

She doesn't answer, just sits like a lump.

"How can I help if I don't know what's going on?"

Her head whips up. "They say *why am I different*—but why do they all want to be the same? They dress like her, they wear their hair like her . . ."

"Who, Sarah Lynn?"

"And even if I tried, even if I tried my very hardest . . ." She flings out her arms. "Just look at me!"

Whoa. She said out loud that which should never be said, because it's absolutely true. Sandy will never be a Sarah Lynn. Never, ever, ever.

"I *told* you," she says. "That first day you sat with me? I told you it was your funeral."

I draw my knees to my chest and wrap my arms around my shins. Sandy peeks at me from beneath her eyelashes, which are so blond they're nearly invisible. She catches me looking and stares at the ground.

"Sandy . . ."

"I know, I know. Don't bother."

"What do you mean, don't bother? You have no idea what I was going to say."

"Sure I do."

"No, you don't, Sandy. I was just—" I break off. I guess I myself don't know what I was going to say.

Sandy's features go slack, and yet there's a dumb-animal pain in her eyes that I can't ignore. Who knows how Heather and Melissa have tortured her in the past? Sarah Lynn, too, from the sound of it. To her credit, Sarah Lynn stayed back this particular time, and she seemed uncomfortable at the way Melissa and Heather were hassling Sandy.

Still. I can see how a girl like Sarah Lynn could make a girl like Sandy feel like dirt.

"Go on, say it," Sandy says. "*Sorry, but I don't think I can be your friend anymore.*"

"Sandy, that wasn't what I was going to say," I insist. How strangely her brain works, turning at once to the idea that a friendship could so quickly turn sour. "What I was *going* to say, before you interrupted me"—I lick my lips—"was . . . do you want to come over sometime?"

Her jaw falls open. "And do what?"

"I don't know. Watch TV?"

She scrutinizes me. She pinches her bottom lip between her thumb and forefinger.

"I'm busy almost every afternoon," she says. "I have things to do."

"Okay," I say, not wanting to call her out. It makes me feel sad, though, that she'd feel the need to pretend. I stand and collect my books.

"But I suppose today could work," she says.

"Today?"

"If you meant it. Did you?"

"Of course!"

"Are you sure?"

"Sandy . . ." I can't help but smile, because she is so *Sandy*, and she'll always be Sandy, but that doesn't mean she has to be a perpetual scapegoat. She has the power to change things, if only she weren't so down on herself. "I'm *sure*."

"Fine," she says.

"Fine," I repeat.

And there it is: We're going to have a playdate.

"You have a plastic egg that may have
a thousand-dollar bill hidden in it, or
it may have a lot less. You can either
keep that, or trade it for what's behind
the large box on the display floor where
Carol Merrill is standing."

—Monty Hall, game show host

"Y ou want something to eat?" I ask Sandy in Grandmother's kitchen. A note tells me that Grandmother is once again at the Ladies Auxiliary. Rosie has left for the day, returning to wherever she calls home.

"Yeah, sure," Sandy says. It's odd to have her here, filling up space. She fingers a blue checkered dishcloth hanging from the oven. "You have any Flavor Straws?"

I shake my head. I don't know what Flavor Straws are.

"How about Ritz crackers?"

"Um . . ."

"Popcorn? Please tell me you have popcorn."

I laugh, because she's different away from Crestview. Bossy, even. "Well, let me check," I say in a tone that implies a joking *Your Highness*. I rummage through the cabinet and pull out a glass jar filled with kernels. "Is this okay?"

"I suppose it'll do."

I arch my eyebrows.

"Kidding!" Sandy says. "*Kidding.*"

"You better be," I say.

I twist the dial on the stove, then light a match. The spark catches. I slide the skillet over the heat and pour in the oil.

"Don't forget butter," Sandy says.

"Butter?" We never put butter on popcorn at the commune. Of course at the commune, we cooked popcorn over a fire—not exactly the most butter-friendly environment.

Sandy sighs and strides to the refrigerator. She pulls out a stick of butter, discards its waxy wrapper, and plops it into a small saucepan. Deftly, she lights another burner and slides the saucepan over it.

"For pouring on top," she explains.

"Yum," I say.

The first kernel pops. Then another. Then *pop-pop-pop-pop-pop*, and man, it smells amazing. The butter in the saucepan is an ooze of bubbles around a molten yellow brick. I swish it around to hasten the melting.

When the popping slows, I turn off both burners. I empty the popped kernels into a brown paper grocery bag from under the sink, and then I tilt the saucepan and dribble in the butter. When I'm done, Sandy takes the saucepan and drags her finger around its inside edge. She sticks her finger in her mouth.

"Blech," I say.

"It's just butter," Sandy says.

"I know," I say. Clementine loved butter too. We didn't have it very often, but when we did, she'd sneak slices and eat them whole.

"Then why'd you say 'blech'?"

I tilt my head. Did I actually hurt her feelings by saying "blech"?

"I was just teasing," I say. "I myself don't like to eat plain butter, but hey, it's a free world."

"Have you tried it?"

I glance at the pan, where the leftover butter is congealing into blobs. "Uh . . . no."

"Then how do you know you don't like it?"

"I guess I don't. I was wrong. Wrong, wrong, wrong."

"In Malaysia they eat dogs," she says. "You think that's gross just because you've never had it?"

I roll my eyes. I've already let her win, for heaven's sake.

"Is it because they're cute?" she goes on. "Cows are cute too, you know."

"Not that cute. Anyway, I'm a vegetarian."

"Bullshit," she says. "You eat meat loaf! I've seen you." She leans back on the counter, and her shirt stretches tight at her chest. Her breasts are enormous. "Face it: If you were born in Malaysia, you'd eat dog. If you were born in Tibet, you wouldn't eat meat at all, because you'd be a Buddhist. People do what they're told, plain and simple. They follow meaningless, boring rules and live meaningless, boring lives."

"*Ahh,*" I say. "Except for you, of course."

"That's right."

"Because you eat butter straight from the pan."

She arches her eyebrows, like *Hey, I call it like I see it.*

124

"Whatever," I say. "I'm not going to eat Snoopy just to make a statement."

Sandy laughs. It catches me by surprise, and pleasure bubbles up inside me.

"You are so weird," I say.

I take the popcorn and head for the living room, and we both plop down on the sofa.

"Nice pad," Sandy says, surveying the room. "Your grandmother's loaded, huh?"

"Not *loaded*," I say. It's so embarrassing to talk about money.

"Sharon Tate was loaded," Sandy says. "Well, her husband was, I guess. And so were the LaBiancas."

"You mean the people in California who were murdered?" I ask.

"No, I mean the *other* Sharon Tate and the *other* LaBiancas." She grabs a handful of popcorn. "You see the article about them in the paper this morning?"

I shake my head. "My grandmother doesn't want me reading about stuff like that."

"Why, because if you read about it, you might do it?" She snorts. "Yeah, you're such a killer."

"I could be," I say, for the sake of my self-respect. "I'm certainly as much a killer as *you* are."

"Pffft," Sandy says. "You're soft."

"I am not soft!"

"Bliss. You're a marshmallow. But maybe if I work with you, we can toughen you up."

"Oh, thank you so much," I say. "That's just what I want—to be a tough marshmallow. So, are you going to tell me about the article?"

"You sure you can take it?"

I shove her, and she smiles goofily. My intuition tells me that she hasn't been touched in a while.

She munches more popcorn and fills me in on the latest developments in the murder investigation. While the cops have asserted loudly and repeatedly that "counterculture influences" were at play in the slayings, they've been coy about naming names. But at last they've identified an official suspect, Sandy tells me. His name is Charles Manson. He's the leader of a cult called "The Family," and the cops think he came up with the idea of the murders and then commanded his followers to carry them out.

Charles Manson—or Charlie, as Sandy calls him—has a pretty rough past. He's been jailed for assault before, and also for stealing cars and passing stolen checks. Also for raping a prostitute.

"Which is ironic, because Charlie's mother was a prostitute," she says. "You knew that, right?"

"Um, no," I say.

"A third-rate whore, and a drunk to boot. When Charlie was a kid, she sold him for a pitcher of beer."

"Sold him? To who?"

She props her feet on Grandmother's coffee table. "And when he was in juvie? Like, ten years later?" She looks at me as if to say, *Get ready, because here comes the big one.* "He himself was raped."

"Raped? By *who*?" I'm not an innocent—Mom and Dad were pretty frank about sex—but I can't get my head around how a boy could be raped.

Sandy looks at me. Her eyebrows go up and stay up.

I still don't get it—and then I do.

"Oh," I say, feeling my face get hot.

"Uh-huh."

"That's awful."

"Uh-huh."

"But even so, even if he had the worst childhood in the world . . . that doesn't justify murdering those poor people."

"*If* he murdered those people. Innocent until proven guilty, remember?" She spits a kernel into her hand, leans forward, and places it on the coffee table. "I'm just saying it's *predictable*, that's all. It's *logical*. Pick on someone all his life and eventually he's going to fight back."

My eyes stay on the lone popcorn kernel. I've got to remember to clean up it before Grandmother gets home. Also, I should tell Sandy to take her feet off the table, or at least take her shoes off.

"Thou shalt not kill," I say softly. I get a flash of Flying V's shiny face. She used to read to me and her girls from the Bible. "It's one of the Ten Commandments."

"Uh-huh," Sandy says. "Just like 'Thou shalt not covet thy

neighbor's oxen,' which I'm sure plays an equally big role in your life. And don't forget 'Thou shalt not steal.' Don't tell me you've never stolen anything before."

This, at least, I have an answer to. "When I was nine, I stole three lemons from a neighbor's tree."

"Three *lemons?*" Sandy says. "You've got to be kidding."

"I gave them back, though."

"You gave back three lemons."

"They weren't mine. I felt guilty." *Lemons, lemons,* I think. *There's something else about lemons . . .*

"You're such a freak," Sandy says happily. "And what do you mean, 'neighbor'? I thought you lived on a commune."

"Before that, we lived in a halfway house. My dad was the social worker."

Sandy makes a sound that shows she's impressed, but she doesn't push for details. She rustles her hand in the popcorn and says, "Last year, I stole a necklace from Alice Sommersby's locker during P.E. It had a solid-gold teddy bear hanging from it. An eighth-grader wearing a teddy-bear necklace—can you imagine?"

I can't. Or maybe I can. Alice Sommersby is in my geometry class, a snub-nosed girl who wears an armband to show she's a hall monitor. She wears her hair in pigtails.

"So . . . you took it to punish her for having bad taste?" I ask.

"No, I took it to punish her for marking me tardy one day. What'd she have to do that for?"

I push off my shoes, draw my legs to my chest, and wrap my arms around my shins. I don't know what we're talking about anymore. *Yes, people should challenge conventions. No, Sandy shouldn't steal teddy-bear necklaces from snub-nosed girls named Alice.*

"Okaaay, I didn't really," she confesses, perhaps sensing my unease. "But I wanted to." She nudges the bag into my line of vision. "Popcorn?"

"No, thanks."

"Fine, more for me. *Anyway,* the man who was murdered the second night—Leno LaBianca, remember him?"

"I guess," I say.

"Well, the killers left a *carving fork* stuck in his chest. No, wait, his stomach. And they used his blood to write 'Rise' on the wall of his house."

Queasiness churns inside me. Why would anyone do that?

"As in, 'Rise up and revolt,'" Sandy elaborates. "That's what it meant. And 'Helter Skelter'? Which they wrote in blood on the refrigerator? They were saying, 'It's all going to get turned upside-down, the entire social order. Just because you're rich, just because you're beautiful . . . don't think that means you're safe. 'Cause you're not.'"

I shiver. I don't want to be the kind of girl who can't talk about this. I don't want to be a marshmallow, especially when I've already been accused of being soft. At the same time, it brings me no pleasure to imagine some poor man with a fork embedded in his stomach.

"But you don't think it *was* Charles Manson," I state slowly.

"Or his cult, or whatever. You don't think they were the ones who did all the . . . blood stuff and all that."

"Did I say that? No. I just said 'innocent till proven guilty.' If no one can prove anything . . ." She shrugs. There's a smear of butter on her lip, and her tongue flicks out to swipe it up.

"Sharon Tate, the first victim?" Sandy says. "She was pregnant."

I run my finger along the corded trim of the sofa cushion. "I know. So sad."

"I think of that baby, of that brand-new life, and I just think, 'What a waste.'"

Heaviness presses down on me. What I think of is the violence and the terror and the senseless wrongness of it.

But yes. A waste.

"You okay?" Sandy says.

I lift my head. She's gazing at me—no, staring at me, her eyes boring into me—but beneath the glitter of her pupils is pain, hot and raw. She feels the suffering of the world too, I realize. Just like me. And just like me, she hates it.

The weight on my heart doesn't go away, but I'm grateful to share this moment with her, in the way that humans do.

"So, didn't you say something about watching TV?" she asks.

Puzzled, I draw my eyebrows together.

She jerks her chin at the remote. "You have to turn it on for it to work."

"Ha, ha," I say. It dawns on me that she's kindly changing the subject, and I wonder if it's that obvious how discomfited I am by the notion of death. Guess I wouldn't make such a good killer after all.

I unfold my legs so I can stretch toward the coffee table. "Um . . . do you like *Let's Make a Deal?*"

She does, and we watch as a lady with poufy hair gives up a crisp hundred-dollar bill for what's behind a closed door, which turns out to be an oversize high chair. One of the prize models is sitting in it, dressed like a baby and sucking a pacifier. Sandy cackles.

"Did you see the one where the man gave up a thousand dollars for an ornery old goat?" she asks. "Boy, was he steamed."

"They should know not to choose the door," I say. "They should stick with what they've got."

"Ehhh," Sandy says. "You never know. Could be a zonk, could be something great."

I suppose she's right. It's like a metaphor for life: No one wants an ornery old goat, but we can't resist opening the door anyway. We can't keep from hoping.

When chained in such a way that she's unable to reach her food and water, Regular will butt her head against my hand and nip at my fingers in a near-demented frenzy. Twice she's drawn blood, and twice she's lapped eagerly at my open wound. It's as Agnes said during our most recent visit: Blood has a power that can't be denied.

"It has a name, this power," she said. "She called it blood magic."

"Who called it blood magic?" I asked. I knew already, of course. I just enjoy hearing her name.

"Liliana," Agnes confirmed. Then she took on the manner of a Sunday-school teacher, warning me from blood magic the way you'd warn a toddler from matches. So I left her in her small room, which is like a cell.

My room is also a cell, and its limitations press insistently into my awareness. The smell is of particular concern. There have been complaints.

I need a space more private, a sanctuary all my own.

I could do much with such a place.

ver the next several weeks, Sandy takes to phoning me almost every evening. Sometimes I hear a woman calling out in the background, and Sandy has to get off. Other times, Sandy talks and talks. On those occasions, I have to be the one to end the conversation, and she doesn't like it.

"You say, 'Well, I should let you go,' as if I'm the one who wants the conversation to be over," she said to me once. "Why do you do that?"

"I don't know, Sandy. Sheesh."

"If you want to get off, you should just say so. If I'm boring you, you should just say so."

"You're not boring me!" I said automatically. After that, it was even harder to end our chats. Although . . . why? Why is it so hard for me to say, "Well, gotta go"?

And Sandy isn't boring. Sandy is many things, but boring isn't one of them.

Tonight she tells me about a reward that Sharon Tate's husband has offered for any information that might lead to her killer.

"You know who her husband is, right?" Sandy says from her end of the line. "Roman Polanski?"

"A movie director?" I say. I think that's what I've heard.

"Not just any movie director. A *famous* movie director. He directed *Rosemary's Baby*, which is about a woman who's impregnated by the devil."

"Ick," I say. "Bad idea on the woman's part."

She trumpets a laugh. "Maybe—but her kid's going to have a hell of a legacy."

"*Hell* of a legacy?" I say. "Ha, ha."

"Oh, man, I didn't even mean that. It just came out."

"You're a genius."

"Aren't I?"

I shift positions. It's after nine o'clock, and I need to get off. I'm already in my nightgown.

"Do you think it's possible?" she asks. "The whole idea of devil's spawn?"

"Devil's spawn?" I say dubiously.

"Satan planted his seed in Rosemary's womb without her knowing it," Sandy says. "He made her his vessel so that his child could be brought forth into this world."

"Immaculate conception," I say, thinking of Jesus and Mary.

"Exactly! If God can do it, why can't Satan?" Sandy is getting excited. "And don't you think it's weird that the woman who was killed after Sharon Tate was named Rosemary? Don't you think that's *weird*?"

"For real?"

"For real. Leno and Rosemary LaBianca." She pauses. "I think it's a sign."

"Of what?" I say.

"I don't know. Just . . . a sign."

"I think it's sick," I say. "I hope Charles Manson gets the death penalty."

Sandy snorts, and I know her well enough to interpret its meaning.

"You don't think it'll happen?" I say. "I disagree. They said on the news that they're sure he's the one behind the murders."

"But they'll never prove it. Even if they make an arrest, the trial will go on and on. It'll last forever."

"You sound glad," I say.

"No, I'm interested, that's all. And you are too. Admit it."

"Maybe . . . but I don't want to be. And before you say it—yes, I'm soft, fine. I think we should focus on what's good in the world, that's all. People are basically good."

She makes a raspberry sound. It reminds me of the bluh-bluh day, and it must remind Sandy too, because she says, "What about Melissa and Heather? You think they're basically good?"

"Well . . . sure."

"What about your peer mentor, Sarah Lynn Lancaster?" Her voice frays, the way it always does when she brings up Sarah Lynn.

"My ex–peer mentor," I say wearily. "And I don't know, Sandy. I hope so, don't you? Maybe she—" I break off.

"Maybe she what?" Sandy says.

Maybe she was mean to you, maybe she's self-absorbed, but that doesn't make her evil. That's what I want to say, because I just don't think Sarah Lynn Lancaster falls into the same category as Charles Manson, no matter what she did to wound Sandy so deeply.

Instead I say, "Well, listen, I should probably let you—"

"Oh, come on," Sandy says.

"It's late," I plead. "I have to go to bed."

"No, you don't. Don't you want to keep talking?"

I tilt my head back on the sofa. She makes it so hard sometimes!

"You don't like it when I talk bad about people," Sandy says. "I know. But that's because you're too nice for your own good."

"Whatever," I say.

"It's okay to be honest," she goes on. "You don't have to be sweet *all* the time. And anyway, you don't know the whole story. You don't know what she . . ."

"Who? Sarah Lynn?"

Sandy pauses. Then she says, "Never mind, it's nothing. Like you said, I shouldn't talk bad about people, even people who do sick, nasty things."

I could strangle her, because of course I'm now dying to know. Sick, nasty things?

But two can play at this game, so I say, "You're absolutely right. I'm proud of you." Grandmother's slippers whisper down the stairs. "And now I've seriously got to go."

"Wait," she says. "Do you want to have a sleepover on Saturday?" She runs the words together, a train rushing past.

"Oh, Sandy . . . I wish I could."

"Never mind," she says quickly. "Stupid. Stupid!"

"It's just that I have to go shopping with my grandmother, and Saturday's the only day she has free. Afterward, we're going to go to Herrin's for dinner."

"Uh-huh. I don't care."

I feel a pang. She obviously does. "Well . . . how about Sunday? Want to do something on Sunday?"

"I'm busy," she says sullenly. "I have volunteer hours at the nursing home."

"You volunteer at a nursing home?"

"I play the harp for the residents."

"You play the harp? That's so cool." I cannot for the life of me visualize Sandy playing a harp, but I love that she does. I love that there are hidden facets to everyone's life.

"You could come with me, I guess," she says.

"I could? Um . . . okay."

"Really?"

Grandmother glides into the living room in her long pink housecoat. "Bliss, it's past your bedtime."

I cover the bottom half of the phone. "Can I volunteer at a nursing home on Sunday?"

Her eyebrows form surprised peaks. Then she nods. "I don't see why not. Do you need transportation?"

"Do I need transportation?" I ask Sandy.

"No, my mom can pick you up." She's happy now, and I think what a difference it makes in how she sounds.

"Okay, groovy. But I *have* to hang up now—my grandmother is standing right here."

"You're the one who's been talking and talking," she says.

"I am not!"

She giggles. "Good night, Bliss. Sweet dreams."

As it is the time of my monthly bleeding,
I have taken special care with my bed linens.
The bottom sheet, which was soiled, I folded
thrice upon itself and placed in Regular's
napping spot, after removing the soiled sheet
from one moon past. From the sheet removed,
I collected Regular's matted fur and placed it
in the designated container.

I think warmly of the quote from
Plutarch, in which he notes the moon power
of felines: "Though such things may appear
to carry an air of fiction with them, yet it
may be depended upon, that the pupils of her
eyes seem to fill up and grow larger upon the
full of the moon, and to decrease again, and
diminish in their brightness on its waning."

I am fortunate to have my own cycle
aligned with these tides.

helma has decided to help me with Mitchell. While Mitchell is too counterculture for Thelma's taste, she thinks it's sweet that I'm sporting such a crush. She also thinks it's ridiculous (her word) that I've had a crush on him for practically two months and have yet to make my move.

Not that *she* would ever put the moves on a boy.

"I'm just not that forward," she explained. "But you, you're more of a . . ." She struggled, biting her lower lip. Then her expression cleared. "Individual."

I wonder what other labels she considered and rejected.

"Let's review," she says today. We're at lunch—it's my day to sit with her and the girls—and Thelma folds her hands and places them on the table. "He's new this year, just like you. He's into politics. We can assume he's smart, because he takes calculus and honors English."

"He slouches," DeeDee contributes.

"True—he needs to work on his posture," Thelma says.

"You guys," I say.

"I'm serious," Thelma says. "What if you get married?

Don't you want to go to fancy dinners with him and feel proud?"

"You guys. We are not getting married!"

"I love his eyes," Jolene says. "If your kids get his blue eyes and your dark hair—wouldn't that be fabulous?"

"The thing is," Thelma says, "and yes, I know, this is the tricky part—but I'm thinking Bliss has to actually talk to him. Am I right? Before they have their brood of brown-haired, blue-eyed children?"

I swat her. "I'm not having Mitchell's children!"

"I'm sorry—what?" Thelma says.

Jolene is shaking her head and pressing back laughter. Her expression says, *Shhh, you crazy girl!*

But I don't care. If they're going to embarrass me, then I'll embarrass them right back.

"I said"—I raise my voice—"*I am not having Mitchell Truman's children!*"

Jolene turns beet red, and she and DeeDee dissolve into mad giggles.

"Um, Bliss?" Thelma says. Her gaze travels upward to someone behind me. The way she sucks on her lip makes me nervous.

"Okaaay, I think maybe I won't turn around," I announce.

A person of the male persuasion clears his throat.

"Definitely not turning around," I say. My cheeks are burning. It's freaky and alarming how much heat is radiating from one little me.

"If you change your mind, we might be able to work something out," the person of the male persuasion says.

"About the children?" DeeDee asks. "Or the turning around?"

"DeeDee!" Jolene says.

"Both," says the male-persuasion person.

I shrink in my chair, but I raise my hand over my head and wave.

"Um, hi," I say to the person behind me whom I'm still not looking at. "I'm Bliss."

Warm fingers clasp my own.

"Pleased to meet you," says the male-persuasion person. "I'm Mitchell."

"Hi, Mitchell." I try to pull my hand from his grasp, but he won't let go. "Um, bye now!"

"Not till you turn around," he says.

I tug harder. No luck. Thelma, DeeDee, and Jolene are close to peeing their pants.

Fine. I twist around and give Mitchell the quickest of glances. His expression is amused, and I grow even hotter.

He squeezes my hand, then lets go. "Just keep me in the loop if you *do* decide to bear my children. I'm happy to help out." With that, he strides jauntily to the food line.

Once he's gone, we lose it. Peals of laughter resound from our table, and the others in the cafeteria look at us funny. We laugh harder.

"Did you see?" Thelma gasps. "Did you see how *proud* he was?"

"You improved his posture!" Jolene says.

"I'm so glad, since that was my deepest desire," I say. "Oh my God, I'm going to have to quit school and become a nun."

"I can't believe you waved at him," DeeDee says.

"Your hand was like a little periscope," Jolene says. "Or, no—like a white surrender flag."

"It *was* a surrender flag. I was surrendering myself to abject humiliation."

"Oh, please," Thelma says, pulling me into a sideways hug. "Think of it this way: Now you've officially talked to him."

FROM *THE ANDY GRIFFITH SHOW*

"Fly away buzzard, fly away crow, way
down south where the winds don't blow.
Rub your nose and give two winks and
save us from this awful jinx."

—Deputy Sheriff Barney Fife

"hy'd you ditch me?" Sandy asks on the phone that night.

"I'm sorry . . . what?" I say.

"You ditched me. You sat with your girly-girl friends and talked about *boys*." She sounds like an old biddy, and I can't help but laugh.

"You're laughing at me!" she cries.

"No, Sandy, I'm not," I say. "I'm just in a good mood, that's all."

She sniffs. At first I think it's a sniff, but then it happens again, with more quiveriness, and I realize it's a *sniffle*.

"Sandy?" I ask. "You okay?"

"No. But who cares? Not you. I could fall into Satan's grave and you wouldn't care."

Satan's grave? Who says things like that?

Please let me never be so needy, I pray.

"Sandy, I don't know what you're talking about."

"You didn't sit with me."

"Yes, but I sat with you yesterday," I point out.

"You have more fun with them."

"That's not true."

"You guys were laughing at me."

"What? Sandy, we weren't. I swear!"

"Yeah, sure."

"*Sandy.* You didn't even . . . enter our realm of consciousness!"

"Oh, gee, well *now* I feel better."

I'm exasperated. "Sandy, listen."

"What?" she says belligerently.

I struggle with how to put it, because how do you tell someone that her very neediness is what makes people resist her? Sandy clings and clings, and yet—because humans aren't always the nicest—there is the urge to pry free her fingers.

"Do you think . . ." I try to be gentle. "Do you think people like it when you, you know, get so . . . ?"

"So *what?*"

"Defensive? Possessive? I don't know."

She's silent. Great, I've hurt her feelings.

"Never mind," I say.

She's *still* silent.

"Sandy?"

"They're not as *perfect* as you think they are," she says.

"Perfect? Thelma and DeeDee and Jolene?" I laugh. "I'm not either. No one is."

"*Bluh* bluh bluh," she says.

"Oh no, that again?"

She huffs.

"You have to work with what you've got," I say. "And not get so upset, or jealous, or . . . needy."

"Sarah Lynn Lancaster is perfect," Sandy states flatly.

"Huh?" She's taken the conversation in a new direction, and I have to catch up. "I thought you hated her."

"But she wasn't *always* perfect," Sandy says. "She used to be a real bitch."

"How?" I say. I'm careful to keep my tone neutral.

"She just was. In fifth grade, she made my life hell."

"Hmm," I say. In fifth grade, Sarah Lynn would have been ten. Some might dismiss the notion of a ten-year-old bitch, but not me.

When I was ten, I had a brief but intense relationship with a girl named Carmen Pagliossi, whose dad was a drug addict. That was when we lived in the halfway house. Carmen and I caught roly-polies together and braided each other's hair. We put our hands to each other's ears and whispered secrets.

And then, one day, Carmen stopped being my friend. Just like that, with no explanation. She switched to hanging out with Lucia, who'd just moved in with her hugely pregnant mother. Carmen and Lucia stole the other residents' food stamps and made greeting cards with them, which they delivered to each other through the cracks beneath their doors. I used a ruler to slide one back into the hall when no one was looking, and I pried open the envelope and read the message. It was about old Mrs. Zevin and how she smelled like fish. I'd thought maybe it would be about me.

Carmen never told me why she stopped liking me. Did I do something wrong? Was I too silly? Not silly enough? Was it bad that I liked bugs? Forever after, until Carmen and her dad left, I felt anxious whenever I saw her, like anything I did would be wrong.

So, yeah. Ten-year-old girls could be cruel.

"What did she do?" I ask, getting back to Sarah Lynn.

"She made everyone hate me, that's all," Sandy says. She breathes heavily over the phone. "She whispered about me. The teachers . . . I told them what was going on, I told them! But they said, 'Not Sarah Lynn. I don't believe it.'"

"Well, that's awful," I say. "But Sandy, that was four years ago."

"She told people things," Sandy insists. "She said things."

"Like what?"

I hear a moist sound, as if Sandy is wetting her lips. I switch the phone to my other ear.

"I had a slumber party," she says. "I sent out invitations and everything, with buttons glued on them, and bows. I invited every single girl in my class. Guess how many came?"

Uh-oh.

"Zero," Sandy says.

"Oh, Sandy."

"For our activity, we were going to make garlands out of flowers. I was going to let Sarah Lynn be the princess, and we'd be her ladies-in-waiting."

"Even though she was so mean to you?"

"But no one came. She *told* them not to."

I grip the phone. I'm sad for her; I'm sad for me. My Mitchell-giddiness is gone with the wind.

On the other end of the line, I hear a woman calling out.

"Hold on," Sandy says to me. Then she raises her voice. "Just a sec—I'm almost done!"

"I've been waiting and waiting," the woman says querulously.

"Five more minutes? Please, Mam?"

"*Waa!* I'm ready for my bath!"

"Sandy, it's totally fine," I say uncomfortably. "Your mom needs you. You should go."

Sandy doesn't respond.

"*Is that your mom?*" *And why does she need you to give her a bath?* I want to add.

"Are you still coming to the nursing home with me on Sunday?" she asks.

I sigh. "Yes, Sandy, I'm still going to the nursing home with you on Sunday."

"Promise?"

"I *promise*. The only reason I won't will be if you keep bugging me about it." I laugh a little to show I'm joking— except I'm kind of not.

She must sense my impatience, because she says, "It's just . . . you don't understand."

"I don't understand what?"

Her tone turns whiny. "What it's like to be different."

At that, I laugh for real. "Are you kidding? Sandy, I lived on a commune, and before that, in the basement of Oregon State University. Before that, in a halfway house full of druggies and pregnant women."

"You lived in the basement of Oregon State University? You never told me that."

"That's because there's nothing to tell." I think of the lab rats in their cages, which my parents were so determined to free. "It was dark and it smelled. End of story."

"*Sandra Lurlene Lear!*" comes the voice in the background. "You will *not* disrespect your mother!"

"Bye," Sandy says quickly, and hangs up.

The sudden silence is a relief, but as I return the phone to its cradle, I consider what it says about me that I'm glad to get off the phone with my friend. Back on the commune, I would have fainted in happiness at the thought of having a friend to chat and gossip and giggle with. Now I have not one friend, but several, and I seem to find fault with all of them.

How ugly that knowledge is. How shameful. And my eagerness to hear the details of Sarah Lynn's bad behavior? Now that I'm out of the moment, I'm sickened by myself.

It's been a long time since I've thought about Flying V's hazy warning, but as I slump against the sofa, it resurfaces. *Girls your age can be cruel*, she said. I assumed she meant other girls, but now I see that there's more than one way to interpret her remark.

For the first time, I wonder if coming to Atlanta has changed me—not just in surface ways, but deep down at the core. There's a hardness inside me I'm not accustomed to. Or, not a *hardness*, exactly. More like a new level of awareness, an awareness that involves passing judgment.

On the way home from school today, I saw a girl (not from Crestview) who wasn't wearing a bra. Who *clearly* wasn't wearing a bra, as in lots of bouncing action and look-at-me nipples. And it shocked me, and I wanted to say to her, *What are you doing strolling down Peachtree Road like that? This is Atlanta, not Woodstock!*

I also thought she should wash her hair, and that her leather sandals looked embarrassingly rough-hewn.

Two months ago, that could have been me.

If a female is bold, should she quell her assertiveness? If a female is strong, should she hide her strength?

Not so long ago, females of power were branded as witches and burned at the stake. But before that, they were known as goddesses. Note the correspondence: Goddesses were intimately linked with felines; witches, too, had "familiars" who took the form of cats.

Regular is my familiar. She suckles my blood. On one occasion, as we lay together in the night, she attempted to suck from my nipple. It tickled but didn't hurt.

"One: Don't play leapfrog with elephants.

Two: Don't pet a tiger unless his tail
is wagging.

Three: Never, ever, mess with the Ladies
Auxiliary."

—Mayberry Rules for a Long, Happy Life

n Saturday, Grandmother and I head off for our day of shopping. We take the Cadillac. I ride in the front seat like a princess, which makes me think of Sandy and her failed slumber party, which I promptly cast from my mind. No sadness today—today is all about fun and money-spending.

When we get downtown, I marvel at the impossibly tall buildings. My neck pops as I take in the shiny surfaces and the blue sky way far up. Men in sport coats stroll along the sidewalk with ladies in pastel skirts and matching heels. The men look tolerantly amused, while the women sparkle with the excitement of being on an outing. The women all have bouncy hair.

"Come along, Bliss," Grandmother says. "Regenstein's first. I need to exchange a scarf."

I follow her into the store. Then I stop, stunned by its grandeur.

"Bliss?" Grandmother calls. She pauses by the jewelry counter. "Bliss! No dilly-dallying, please."

"Oh! Sorry!" I say. It's just . . . it's so huge! The ceilings are twenty feet high, and there are mannequins and clothing displays everywhere. The salesclerks are lovely. The air is perfumed.

I trot to catch up, and Grandmother leads us to the accessories department.

"What about this?" she asks, lifting a chiffon scarf that looks nearly identical to the one she's brought with her.

"It's pretty," I say.

"Isn't it?" She shifts the fabric so the threads catch the light, then smiles at me. I feel a glow of pleasure.

After she makes the exchange, we go to Rich's, which is even grander then Regenstein's. It's four stories high, which boggles my brain. Cosmetics, fragrances, shoes. Linens, towels, housewares. Anything you could possibly want!

The junior-miss department is on the third floor; we take two separate escalators to get there. On each, Grandmother checks her reflection. She's funny how she does it. She steps onto the escalator, then glances oh-so-casually to the right, where a long, shiny mirror extends from floor to ceiling. Her eyebrows arch—*Why, look, it's me!*—followed by a trained pat to her hair and smoothing of her dress. Strangely, these grooming rituals make me like her better. Or maybe what I like is her eyebrow gesture, as if she happened on her reflection by accident and was just as surprised as anyone.

When we reach the third floor, Grandmother steps confidently off the escalator, while I worry about catching the toe of my shoe and give a last-minute hop. I'm not so good at escalators. The disappearing metal slabs seem beastlike with their sharp teeth.

"Let's start with the sales rack," Grandmother says, weaving through the carpeted aisles. She holds up a fitted white blouse with tiny pearl buttons. "How about this?"

"Um . . ." It's almost identical to my school uniform blouses, and I'm not sure why I'd get the same exact thing as I already have. "I guess I was hoping . . . could I get some jeans? New ones—not all tattered—and maybe a peasant blouse or something?"

"It would be precious with this skirt, don't you think?" She checks the tag and frowns. "Well. Better keep looking; they've only got it in a two."

She's so sure of herself in this land of feminine attire. She knows the language, and she knows how to slide the hangers against the steel rod so that they whisper shh, shh, shh.

Mom and I shared few shopping excursions, and I can't recall ever going to a store where you handed over money and were in return given a crisp paper bag with curved paper handles, like Grandmother's Regenstein's bag. Mom and I got our clothes at festivals, where men and women spread out their wares on quilts. We did a lot of trading, which is how I got my jingle bell skirt. Also, I got a lot from the Goodwill bins, where we paid a quarter for five pounds of clothes.

"How about this one?" Grandmother says, freeing a light green blouse.

I glance at the shirt, which also has a Peter Pan collar and capped sleeves.

"It would look pretty with your eyes," she says. The unexpected compliment triggers a wave of loneliness, and I edge closer, craving . . . something. I don't know what.

Grandmother awkwardly pats my arm. "You have lovely eyes, Bliss. Just like your mother."

"Do you miss her?" I blurt. I know this is against the rules, but I can't help it.

She takes her time putting back the blouse, and then she says, "Of course I do." She searches my face. "Do you?"

Tears burn my eyes. Grandmother sees, and her own eyes respond in kind, tears to tears.

A woman pushing a stroller cuts through the aisle to our left, and our bubble of connection pops. I swipe my eyes as the toddler reaches for me.

"I'm sorry," the woman says, attempting to pry her daughter's chubby fingers from my skirt. The moment she succeeds, her daughter grabs me with her other hand.

"Nancy," her mother says. "Let go."

Nancy clutches tighter. "Me say hi."

Her mother rolls her eyes, but it's clear she finds her daughter utterly adorable. "Go ahead, then. Say hi."

Nancy beams at me. "Hi, puppy."

"She's not a puppy. She's a girl," Nancy's mother says.

Nancy pats me and says, "Good puppy. Nice puppy." When her mother bends down to pull her away, she wraps both arms around my leg and wails. "No! *My* puppy!"

"Oh, Nance," her mother says. To Grandmother and me, she says, "I'm so sorry."

"No problem," I say. I like this goofy kid. I like her warm, sticky hug; I haven't gotten many hugs recently. My smile feels wobbly, but probably in a way that only I can sense.

"Nancy, let go of the nice girl *now*," her mother says. Above Nancy's head, she gives us a look that conveys loving exasperation. "What can I say? She's a spirited child."

"Bless her heart," says Grandmother, which in the language of the South implies not one ounce of actual blessing. She turns to me with pursed lips. "Bliss?"

Reluctantly, I extricate myself from Nancy's grasp. Nancy wails, and Nancy's mother, who has discerned Grandmother's lack of approval, quickly wheels her off.

Grandmother follows them with her gaze. "And there are things about your mother I *don't* miss," she says.

It takes me a minute to understand. When I do, I grow hot with shame. Mom isn't a toddler, and neither am I.

Grandmother selects another blouse. "Now," she says, "what do you think about this one?"

FROM A TV COMMERCIAL FOR LADY CLAIROL
CRÈME HAIR LIGHTENER

"If I've only one life . . .
let me live it as a blonde."

After purchasing my new clothes—two blouses, two skirts, and, astonishingly, one pair of flared jeans—Grandmother treats me to the Ladies' Luncheon in the Magnolia Room. We have frozen fruit salad, fried chicken, and homemade yeast rolls. We wash it down with sweet tea. The meal restores Grandmother's mood, and she suggests we stop by the Lancôme counter before going back home.

"I always enjoy seeing what their bonus is," she says.

I don't know what that means, but I say, "Sure, okay."

"Hmm," Grandmother says when we reach the cosmetics department. She sorts professionally through the contents of the black-and-white pouch on display by the "Gift with Purchase" card. "The blush isn't a shade I would use. The lipstick might work."

"Have you tried our new foundation?" the salesclerk asks. She reaches over and takes the sample from the pouch. "It's formulated with vitamin E, which is excellent for maintaining elasticity."

I lean against the counter. Flying V was a big fan of vitamin E, squishing it from golden capsules and smearing it on Daisy and Clementine's cuts.

"And what's the minimum purchase?" Grandmother asks.

"Eight dollars."

"Well, I hate to spend so much on myself . . ."

The saleslady brings forth other products. She squeezes a dollop of lavender-scented lotion onto the back of Grandmother's hand, and Grandmother brings her hand to her nose and inhales.

Grandmother and the saleslady discuss, their voices like hummingbirds. Grandmother turns to me. "Bliss, why don't you pick something?"

"I'm sorry . . . what?" I've tuned out and have no idea what's expected of me.

"Go on, Bliss," Grandmother says. When I hesitate, Grandmother makes a tch-ing sound. To the saleslady, she says, "Bliss is my granddaughter. Her upbringing has been . . . unconventional."

"I see," the saleslady says. Her expression suggests she doesn't.

"I wonder if we could do a full work-up," Grandmother says, "given that I doubt she's had a makeover in her life. What do you think, Bliss? How does that sound?"

It sounds terrifying. A full work-up?

But Grandmother is waiting, and I sense that she sees this as a treat she's offering.

"Hop on up here, sweetie," the saleslady says. She pats a stool in front of the counter. "This will be fun."

I climb up and smooth my skirt over my legs. "So . . . what do I do?"

The saleslady laughs. "Just sit and enjoy! That's all there is to it."

She clips my hair back with two large bobby pins. "This toner will remove excess oil without stripping your skin of essential moisture," she says, dabbing my forehead with a moist cotton ball. "Are you currently using a cream-based cleanser or a gel?"

"I just use Ivory," I say.

"My, my," she saleslady says. She studies me and says, "I would recommend our creamy cleanser for combination skin. Your T-zone is one of your challenge areas, but you don't want to overdry the skin around your mouth."

"I don't?"

"No, dear."

"Absolutely not," Grandmother confirms.

"Oh," I say. And here I've been so pleased with the Ivory I discovered in the bathroom cabinet. It's a vast improvement on Flying V's homemade lye soap, that's for sure.

The saleslady dots moisturizer on my cheeks and around my lips. "There. That will address the patchiness without promoting further breakouts."

Patchiness? Further breakouts? I look at myself in the mirror, which magnifies my face to three times its normal size. My nose is shiny from the toner, and there does seem to be some flakiness around my mouth. Gross.

"Shall we try some concealer?" the saleslady says. "Even out those skin tones?"

I try not to fidget as she layers on concealer, foundation, and blush. Grandmother watches from over her shoulder and supplies a stream of commentary.

"*Vast* improvement," she says to the saleslady after she strokes on a second coat of mascara. "She's got such funny, stubby eyelashes, doesn't she? She gets them from her father." And later, "Such a pretty girl, if only she'd take advantage of it. These women's libbers, they forget what power a woman can have. A woman's looks are a woman's best weapon, if only she's smart enough to use them."

Grandmother brushes back a wisp of my hair that's escaped from the bobby pin, and I feel a mix of emotions. I'm pleased she thinks I'm pretty, but I'm dismayed by the thought that being pretty is a woman's best weapon. Weapon against what?

The saleslady fills in my lips with a pink lipstick that smells like bath beads. I need a break from my oversize reflection, so I glance out at the growing number of people browsing the aisles. I spot a familiar face, and my heart skips a beat. It's Sarah Lynn Lancaster. She's with Melissa and Heather, the girls from the quad that day.

Sarah Lynn is laughing, her eyes bright, and I watch as she nudges Melissa and points at a mannequin wearing a plaid miniskirt. Heather says something that makes Melissa squeal, and Sarah Lynn laughs harder.

My shoulders scrunch in, as does the space behind my breastbone. I watch Sarah Lynn strike a pose beside the mannequin, jutting her hips and pursing her lips, and I don't know what's going on inside me, just that it's twisty and confusing. Then, with a jolt, I recognize it for what it is: jealousy. I'm *jealous*, and I absolutely didn't see it coming.

I've noted her beauty, of course. I've wished my hair was as glossy as hers. But my primary response to Sarah Lynn, until this moment, has been fascination combined with disdain.

Looking at her now, I feel . . . *less than*, and it dawns on me my jealousy is related to the whole "being pretty" conversation. Sarah Lynn is what "being pretty" is all about, and it's so much more than her features, her makeup, her clothes.

That's why Lawrence looks at her with such piercing intensity, as if he would die for her. That's why Melissa and Heather act as her handmaidens. That's why Thelma claims to be her "pretty much best friend," when their interactions have been few and far between.

Is that why Sandy hates her so? Hatred can certainly spring from jealousy—and such jealousy isn't *pretty* at all.

"Don't jerk," the saleslady chides. She steps back, lipstick held aloft. "So do we like this shade, or do we want to try something more dramatic?"

I don't respond, because somehow, unbelievably, Sarah Lynn is walking toward me. She lifts her hand and calls, "Hey, what's up?"

My pulse quickens. "Um, not much," I manage. "What's up with you?"

Her brows draw together. Then she widens her eyes and says, "Oh. Hi."

Her gaze flickers to a spot behind me, and I twist around to see Lacy McConnell at the perfume counter. Lacy of the briefly pierced ears. Lacy who goes out with Burt, the captain of the football team.

Lacy hides her smile with her hand. But good breeding dictates politeness, at least on the surface, so she comes over to the Lancôme counter. Pretending my faux pas was no big thing, she says, "Hi, I'm Lacy."

"I'm Bliss," I say, wanting to melt into the chair. Having Grandmother here does not help. Sarah Lynn joins us, and having her here doesn't help either.

"Bliss," Sarah Lynn says. She makes a face. "I'm so bad with names."

Now Melissa and Heather come over. They don't make eye contact with me.

"Come with us to Woolworth's," Heather says to Lacy. "I'm absolutely aching for a cherry Coke."

"Sure," Lacy says. "Just let me pay for my perfume."

The four of them head for the cash register. Halfway there, Sarah Lynn turns around. "Bliss? Want to come?"

Her invitation is genuine, I'm almost positive. I know her motivation has little to do with wanting to spend time with me and a great deal to do with wanting to make me feel less stupid about my gaffe. But even so, it's an act of kindness, isn't it?

It is. Her expression, as she waits for my reply, is friendly.

"No, thanks," I say nonetheless.

Sarah Lynn hesitates, and Heather grabs her arm. "She said she doesn't want to. Come on."

I turn back toward the makeup counter, telling myself I was right to decline.

It was nice to be asked, though. And maybe it wasn't just kindness. Maybe Sarah Lynn saw something in me that made her think she *might* want to hang out with me, and not just out of pity.

Then I see my reflection in the round mirror. *Oh, God.* Wide, startled eyes and shiny pink lips, plump as jellied candies. Hair clipped back. Forehead paler than a night crawler.

I feel sick all the way to my bones.

"Shall I ring up the concealer?" the saleslady asks.

"I think yes," Grandmother says.

"Excellent. And what did you decide about the mascara?"

"Bliss?" Grandmother asks. "What do you think?"

I reach into my hair and tug at the bobby pins. One of them sticks, and I have to yank it free before flinging it on the counter.

Grandmother and the saleslady share a glance.

"Bliss," Grandmother says.

Humiliation burns through me.

"Oh, why not," Grandmother says. "We'll take the mascara and the lipstick, too. And of course my gift-with-purchase."

"I'm trying to say that this period of life which we all go through, the teenage period, is a very frightening time."

—Miss Helen Crump, Opie's teacher and Andy Taylor's girlfriend

"Scoot over," Sandy says.

"I *am* over," I say.

Sandy glances over and sees that sure enough, I'm squished to the size of a flea against the passenger-side door of her mom's station wagon. She laughs her man-giggle.

"Oh," she says. "Sorry."

Mrs. Lear, Sandy, and I are crammed together in the wide front seat of Mrs. Lear's station wagon, along with a bag stuffed with buttons, felt, and fake fur, which somehow ended up in my lap. Behind us—the backseat folded down to make room for it—lies Sandy's harp. Also, Mrs. Lear's walker. Mrs. Lear is a sour-faced woman, thin and hunched, and she smells of whiskey, though I could be wrong.

Be nice, I tell myself. I clear my throat and say, "So, Mrs. Lear, you're going to a crafts class?"

"*Waa*," she says. It's the scolding caw of a crow. "Yes, yes, I already said that. Pint-size teddy bears. I plan to make three."

"Oh," I say. "Um, cool."

"I'll put them in the bathroom." She shoots me a sidelong glance. "Last week, we carved radishes into tiny rosebuds."

"Yeah?"

"Week before, we made Bibles out of bars of soap." She sounds angry about it. Not just the soap-bar Bibles, but all of it.

"Well, um, that's nice."

"*Waa*," she says, disgusted.

Beside me, Sandy turns deliberately from her mother and says, "Tell me again what Sarah Lynn said to you."

"Oh, I don't know," I protest.

She makes praying hands, a feat in this cramped space. "Please?"

The story of my run-in with Sarah Lynn has proven quite a hit. Sandy's the ideal audience, and I'm not so dumb as to take her gleeful indignation as an accurate read of the incident. But I guess my ego needs nursing.

"She said she was bad with names," I say, trotting out the critical details one more time.

Sandy chortles. "Yeah, sure, like 'Bliss' is a name you could forget. And then she asked if you wanted to get a Coke?"

"A cherry Coke," I confirm. "But Heather was the one who brought up Woolworth's. Sarah Lynn just asked if I wanted to come too."

"All sticky-sweet, 'I'm-so-nice, I'm-a-little-princess,' right? When she didn't even know your name. Good one, Sarah Lynn! Real believable."

"*Waa!*" Mrs. Lear interrupts. "This is why you have no friends. So judgmental!"

Sandy blushes, yet she keeps on as if she didn't hear. "What was she wearing? A micromini?"

"Um . . ." I remember Sarah Lynn's kind expression, but I don't remember her outfit.

"If she wore a micro, it was probably Heather's or Melissa's. I bet she had to sneak it on after she left her house."

"So *catty*," Mrs. Lear rebukes. "What do you care what she wore?"

"I think she wore just a normal skirt," I say.

Sandy leans close and breathes into my ear. "Bet she wears fancy little panties, don't you? With ruffles along her ass, and when she bends over to pick up a lipstick that she *accidentally* dropped—*oops!*" She pitches her voice to a falsetto. "*Oh my goodness, oh my gwacious! Did anyone see my widdle bottom?*"

Mrs. Lear smacks her. "Nasty!"

I sink in the seat. This is the first time my story has prompted references to Sarah Lynn's "widdle bottom," and I vow not to tell it again.

"I was just teasing," Sandy says petulantly. She points out the window. "There's the turn." She raises her voice. "I *said* there's the turn!"

The tires squeal as we veer into the Eternal Fountains parking lot. For a long second Sandy is thrown against me, and then we rock back into place.

Mrs. Lear stops the car, and Sandy nudges me with her thigh. "We're here. Get out."

I open the door and step into the sunlight—oh, it's good

to be free of the car—and Sandy pushes past me to the back of the station wagon. First she unloads a special wheeled cart. Then she tugs at her harp. Mrs. Lear's walker thunks as it's dislodged.

"A little help, please?" Sandy says over her shoulder.

I dart forward and grab the harp's base, and we maneuver it onto the cart. Sandy shuts the trunk, and Mrs. Lear roars off.

"Um, thanks for the ride!" I call.

The station wagon expels a cloud of smoke.

Sandy pulls the cart toward the nursing home, and I jog to catch up.

"Why does your mom use a walker?" I ask.

"To help her walk," Sandy says.

"Yes, thanks," I say. "But why does she need help walking?"

She steals a glance at me. "You really want to know?"

"Yes." I hesitate. "I mean, why wouldn't I? Is it bad?"

"'Course not. Charming story, sure to delight."

"If it's something private, then never mind."

Sandy sighs. "If you must know, she has chronic back problems from a car accident."

"Oh, I'm so sorry."

"Yeah? Well, get ready to be even sorrier: It was my fault."

"It *was*? How?"

"I was six, and she and I were on the way to the grocery. Except we hadn't left yet. Mam's door was still open."

Her tone stays light, as if we're discussing a new hairstyle. Not that Sandy and I would ever discuss hairstyles, unless it was Sarah Lynn's, and unless Sandy was making fun of it.

"You don't have to tell me," I say.

"You asked, didn't you?" She heaves the front edge of the cart over a cement step. "Mam dropped the grocery list. She leaned to get it, and while she wasn't looking, I shifted the car into reverse."

"Oh, no."

"Mam fell out. The car rolled over her."

I suck in my breath, and air whistles over my teeth.

"It gets worse," Sandy says. "I just sat there, see? With Mam pinned beneath the car."

"Well . . . you were six," I say.

"Six-year-olds know how to go inside and use the phone," she says. "Six-year-olds know that when someone's screaming in agony, chances are that person needs help."

"You were a kid! Oh, Sandy, you must have been terrified."

"I suppose. I don't really remember."

"But your mom . . . she can still walk and everything?"

"As long as she uses the walker," Sandy says. "But she doesn't like it. Can we stop talking about it now? It's so embarrassing."

Embarrassing—not the word I would have chosen. Her attempt at bravado makes me feel tender toward her, and I think, *No wonder she hates life's cruelties. No wonder she helped Gayla that day.*

182

We reach the entrance to the nursing home, and Sandy shoves open the door with her shoulder. The cart gets lodged in a metal ridge at the door's base, and the harp totters.

"Whoa," I say. I hurry to her side, and together we steady the harp and ease it over the hump.

FROM A CANDY PRINT ADVERTISING CAMPAIGN

"The really GOOD
five-cents caramel bar!"

—Snirkles

Sandy signs in at the front desk, and the receptionist says, "Knock 'em dead, doll." I follow her down a wide hall to the recreation room, where twenty or so old people sit in a semicircle. Most of them seem out of it, staring into space or slumping in their wheelchairs. One old lady gazes at the floor with her mouth half open. With a sudden twitchlike motion, she flings her leg up and over the arm of her wheelchair, exposing the flesh of her thigh. An aide steps over and coaxes the leg back down. I look away.

I guess I'm not so accustomed to old people, other than Grandmother.

Then again, I'm not completely accustomed to Grandmother. So never mind.

Sandy wheels her harp to the center of the room, and the more alert residents shift and stir.

"Wake up, Doreen," one lady says, shaking the arm of her friend. "It's Sandy, here with her harp."

"Oh, Sandy," says another lady. "Will you play the Pachelbel, dear? So lovely. A gift from sweet Jesus."

One of the few old men, skinny and frail with pants that come up to his rib cage, puts his fingers to his mouth and whistles. "One hunner percent woman," he calls out.

Sandy grins. "You got that right, Oscar."

"Sandy!" I say in a scandalized voice. But of course I'm delighted.

"Oscar, hush," says the Jesus lady, who isn't. "Go bother the nurses if you're after a ruckus."

Sandy sets up her harp, then strides to the side of the room and grabs an empty chair. She's more confident here than she is at school. She plunks the chair behind the harp, sits down, and spends a few minutes fooling with the strings. Then she starts to play.

I find a place against the wall. Sandy pushes her tongue around in her mouth while she plucks, but the sounds that rise from her harp . . . they're lovely. Again I'm struck by how unpredictable our world is, a world in which lumpish girls make beautiful music while beautiful girls turn others into lumps.

I slide my spine down the wall until I'm sitting on the floor. I close my eyes and listen, and it's such a release to be transported from my humming, overworked brain. I'm a transparent dot floating in the universe. I'm not thinking about fancy panties; I'm not thinking of cherry Cokes. Or fine, maybe I *am*, but not with the same urgency as before. *Good-bye, panties! Fly away! Fly away, thirst-quenching cherry Cokes!*

I'm glad for Sandy, that she has this inside her.

Sandy plays four songs. The notes of her last selection flow out in a rich, final-sounding succession, and her hands hover above the strings until the tones die away. There's a moment of stillness, and then Sandy smacks her hands to her knees.

"That's it," she says. "Time's up."

The residents who are still awake beam and clap their hands. The others jerk upright, blinking and stirring. An old lady plucks at the blanket in her lap and says, "It's too cold in here. Somebody turn up the heat."

I stand and go over to Sandy, who's wrestling her harp back onto its cart.

"Heavenly, heavenly," the Jesus lady says, hovering by Sandy's side. "Our own dear angel."

Another resident tugs Sandy's sleeve. "My granddaughter plays the flute," she says.

"No, Doreen," scolds the Jesus lady. "That's *Larissa* who plays the flute, my oldest boy's girl. You don't have any grandchildren."

"So selfish," Doreen tells the Jesus lady. "Selfish, selfish, selfish."

"I'm selfish for telling the truth?" the Jesus lady says.

"And you cheat at bingo, always stealing the banana."

"I don't *steal* the—" Jesus lady breaks off. She huffs. "If there happens to be a banana on the prize cart, I take it. Is that a crime?"

"Selfish banana-stealer," Doreen says.

So this is what it's like to be old, I marvel. *Why, it's no different from high school.* But I get plenty of high school on my own, so I tear myself away from their conversation and focus on Sandy.

"That was great," I say. I pause, wanting to give more. "You were great."

Sandy shoulders the harp toward the hall. I trot along behind her. She pulls up short to avoid a nurse carrying a high stack of towels, then starts walking again.

"You liked it?" she says. "Really?"

"You were amazing," I say.

"Hah," she says. "Shows how much you know."

Leave it to Sandy to flip a compliment upside-down.

"So . . . what now? Are we done?"

"Not yet. Some of the residents can't get out of bed anymore, so we're going to do a couple of room visits."

She raps on a half-open door. "Wake up, Elsie. It's Sandy." She pushes through without waiting for an answer.

"Come *on*," she says, looking back at me.

Inside the room, the lady in the bed smoothes her quilt with nervous pats. Her white hair sticks up in a puff around her head, and pale pink earrings hang from her ears like oversize buttons. "Sandy," she says. "I'm a bit tired today."

"Want me to leave?"

"No, no. Stay." She gestures at me. "Who's this?"

"No one," Sandy says, and I make a sound of indignation. I'm a little stung, to tell the truth. That's who I am to her? No one?

"Just someone from school," she says, shooting me a look that says, *Don't get your knickers in a wad. Geez.* "I'm going to play now, okay?

Like in the recreation room, the music takes over when Sandy starts plucking. She plays Pachelbel's Canon for a second time, but she plays some new songs too. Hymns, I think.

Elsie flutters her fingers along with the music. Her eyelids droop as Sandy comes to the end of her set, but snap open the instant Sandy stands to go.

"One more," she says.

"Sorry," says Sandy. "I've got other residents to play for."

"Hmmph," Elsie says. "I know who you mean, and I don't know why you bother."

Sandy tightens her jaw.

Straining forward, Elsie fumbles with the drawer of her bedside table. "Here, have some candy before you go."

She holds out a cardboard box of Snirkles candy bars, and Sandy takes one despite her apparent irritation. I take one too.

"Thanks," I say.

But in the hall, after I've ripped mine open and taken a bite, I spit it into a trash can.

"Igh," I say. "The caramel is *crusty.*"

"Because it's about a thousand years old," Sandy says. She chucks her candy bar into the trash as well, then reaches into her pocket. "But check this out."

In her hand is a twenty-dollar bill. I look at it, then at Sandy.

"Don't worry," Sandy says. "She didn't notice."

"Who?" I ask. Then comes the bad feeling. "Elsie?"

Sandy smiles triumphantly.

"*Please* tell me you didn't steal from that sweet old lady," I say. "Twenty dollars, that's like . . ." I swallow. "That's a lot of money, Sandy!"

"Elsie doesn't care." She stuffs the bill back in her pocket. "And she's not sweet."

"Sandy, go give it back."

Sandy takes both of my hands, which utterly shocks me. Her palms are moist.

"Bliss, don't you ever want to be *more?*"

I try to pull away. "What do you mean? More what?"

"More. Just . . . *more.* More than what society says you should be, more than a stupid rule-follower. You know who the rules are made to protect, right? Not me. Not you. They're made for the people who already have everything, that's who."

"Like Elsie?"

Anger darkens her face. "You don't know her like I do."

"She's an old lady, Sandy. An old lady you just *stole* from." I free my hands.

Sandy starts down the hall with the harp. The set of her shoulders tells me she isn't pleased with me. Well, I'm not pleased with her, either, and I press my lips together as I take a loping step to catch up with her.

"Bliss, listen," she says.

"Give Elsie her money."

"You know that expression, 'The scales fell from his eyes'?" she asks.

Of course I do. It's from the Bible, which means I heard it from Flying V on more than one occasion. I'm not interested in discussing it now, though.

"For real, Sandy," I say. I follow her, but only to make her do the right thing. "Turn around."

"It's what you say when someone's blind to reality, and then something happens and they're not," Sandy says. "The scales fall from their eyes and they realize how . . . *illusory* everything is."

"So that twenty-dollar bill was an illusion? Wow, good trick."

She draws up short, and I nearly run into her. "You're deliberately not understanding," she says. "All the rules we're taught, the only reason they exist is so the people in power can keep the rest of us down. But the rule-makers don't follow the rules themselves, because why should they? Rules are just words. That's all. And once you realize that . . ."

Her expression is no longer angry, but beseeching. "Bliss, it liberates you."

"I don't need to be liberated."

"But you do." She says it with the fervor of a visionary, and for a disjointed second I doubt the certainty of my position. Is it possible she sees something I don't?

Then I reclaim my sanity and think, *She is so full of it.*

"Kitten?" a weak voice asks. I turn toward the sound, which is coming from inside room 13. On the door is a construction paper heart that says "Agnes Nutter."

"One sec," Sandy calls. To me, she says, "That's Agnes." Her tone is admiring, a quality I don't often hear in Sandy. "You're going to love her."

"Actually, I'm going to go," I say.

"What? No! You've got to meet Agnes. You *have* to!"

"I can meet Agnes another time," I say, knowing full well there won't be another time.

"Wait. I'll return the money, okay?" She abandons her harp and drags me back the way we came. She plants me in front of Elsie's room and pulls the twenty-dollar bill out of her pocket. She waves it in the air. Then she goes into Elsie's room, pushing the door wide so I have full view of her actions.

"Me again," she says, slapping the bill on Elsie's dresser. Elsie startles awake and strains to sit up, but Sandy pushes her back against the pillow. "Just wanted to say 'Have a great day.' Bye!"

"Sandy?" Elsie calls in confusion, but Sandy's back in the hall with me.

"Are you satisfied?" she says.

I stare at her. I struggle for words, coming up at last with, "You are such a dingbat."

"Takes one to know one," Sandy retorts. Her relief is palpable. A smile trembles across her face, and she seizes my wrist and tows me back to Agnes's room. "Now, come on, you promised you'd meet Agnes."

"No, I didn't," I say, feeling like a rag doll, or maybe a puppet.

"She was a novice at Crestview, back when it was a convent, and she's got the absolute best stories. She knows practically *everything*."

"Kitten?" Agnes calls.

Sandy propels me into Agnes's room. I trip over my own feet, and I nearly laugh. This whole situation is just that ridiculous.

Then I see Agnes. And her birthmark. I see Agnes's birthmark, which is the color of fruit punch. It's as if someone splashed a cup of punch right in her face, and the punch congealed in a slippery mass that couldn't be wiped off. My laughter dries up.

"This is Bliss," Sandy announces. She ducks back for her harp, which she wheels in and parks in the corner of the room. "Bliss is my best friend."

"Best friend?" I say to Sandy, mainly because I don't want to look at Agnes. "Five minutes ago, I was no one."

Sandy frowns as if she has no idea what I'm talking about. Then she shifts all her attention to the woman in the bed, her manner reverent. "And Bliss, this is Agnes."

Awkwardly, I meet Agnes's gaze. The birthmark is still there, a violent, purplish lesion that disfigures half her face. It runs from the left side of her forehead to the left side of her chin, splitting her in two. I don't want to stare, but I also don't want to *not* stare.

"Some of us hide our differences on the inside," Agnes says to me kindly. "Others wear them on the outside, for all the world to see. Don't be scared, pet."

I feel myself flush, my skin growing so warm that I, too, probably look diseased.

"Just take a good, long look," Agnes says. "You won't hurt my feelings."

I'm shamed by her grace, and I lift my eyes. The affected skin is mottled with swollen capillaries. In some places the surface is tight and shiny; in other spots, its texture is thicker. The left side of her upper lip swells out in a bulbous lump, as if a caterpillar is nesting inside. That's the shape of it, anyway. I fight a wave of nausea and keep looking. I will look and look until my queasiness passes. I *will*.

Agnes laughs, a faint chuckle like rustling leaves. "You see? I'm just like you."

I meet her eyes, which are a dark, twinkly brown, and I *do* see. I give her a sheepish smile.

"Oh my, how happy you've made an old woman," she says to the two of us. "What a lonely day it's been. But now you two are here. I'm *glad*."

"Bliss goes to Crestview with me," Sandy says. "She wants to hear what it was like in the olden days."

"Do you, now?" Agnes says. She takes my hand, and I let her. Her skin is papery. She gives me little pats.

"Only if you feel like it," I say. "We don't want to bother you."

"Sweet girl, there's nothing I'd like more. Otherwise they'll come for me and make me play bingo, and that foolish Elsie will get all worked up, as she always does." She clucks. "She thinks I bear the mark of the devil."

"You see?" Sandy says to me. To Agnes, she says, "Elsie is an idiot. You were a nun, for God's sake."

"'*For God's sake*,'" Agnes repeats, amused. "Yes, that was my intent. It didn't always feel that way, however."

"What do you mean?" I say.

Agnes pulls at me, coaxing me to sit. I perch beside her on the thin mattress.

"I'll tell you," she says, "but you need to know, it's not a pretty story. It's not . . . a *comfortable* story. Are you brave of heart?"

"Um . . . I think," I say, though I'm suddenly not. I'm suddenly certain that her story has to do with the dead girl. I want to hear it, though. "At least, I try to be."

She scrutinizes me. I try not to fidget, and at last she nods.

"Sandy, dear," she says, "would you be so kind as to close the door?"

"Unfortunately, the trickiest deodorant problem a girl has *isn't* under her pretty little arms. The real problem, as you very well know, is how to keep the most girl part of you fresh and free of any worry-making odors."

gnes is a good storyteller—that, and she has an excellent story to tell. When she was twelve, her parents sent her to be a novice at the Holy Order of Perpetual Chastity, which is what Crestview was called back then. She took her vows of obedience, poverty, and chastity, and she lived inside the convent walls with the other members of the order. Mother Mary Josephine was her Mother Superior.

"Was she nice?" I ask, recalling my image of Hamilton Hall as a grim and disapproving mother.

"I wouldn't say 'nice,'" Agnes says. "She did what she needed to do. She kept us girls under control. And for the most part, we lived in harmony." She tsk-ed. "That all changed when Liliana came."

"Liliana?" I ask.

Sandy joins us on the bed, sitting on my left. "Liliana is who I want to be when I grow up," she says.

"Sandy," Agnes says in a warning tone.

"Well, she is!" Sandy insists. To me, she says, "Agnes has told me all about Liliana, and she's pretty much my hero. She was a novice just like Agnes—except she wasn't anything like Agnes, because Agnes was a rule-follower and Liliana was the original bad girl." She giggles. "Isn't that funny, to think of a nun being bad?"

"It's not funny," Agnes says. "And if you recall, Liliana never got to be a nun."

"Oh, yeah," Sandy says. She rolls her eyes as if to make fun of herself. "*Oops.* Anyway, tell her, Agnes."

Agnes fixes her deep eyes on me. "Liliana came to us when she was fourteen. She'd had a troubled past, I'm afraid."

"She was an orphan," Sandy says. "Her parents immigrated to America when she was a baby, but then they died. Tell her, Agnes."

Agnes gives Sandy a look.

"Sorry," Sandy says. She makes the motion of zipping her lips.

Agnes waits. Sandy stays quiet. Agnes turns to me and says, "Yes. Liliana's father died in a factory accident, and six months later, her mother died from a disease she contracted in their unsanitary living quarters."

"So Liliana was put on an orphan train," Sandy says. "That's what they did back then."

"What's an orphan train?" I ask.

"Orphan trains took children like Liliana to new homes," Agnes explains. "Homes with God-fearing parents, ample food, and plenty of fresh air."

"Plenty of work too," Sandy butts in. "The orphans were slave labor, that's what they were. Only Liliana was too smart to go along with it, so she got herself kicked out. See why she's my hero?"

"Hmm," Agnes says. "I believe that's your own interpretation, Sandy dear. As I understood it, the couple who took in Liliana was unable to care for her, good as their intentions were."

"Yeah, sure," Sandy says. "Likely story."

"On the farm where she was sent, carcasses of animals began showing up, drained entirely of blood," Agnes says.

"Ick," I say.

"Blood magic," Sandy says, almost under her breath, but not quite.

"Blood magic?" I say.

Agnes shoots Sandy another look of warning, then turns back to me.

"And though her foster parents were loath to assign blame," she says, "they decided that sending Liliana to the Holy Order of Perpetual Chastity might better meet everyone's needs."

"Because they were expecting their own child," Sandy says. "The lady got pregnant and said to Liliana, 'Okay, done with you, bye-bye.'"

"But if it was true," I say. "If Liliana was experimenting with . . . blood magic—"

"Oh, she was," Sandy assures me. "But not in, like, an evil way."

"I wouldn't have wanted her around my baby either," I finish. "And how could killing animals and draining their blood not be evil?" I turn to Agnes. "*Was* Liliana evil, Agnes? And what is blood magic? And was Liliana . . . is Liliana . . . is she the girl who killed herself?"

"You know about that?" Sandy says. I can almost see her mind working. "Oh. The Crestview ghost story." She presses her lips together derisively. "Yes, that's Liliana, but the story that's passed around is just stupid. I never told you because I wanted you to hear it from Agnes. I wanted you to hear the truth."

"So what is the truth?" I ask.

Agnes sighs. "These are not pleasant things I speak of," she says. "And though I was Liliana's friend, I *never* . . ." She falters and breaks off.

"I know," I say. "I can take it."

Agnes focuses on her wrinkled hands, which rest upon the sheet. "Liliana had certain . . . beliefs. She believed that under the right circumstances, our world could be opened up to that other world. Spirits could communicate with humans, the future could be foreseen, the dead could return to life."

I'm watching Agnes's face, but I'm thinking of Flying V. Flying V believed in an unseen world too, but she never spoke of the dead returning to life.

"It came at first from a longing for her parents," Agnes says. "At least, that's what I suspect. To talk to them again. To somehow bring them back. But then the blood took ahold of her."

I shiver.

"Go on," Sandy tells Agnes. "Get to the juicy part already."

"Do you want to hear it?" Agnes asks me.

Do I?

Oh dear, I do. I nod.

Agnes shifts in her narrow bed, and a musty smell wafts up from the sheets. "Well, as you know, Liliana came to us as a motherless child. Some such children might turn to a surrogate . . ."

"Like Mother Mary Josephine," I say.

"Yes, like Mother Mary Josephine. But Liliana wanted nothing to do with Mother Mary Josephine. Indeed, she had no interest in being taken care of by anyone. She far preferred to do the 'taking care' of herself, though not always—or rather, never—in ways condoned by the convent."

"Meaning what?" I ask.

"Well, Liliana was quite charismatic. She was a favorite with the other initiates. Fearless, dynamic, completely ungovernable—she brought life to the convent, and we girls adored her for it. I, especially, adored her, for unlike the others, Liliana never made me feel unwelcome. Indeed, she cultivated my devotion."

I bite my lip, seeing how potent such attention could be.

"Quite simply, Liliana supplanted Mother Mary Josephine," Agnes says. "*Liliana* became our Mother Superior."

"How did Mother Mary Josephine take to that?" I ask.

"As you'd expect. I found it foolish that a grown woman was so threatened by a fourteen-year-old girl, until I realized that Liliana wasn't like other fourteen-year-old girls."

"What do you mean?" I ask.

For a moment, Agnes doesn't answer. She plucks at the sheets just as Elsie did, and I remember that Agnes is an old lady. A very old lady.

"It started off innocently enough," she says at last. "Simple pranks, like resetting all the clocks, or stealing apples from a nearby orchard and dropping them all at once during Mass."

I wait. Dropping apples during Mass doesn't sound so awful.

Agnes stills her hands. "For us, it was the first fun we'd had since we arrived at the convent. For some of us, it was the first fun ever. We all wanted to be near her . . . to impress her . . . But as I said, Liliana had an unhealthy obsession with subjects best left alone."

"Like blood," Sandy says.

"Why blood?" I say. "What's so great about blood?"

Sandy laughs contemptuously. "You're kidding, right? *What's so great about blood?* We'd only die without it, that's all."

"'For the life of the flesh is in the blood,'" Agnes says in a quoting voice. "Leviticus seventeen, verse eleven. Liliana believed blood could give life to the dead. A creature who comes back to life—for that is what such a being would be, no longer a man or woman but a *creature*—would possess great power," Agnes goes on. "And Liliana was always . . . eager for power."

"Who isn't?" Sandy says. When I look at her, aghast, she says, "Oh, come on. Pretty pretty pretty, nice nice nice." She exhales with a *pfffff.*

"So . . . what happened?" I say uneasily.

"There was a girl in our class named Nanette," Agnes says. "Nanette was feebleminded, so she was given the simplest chores, such as slicing potatoes." She briefly closes her eyes. "One day, Mother Mary Josephine found Nanette in the kitchen, covered in blood. Nanette wouldn't stop screaming. She wouldn't—or couldn't—tell Mother Mary Josephine what had happened."

"Was it . . . Liliana?" I ask. "Did she hurt Nanette?"

"Nanette never said. In fact, she never spoke again. But the blood wasn't hers; it came from a newborn lamb. Mother Mary Josephine found the carcass behind the woodpile."

"Did Nanette do it, or did Liliana? Or did Liliana make Nanette do it?"

"How do you *make* someone do something?" Sandy says contemptuously. "Only if that person doesn't have a mind of her own."

Which Nanette didn't, I think.

"Mother Mary Josephine suspected that Liliana was responsible for what happened. But since she couldn't prove it, Liliana went unpunished."

"Not for long," Sandy says in a singsong voice.

"No, not for long," Agnes says. Unlike Sandy, she sounds sad. "Liliana grew more audacious with every day that passed. She thought she was invincible, and for the most part, she was."

In my mind, I see a young girl tumbling from a third-

206

story window. I see blood on the flagstones below. I'm starting to get the lightheaded feeling of being outside my body, and I put my hand on the mattress to steady myself.

Agnes, who is watching my face, seems to intuit this isn't fun and games and a yummy ghost story for me. In a voice that's carefully neutral, she says, "Sandy, dear, can you get me some water?"

"Huh?" Sandy says.

"Water, please. I'm feeling a bit parched."

"Oh. Sure." She heaves herself up and goes to Agnes's bureau, where she picks up a pink plastic pitcher. "It's empty."

"Will you fill it for me, dear? The water fountain's in the hall."

"I know where the water fountain is," Sandy says. "Geez." She strides out of the room, plastic pitcher swinging by her side.

The moment she's gone, Agnes's whispery fingers tighten on mine. "You have it too, don't you?" she says. "The gift to see beyond our world."

I open my mouth to deny it . . . but why bother? Liliana obviously wants something—wants it from *me*—and maybe Agnes can explain.

I nod.

"Quickly then, pet," Agnes says. "There's something I'd like to show you."

FROM "HAPPINESS IS A WARM GUN"

"Mother Superior jump the gun,
Mother Superior jump the gun!"

—The Beatles

pen the top drawer of my bureau," she instructs. She glances at the open door. "Hurry."

I rise and do as she says, tingling with apprehension. This is a peculiar turn of events.

"In the very back corner—do you feel it?"

I pat the soft and silky garments, assuming a nightgown isn't what she wants. In the corner, beneath a beige slip, I feel something hard. I pull out an exquisite cloisonné box and say, "Is this what you mean?"

"Bring it to me," Agnes says.

I deliver it to Agnes, and she draws it to her chest. Her eyes close as if she's praying. Then she opens her eyes and speaks intently.

"Liliana wanted a blood sacrifice. She wanted it from . . . a human."

"That's crazy," I say.

"Yes, indeed. But as I've told you, she could be quite persuasive."

I sit back on the bed.

"There was another girl in our class," Agnes says. "A very devout girl. Her name was Elizabeth."

Uh-oh, I think.

"Liliana spent a great deal of time with her. We were all jealous. She whispered to Elizabeth endlessly . . . and Elizabeth listened. One day, Liliana and Elizabeth went off together into the woods, and when, by evening, they hadn't returned, Mother Mary Josephine sent me to find them. Which I did."

"What were they doing?"

"Elizabeth was bound to a roughhewn cross. She seemed to be experiencing a sort of rapture."

I grow cold.

"Liliana had a knife. Nanette's knife, from the potatoes. I screamed. Elizabeth startled from her trance. She screamed as well." Agnes trembles, and I take her hand.

"But . . . she was all right?" I say. "Elizabeth?"

"All right?" Agnes repeats. "No. She was never the same. As for Liliana . . ."

I squeeze her frail fingers.

"Liliana was to be locked away until she repented," Agnes says quietly. "Locked away for life, if need be, and Mother Mary Josephine would have the full support of the Church."

"That's terrible," I say.

Footsteps sound in the hall. Agnes and I glance up, and there's Sandy with the pink plastic pitcher.

"I'm baaaack," she says. "Miss me?" As she pours Agnes her water, Agnes slips the still unopened cloisonné box beneath the covers, where it makes a small bump.

"Thank you, dear," she says. She takes a long sip, telling me with her eyes that the box is our secret.

"Did you get to the end?" Sandy asks. "Did you tell her about the cage?"

Agnes hands the cup to Sandy, who puts it on the bedside table. "The room Liliana was kept in was called the isolation chamber, but yes, it was little more than a cage. Four walls, a hard floor, a single, cramped window."

"No human contact," Sandy says. "We're talking a tiny room on an empty third-floor corridor, no light except what came from the window, and the only people who could visit her were Mother Mary Josephine and you. Right, Agnes?"

"It was my job to deliver her meals," Agnes affirms.

"Guess what Mother Mary Josephine's job was?" Sandy says. "Agnes came in the day; Mother Mary Josephine came in the night. And she brought her whip."

"Her whip?" I say.

"*Miserere mei, Deus,*" Agnes murmurs.

"For months Mother Mary Josephine kept her there," Sandy says. "For months she told the others that Liliana required further mortification of the flesh before she could be released."

I have mixed feelings for this long-dead girl, who in my imagination I see tensing at the nightly rap on her door. Or, no. Why bother with a rap? The slither of iron slipping into iron, the thunk of a bolt sliding free.

My key. From the third floor of Hamilton Hall. Of course.

I rub my temples.

"Liliana came up with a plan," Agnes says. Tears well up, round and glassy, and she swipes them away. "Ghosts in my eyes. Forgive me."

"She wanted to poison Mother Mary Josephine," Sandy informs me, and though she tries uncharacteristically to be solemn, there's pleasure in the telling. "She hid a piece of rye bread in the corner of her chamber and added her own saliva. The mold that grew was called *ergot*. Agnes was to mix it in Mother Mary Josephine's nightly glass of warm milk."

"Ergot?" I say.

"First would come convulsions, then blindness, then death," Agnes says.

I blanch.

"But I couldn't do it," Agnes says. "I couldn't!"

"I'm *glad* you couldn't," I say.

"Liliana wasn't," Sandy says. "Liliana was P.O.'ed. When she realized Agnes had failed her, when Mother Mary Josephine came yet again with her whip . . . that was the night Liliana flung herself from the window."

On the pillow, Agnes's head lolls toward me. "I was the one who found her," she says. "I couldn't sleep . . . I knew

Liliana would be displeased . . ." With her eyes, she pleads with me. "I heard the sound when her body—when her skull . . ."

"Shhh," I say. "It's over. It happened long, long ago, and now it's over."

"So sad," Sandy says. "So sad. So, so sad." She shifts positions and frowns. She rummages under the sheet, and it's just like Sandy to fail to realize how inappropriate she's being. "Hey, what's this?"

It's the cloisonné box.

"Give it to me," Agnes says, pulling her hand from mine and holding it out to Sandy.

Sandy lifts the lid. "Eww. What is it?"

"Give it to me," Agnes demands.

But Sandy doesn't, and I lean close and peer inside. I can't help myself. And then I recoil, because what lies within is shriveled and black. It's small, maybe an inch long, and it looks like a finger, the way it's curled in on itself. Only it can't be a finger, for attached to it are long strands of hair.

Human hair?

"I couldn't just walk away," Agnes says, as if imploring us to understand.

Sandy moves to pluck the thing from the box, and Agnes cries, "No!"

I give Sandy a hard look and snatch the cloisonné box. I snap the lid shut and hand it to Agnes, who clutches it to her chest.

"I had to honor her," Agnes says. "Don't you see?"

"What *is* it?" Sandy asks. "A piece of her scalp?"

Agnes's eyes blaze. "It's what came free. I wasn't . . .
I didn't have time to be picky."

"Agnes, that's disgusting," Sandy says gleefully.

As for me, I'm slogging through the horror of my
thoughts. *Liliana died . . . she jumped from the window and her skull
smacked the ground . . . and Agnes kept a piece of her?*

"Go now," Agnes says. "I need to rest." Her expression—
eyes averted, lips tight—tells me she regrets saying so
much.

"Aw, Agnes, don't be like that," Sandy cajoles. "I think
it's great you kept a souvenir. Really, really *gross*, but great.
Can I see it again?"

"You may not," Agnes says sharply.

I lurch from the bed, afraid I'm going to throw up. I
place both hands on the dresser and bow my head.

"What you girls saw, what I've kept safe for all these
years . . . it is a *relic*," Agnes says. "It should be revered."

I turn from the bureau to see Sandy's fingers twitching
toward the box. Agnes slaps them away.

"Why should it be revered?" I say. "It's a piece of a dead
girl."

"That's where you're wrong," Agnes says. "You see,
Liliana lives on."

My stomach, already hollow, drops to my toes. "What
do you mean? Like . . . as a ghost?"

Agnes offers no denial—and why would she? I already knew it to be true.

"Have you really seen the ghost of Liliana?" Sandy says.

"Don't be absurd," Agnes says.

Sandy's face falls.

"I feel her," Agnes says with dignity.

"For real? Because I want to too. You know I do."

"Other times, I smell her."

"Yuck," Sandy says happily, clearly oblivious to the sudden trace of citrus in the air. Agnes's eyes find mine. She knows I smell it too.

"I snuck her lemons when I could," she confesses. "She always loved lemons."

I press my hand to my stomach. If I had a lemon, I would not suck it. I will never suck a lemon again.

With discernible effort, Agnes composes herself. She holds out the cloisonné box and says to me, "Put this away now."

I shake my head. I'm not touching it.

"I'll do it," Sandy says, nabbing the box. "But first can I . . . ?"

"Put it *away*!" Agnes says shrilly. "In the top drawer of my dresser. Put it there now!"

"Sheesh, have a cow, will you?" Sandy grumbles. She lumbers off the bed, and the mattress springs up. Agnes bobs on the wake.

"Move," Sandy says to me. I step back, but keep a close watch, because I don't want her trying the same trick she pulled on Elsie. The box is enfolded in Sandy's thick fingers, but when she pulls her hand from the drawer, there it is on top of Agnes's undergarments. Silky slips, stiff conical bras, a medieval-looking girdle, none of which Agnes will ever wear again.

Sandy sneezes. She thrusts her hand in her pocket, but comes up empty. "Anyone have a tissue?"

Agnes hands her one from her bedside table.

"Thanks," Sandy says, blowing her nose with a honk. "Too much dust in here."

"Not dust," Agnes says. She closes her eyes. "Go now, girls."

"You don't want me to play my harp for you?" Sandy says.

I'd forgotten all about Sandy's harp.

"Not today," Agnes says.

"Okey-dokey, you're the boss."

Sandy lugs the harp from the corner of the room, pausing when she reaches the door.

"Bye, Agnes," she says.

"Yeah," I say. "It was, um, nice to meet you."

But Agnes has fallen asleep, or she's pretending she has. She doesn't respond.

Something miraculous has happened.

I have, at long last, been singled out for greatness. And now my nights have fallen into a pattern: Once Mam is down, I put my familiar in the closet and draw out the relic. I stare at it until a trance descends, and then it speaks. Or rather, She speaks. She speaks, and I listen.

She told me that I am not the one She expected, for I do not hold the key. She told me I must find the key, and when my mind registered confusion, She grew impatient and said, "The key to my room, you ninny. That is the first step if you are to become my vessel."

I am in awe. While I'm not yet certain of what this implies, to be Her vessel would be a higher honor than I've ever imagined.

So I will find the key.

For Liliana, I will do anything.

FROM PRESIDENT NIXON'S SPEECH ON
"VIETNAMIZATION," NOVEMBER 3, 1969

"Good evening, my fellow Americans.
Tonight I want to talk to you on a subject
of deep concern to all Americans and to
many people in all parts of the world—
the war in Vietnam."

—President Richard Nixon

oward the middle of November, our school counselor gets the idea of herding all the students into the gymnasium for a series of lectures on acting responsibly and not doing drugs. In other words, not becoming hippies. The Tate-LaBianca murder trial continues to dominate the news, and Charles Manson is portrayed as the worst sort of hippie of all—a hippie who holds such little regard for rules that he kills for the sport of it.

Also, President Nixon has just instructed the Air Force to place additional B-52 bombers on ground alert, and thousands of hippies demonstrated in protest. I saw footage of the marches and wondered if Mom and Dad were bummed they were missing out.

At any rate, the lecture series isn't much of a success, at least not in the way it's intended. Practically everyone either falls asleep the minute the lights are dimmed or passes the time by writing notes to their friends.

On the last day of the program, the topic is dangerous behaviors. Like if someone sips a beer, the speaker tells us, it's really a cry for help. Or if we have a friend who tries marijuana, or attends an antiwar rally, we should tell an adult we trust.

"Rebelling against society is a sign of disconnection," the speaker says, and I think about Liliana. Does it count as rebelling against society if she wanted to create her own society? Does an obsession with blood constitute a cry for help . . . or does it just mean Liliana was a sociopath?

Let's pretend you're Jesus, I imagine Liliana telling poor Elizabeth.

Charles Manson has claimed, at different times, that he is Jesus.

Stop, I tell myself. I don't want to think about Liliana or Charles Manson. There is nothing I can do about either of them except stay away—and as far as Liliana goes, this has been unexpectedly easy. I haven't heard her slithering whisper for days now. Perhaps she's forgotten about me. Perhaps, now that I know her secrets, she has retreated in shame.

Although based on what I learned from Agnes, Liliana didn't know the meaning of shame.

"If you sense that someone feels disconnected, reach out to them," the speaker urges. "Buy them a soda. Compliment their new hairdo. It'll make them feel better, and you'll feel better knowing you've been a channel of grace."

Jolene leans over and whispers, "My pen is feeling disconnected. Will you be a channel of grace and get it for me?" She points to the floor near the end of the bleacher.

I slide off my seat and kneel, reaching for the pen. I work on a witty retort, something along the lines of how we don't want her pen falling into a bad crowd, now do we?

But when I rise, my seat is taken. Jolene has taken it, and Thelma and DeeDee have scooched over so that there's no room left for me.

"Hey!" I protest.

"There's a seat behind you," Thelma whispers.

I glance back at the next row. I feel myself blush. "No."

"But he's feeling disconnected," Jolene says. "Even more than Pen-Pen."

"Pen-Pen?" I say.

She plucks her pen from my fingers. "Oh, Pen-Pen, I missed you!" She covers it with smooches. Then she drops it into her purse and says, "Go. Sit. Converse!"

I glower, but my crouching posture has caught the attention of a teacher, and she's rising from her spot. I stand, flick Jolene hard, and climb one row up.

"Hi, Mitchell," I say, sitting as far to the right as I can. My cheeks are still hot. I can't bear to look at him.

"Hi, Bliss," he says. "Have you decided to bear my children yet?"

"Sorry," I say. "I've taken a vow of celibacy."

He chuckles, and I risk a peek. And omigosh, he's got the cutest dimple in the world.

"I'm not so impressed with our man here," he says, leaning close. "Does he think Charles Manson wouldn't have murdered those people if only they'd offered him a soda?"

"Well, they couldn't have complimented his hairdo," I say. I've seen pictures of Charles Manson—by now the whole world has seen pictures of Charles Manson—and his long hair is oily and uncombed.

"You don't like the devil-may-care look?"

"I don't like the unbathed look," I reply. "Nor the unbathed smell, for that matter." Mitchell, for the record, smells of pine trees and wonderfulness.

Jolene peeks over her shoulder and grins. She gives me an un-sly thumbs-up, until Thelma yanks down her arm.

"Sheesh! Give the lovebirds some privacy!" she says.

I about die.

Mitchell laughs, and I meet his eyes and grimace as if to say, *Sure, sure, take pleasure in my pain.*

"Relax," he says. "I think you're cute."

"You do?" I squeak. Good heavens, since when am I a squeaker?

"I do. Want to know why?"

My heart races. He shifts positions so that our legs touch, and I try not to faint. "Um . . . I don't know. Do I?"

"Because unlike the other girls at this school, you're not a beauty queen," he says.

I laugh. "Gee, that's just what every girl wants to hear. Next time say something nice about my hair, would you?"

"Wait, I didn't mean it as an insult. I just . . . what I meant was—"

I pat his leg. I don't think about it; I just do it. "It's okay. I have no interest in being a beauty queen."

His shoulders relax. "My point exactly."

He takes my hand—the one on his thigh—and we sit, fingers laced, through the rest of the assembly. His friends nudge each other and snicker, and when Jolene sees, her smile nearly splits her face. She elbows Thelma and gets her to look, and Thelma's eyes bug out to such a degree that I think they're going to bounce into my lap.

But Mitchell holds on, and so do I. I'm thankful for the war protests, and I'm thankful for President Nixon. For those minutes, I'm even thankful for Charles Manson, though I'm quite content for our relationship to remain one-sided.

FROM *THE ANDY GRIFFITH* SHOW

"Shazam!"

—Gomer Pyle, gas-pump attendant

hen the assembly ends, Mitchell gives my hand one last squeeze, then lets go. *Booooo.* But he winks at me before going off with his friends, which makes everything all right. I'm so giddy, I could fly.

"Chelsea, quit picking at your scab," a girl in front of me says to her friend as we file out. "It's gross." Then she gasps in mock horror. "Or maybe it's a cry for help! Be strong, Chelsea! Stay with the living!"

A guy from my geometry class nudges his friend and says, "Hey man, got any weed?" He makes his eyelids all droopy, trying to look like a stoner. Actually, it's not a bad impersonation, and I grin. I can't stop grinning, to tell the truth.

Thelma, DeeDee, and Jolene catch up to me, enveloping me in squealing delight.

"Omigosh, you and Mitchell are going to get pinned—I just know it!" Thelma says, clutching my arm. "You really *are* going to have his babies. Omigosh!"

I laugh. "Ow, you're hurting."

"He is *so* cute," DeeDee says, wide-eyed. "I mean, I didn't used to think so, and he's not really my type. But he is so perfect for you!"

"I know," I say. "I agree."

"You owe me big-time," Jolene says.

"Meaning what? Next time I get to bump *you* off the bleacher and steal your spot?"

"If that means I end up holding hands with a cute boy . . . then yes!"

Over spaghetti and meatballs, they discuss possible names for Mitchell's and my children. Jolene likes Barbara for a girl and Mike for a boy. Thelma can't decide on a girl's name, but for a boy, she likes Rock.

"Rock?" I say.

"Like Rock Hudson," DeeDee explains.

"Only the hunkiest man on the planet!" Thelma says.

A strange current in the air draws my attention, and I look up to see Sandy standing several feet away, staring at me. Just *staring*, with a wooden expression on her face.

I've neglected Sandy a bit since our visit with Agnes, because to tell the truth, her fascination with Liliana disturbed me. Her outright *admiration* for Liliana, I should say. Likewise, her admiration for Charles Manson. I know that in neither case does she admire their actions; she admires their refusal to play nice just because society said to. Still, I didn't enjoy that time with her in Agnes's room.

I shouldn't ignore her, though. That's unkind. I lift my arm to call her over, but Thelma pushes it back down.

"What," I say, "she's not allowed to sit with us?"

Thelma looks at DeeDee, who looks at Jolene, who looks at the table.

"It's not a good idea," Thelma says.

"Why?"

"It's just not."

I'm exasperated. Do they find Sandy so repellent they can't even bear to share their table with her?

"Fine," I say, pushing back from the table. I pick up my tray.

"Bliss," Jolene says unhappily.

I shake my head. I refuse to lose my good mood over this, but I also refuse to be party to their exclusion. If Sandy hadn't noticed me raising my hand and beckoning . . .

But she did. What's done is done.

Sandy has taken up residence at her customary table, so I walk across the cafeteria and join her.

"Hi," I say. "I didn't see you in assembly. Where were you?"

"Why'd you leave your girly friends?" she says.

"Because I did," I say. "Why weren't you at assembly?"

She stabs at her noodles. "I got sent to the principal's office."

"How come?"

"They made me take a *personality* test. It was so lame."

"A personality test? Why?"

"'I am neither *gaining* nor *losing weight*,'" she says in a monotone. "True. '*At times I have fits of laughing and crying that I cannot control.*' False. '*I sometimes hear voices.*' False." She looks at me from under her pale lashes. "I lied, basically."

"Meaning you *do* hear voices?" I ask, astonished to find that I'm not the only one at Crestivew who does. Liliana, before she receded, spoke with such intensity that I assumed I was the first person she was able to communicate with. Well, that and the fact that no one else ever seemed to react to her blood-drenched utterances.

"Ha, ha," she says, as if she suspects me of making fun of her.

I'm disappointed—and then I'm not. It's just as well that Liliana can't communicate with Sandy. Sandy would prove far too responsive an audience, I'm afraid.

"Seriously, why'd they make you take a personality test?" I ask. "Are we all going to have to?"

"I doubt it. Just the losers like me."

"You're not a loser," I say automatically.

"Just the potential *unstable psychopaths*," she says. "They think I have no friends, but they're wrong. They're *totally* wrong. I told Dr. Evans that, but he didn't believe me."

"What do you mean, he didn't believe you? Why would he not believe you?"

"I don't know." She bites her lower lip.

"Oh, please, you're just being paranoid. And don't worry, you're not a psychopath. You might be weird, but you're not a psychopath."

"I might be," she says peevishly.

I can't help but laugh. "Sandy. My parents had to fill out personality profiles once, and they're not psychopaths."

"Who made them?"

"The psych-ward people, when they were brought to the county jail."

"Your parents went to jail?" she says.

"Yes, but they were released. Actually, they were given a probationary warning and assigned to do community service, but—"

"I don't care about that. Are you going to tell me what they did?"

I consider. The thing is, I know she's going to dig it, what I'm about to say, and with Sandy, that can be a dangerous thing. Like with Agnes and the relic.

I shudder, seeing those hairs still attached to the flap of scalp. Eughh. I force my thoughts in a different direction.

"Um, it was when we lived in Oregon," I say. I exhale. "You remember me telling you that we lived in the basement of Oregon State for a while?"

"Yeah. And?"

"Well, we were living there without permission."

"Meaning what?"

"Meaning no one knew we were there."

Her eyes gleam. "I could use a place like that."

"See, the scientists in the immunology department were trying to develop new methods of chemical warfare," I say. "And my parents were big into SDS, at least that year, so—"

"SDS? What's that?"

"An antiwar group called Students for a Democratic Society."

"Your parents were students?"

"Will you let me finish? The SDS chapter in Oregon didn't like the whole chemical-warfare thing, and my mom and dad were buddies with lots of the students. So they agreed to live in the basement for a few weeks, just to mess things up. Like, they let rats out of their cages and spilled stuff on the data logs, stuff like that."

"*Ah,*" Sandy says. "The warfare folks were experimenting on *rats.*"

"Sick, huh?" I don't agree with everything my parents do. In fact, I don't agree with most of it. But I did agree on this one: Torturing animals is wrong, case closed.

"I don't get why you had to live there, though," Sandy says.

"We camped out in the lab sometimes, that's all. Like on the weekends, when we knew no one would be coming in. There was a faculty lounge, and a drink machine, and it was either crash there or on someone else's floor." I shrug. "The lab smelled like rat poop, but it was air-conditioned."

"How'd you get in?" Sandy asks. "Didn't they keep the lab locked?"

"My mom made a key from a wax mold."

Her eyebrows go up. She makes a circling motion with her hand, like *go on, go on.*

"You take a key and press it into a slab of wax," I explain. "And then you make a copy of it out of Bondo—"

"Bondo?"

"It's something mechanics use. It's an epoxy."

"Bondo," Sandy repeats.

"It's not firm enough to actually use as a key, but it's stronger than the wax. So then you've got a replica. After that, all you have to do is get a blank key and file it down so that it matches."

"Where do you get a blank key?"

"Why, are you planning to do some burgling? Steal from another old lady?"

Her denial is immediate and indignant. "No. *No!*"

I smile a little, because usually it's Sandy giving me a hard time, not the other way around. The tease would be funnier if Sandy didn't have a record, though.

"You can get blank keys at a hardware store," I say. "But just to be clear, we got *caught.* That's why my mom and dad got hauled off to jail, and even though they weren't charged with anything, they could have been."

"Blah, blah, blah," Sandy says.

I shake my head and grin. Whatever else happens, she will always be Sandy.

"Um, hi there," someone says, and I look up to see Sarah Lynn Lancaster standing by our table. *The* Sarah Lynn Lancaster.

The color drains from Sandy's face. She goes from ruddy to tombstone pale in less time than it takes for my own smile to fall away.

Huh, I think, noting almost as a disembodied observer the sweat that's popped out in my armpits. *This is going to be interesting.*

DATE: November 14, 1969

STUDENT: Sandra Lurlene Lear

TEST: Minnesota Multiphasic
Personality Inventory

RESULTS: Test results reveal no
indications of abnormal mental,
emotional, or psychological processing.
Subject was pleasant and compliant.

HANDWRITTEN NOTE TO SCHOOL COUNSELOR,
PAPER-CLIPPED TO REPORT

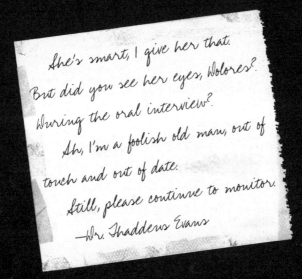

She's smart, I give her that.
But did you see her eyes, Dolores?
During the oral interview?
Ah, I'm a foolish old man, out of
touch and out of date.
Still, please continue to monitor.
—Dr. Thaddeus Evans

Sarah Lynn smiles awkwardly. My own smile blossoms back, more out of reflex than intention. I recall her kindness at the department store.

"So, Bliss, did you like your makeover?" she asks me.

"Kind of," I say, preferring not to think about my jellied Lancôme lips. I'm glad she remembers my name, though.

"You looked really pretty," she tells me.

Sandy snorts derisively. It flusters Sarah Lynn.

"I mean, you look really pretty anyway," she says. "But I love makeovers. They're so fun, don't you think?"

"Um, yeah," I say.

Sandy snorts again. I wish she would be quiet.

Sarah Lynn shifts her weight. "You know what I realized after we got to Woolworth's?"

"What?" I say.

"I never did any of the peer mentoring stuff I was supposed to do with you, did I?" She wrinkles her nose like she knows she's been bad. "I'm sorry."

"It's okay," I say. She's making it sound as if it slipped her mind, when the truth is that she passed me off on Thelma squarely and fully. Still, I appreciate her apology.

She turns to Sandy, who radiates ill will.

"So, Sandy, are you ready for the math quiz?" she asks.

Sandy scowls and fiddles with the salt shaker.

"I hear it's supposed to be superhard," Sarah Lynn says.

Sandy still doesn't reply. The silence is long and obvious, and Sarah Lynn and I share a look, which Sandy sees. Sandy kicks me, and I say, "Ow."

"Well, I know you'll ace it," Sarah Lynn says gamely. "You always do."

Sandy twists her face like rotten fruit. My stomach muscles tense, because I'm afraid she's going to start in with the bluh-bluhs. I try to nonverbally communicate my embarrassment to Sarah Lynn, and Sandy kicks me again.

"Ow!" I say. I reach below the table to rub my shin.

Color rises in Sarah Lynn's cheeks. "Well . . . bye," she stammers, and hurries off.

"Bye!" I call.

A long few seconds tick by, and then I turn to Sandy. I hold my hands out, palms to the ceiling, and choke out a sound that basically means, *What the . . . ?*

"'I know you'll ace it,'" she says in a fussy falsetto. She switches back to her own voice, throaty and full of fury. "Yeah, right. And *you'll* ace it too, Little Miss Priss, because if you don't, you'll burst into tears, and Mr. Carson will rub your shoulders and give you a big, fat A."

"Sandy," I start. I have to shake my head and try again. "Sarah Lynn was perfectly nice just now. You were the one who was a jerk."

Sandy's eyes follow Sarah Lynn as Sarah Lynn joins the food line. "That's right, wiggle your widdle bottom in your fancy panties," she says under her breath. "Your widdle *ham hock*, that is."

My mouth tastes sour. I really wish I'd never told that ham hock story. I also decide that maybe it's time to take a good hard look at myself, and not do the same thing to Sarah Lynn that Thelma and the others do to Sandy. Because yes, Sarah Lynn treated me poorly on the first day of school. Since then, she's been nice. Shouldn't I give her a chance?

"Why are you so intimidated by her?" I ask Sandy. "I get it that she was a jerk to you in fifth grade. I do. But don't you think it's time to let it go?"

An ugly flush mottles Sandy's face. "I am *not* intimidated by her! You think I'm . . . ?" She works her mouth, but no words come out. Then, sounding strangled, she spits, "I can't believe you would *betray* me—for *her*."

"What?!" I say.

She glares. Her chair scrapes the floor with a hard noise, and she strides out of the cafeteria without a backward glance.

I can't believe her. I refused to trash Sarah Lynn for coming over and being friendly. Ooh, I'm *sooo* despicable.

I turn my head toward the front of the cafeteria and look

at Sarah Lynn, who is chatting with another girl in the lunch line. Sarah Lynn's smiling, but it's a tamped-down sort of smile. Is her pensiveness due to the way Sandy treated her just now? For that matter, what in the world made her come over in the first place? Surely she knows Sandy hates her.

I sense someone's gaze, and I glance across the cafeteria. Thelma and DeeDee are absorbed in conversation, but Jolene is staring at me intensely. Her expression is . . . disapproving? Smug?

No, neither of those things.

She's worried.

As Liliana reveals her intentions, my excitement mounts. My one concern is that I want a supplicant. I need a supplicant. Liliana has me; don't I deserve someone too? One day, perhaps, more than one. A sect of followers to quail at my magnificence.

don't let's get ahead of ourselves. and . . . whose magnificence?

Forgive me, Mother of All. Your magnificence.

hmm. you could benefit from a supplicant, i suppose.

Yes. Thank you. I've already chosen who it will be, actually.

i'm fully aware of whom you've chosen. but will she stay true?

Yes, of course. She may have misbehaved at lunch . . . but I forgive her. She's my friend.

and if she misbehaves again?

She won't! Mother, what are you suggesting?

a proper supplicant bows to only one mistress, while a proper priestess—and that is to be your role—is revered by all. for it is the priestess who offers access to Me.

Yes, yes, I understand. You and I shall merge, and those who have scorned me will prostrate themselves at my feet.

you deserve such devotion, certainly. yet if you fail to inspire such devotion . . .

Mother, are you displeased with me?

a high priestess must command absolute loyalty, or she is of no use.

But, Mother . . .

YOU MUST DEMAND PROOF. YOU MUST PUT HER TO THE TEST.

I can hardly breathe. The pen trembles in my hand. I look at the words on this page—this transcript of otherworldly communication!—and I am filled with glorious awe. Great indeed is Her power, She who not only speaks to me but through me!

I will not disappoint Her. I will consider how best to proceed.

"He's going to ask you, I just *know* he's going to ask you," Jolene says, squeezing my arm on Monday. We're sitting out on the quad, and Jolene is uncommonly giddy. "Promise me you'll say yes, okay?"

I laugh. "Uh . . . sure," I say. "If Mitchell asks me to the Winter Dance, I promise I'll say yes." It's like promising to take the money if I won the lottery. Who wouldn't? Only my chances with Mitchell are better than my chances of winning the lottery, and in my gut, I know this. It makes me giddy. It makes me think, *Oh, please please please.*

"Yay!" she says. She gets to her feet. "'Cause here he comes. I told him you wanted to talk to him."

"You told him . . . What?!"

"Bye!" she says, scampering off. I see Thelma and DeeDee waiting for her on the walkway, full of giggles.

I've been set up.

I glance warily behind me, and sure enough, there Mitchell is, strolling toward me with his patented sardonic smile.

"We've got to stop meeting like this," he says. He joins me on the stone bench.

"Hi, Mitchell," I say.

"Hi, Bliss." He nudges me with his thigh, which is lean and strong in his dress-code khakis. "I hear there's something you want to ask me?"

"Um . . ." Oh, gosh. Where do I go with this?

He lifts his eyebrows. His leg is still next to mine. He's sitting that way guys do, feet planted wide, and he reaches over and runs his finger down the sleeve of my cardigan. His expression is questioning and sweet, and all I can think is, *He's touching me on purpose.*

"That's all I get?" he says. "'Um'?"

I blush. "Um . . ."

He grins and slides his thumb up under the cuff of my sweater. Every cell is on high alert, saying, *Me! Me! Stroke me!*

"Sing that 'Little Boxes' song again," he suggests. "The one you were singing with your friends that day."

I snort-laugh. "Yeah, uh-huh. *No.*"

"But it's such a good song."

"I know it's a good song. *You* sing it."

He looks at me appraisingly. Then he leans back, cocks his head, and starts singing. He's doing it to show he's not afraid of taking a dare, but—*whoa.* His voice is as gorgeous as the rest of him. It's low and sexy, and it's just for me.

He sings about the identical people with their identical

249

homes and identical children, and when he gets to the end, he draws it out slow: "And they all get put in boxes, and they all come out the same."

I clap.

He glances down like maybe he's a little embarrassed. But right away his gaze swings back, and there's no way around those long, dark eyelashes. He's so gorgeous. He's so . . . *boy*.

"It's true, you know," he says.

"About people getting put in boxes?"

"About people putting *themselves* in boxes. Everyone's afraid to be an individual. We're no better than sheep."

I lift one eyebrow. "We aren't?"

"Excluding present company, of course."

"Ah. Of course. But don't you think . . ." I hesitate, because I have opinions on this "sheep" business. Only I'm not sure how far I want to go.

"What?"

I blow out a puff of air. "Okay. When I lived on the commune—"

"That's what I mean," he says. "You get it. You've *lived*. For you, it's not all prep schools and bobby socks."

"Bobby socks?" I tease. "I'm afraid you've been watching too much *Andy Griffith*."

"Miniskirts, then."

"You're saying you don't like miniskirts?"

"On the right girl, sure, I appreciate a miniskirt." He

keeps his eyes steadfastly off my legs, which makes me think I'm that right girl and which kindles warmth within me. "But there's more to life than that."

"Well, sure," I say. "But what I'm trying to say is that people on the commune . . . I don't know. Just that there were sheep there too."

"But there's a difference," he insists. "Anyone who makes a decision to live like that, they're doing their own thing. Even though it goes against society."

If I were having this conversation with Sandy, I know how I would feel. I would feel antsy, because I'd wonder at her private agenda. But Mitchell has no agenda. Or rather, Mitchell's agenda is me.

So I flutter my hand dismissively. "Society . . . pah."

"Right," he says. "Yes!"

Confusion pulls his eyebrows together. Then he laughs as if it's just a joke.

It is a joke, but it's more than that too.

"I'm serious," I say. "Yes, it's important to think for yourself, and I never want to be someone who lives in a little box. Especially if I don't even realize it."

"You're not going to end up in a little box," Mitchell says.

"Um, thanks. I hope not." I tilt my head. "In the lyrics . . . you think the little boxes are houses?"

"What else would they be?"

"I don't know. Maybe coffins?"

He weighs the possibility. He nods and says, "If you spend

your whole life trying to be like everybody else, you might as well be dead. Conformity equals coffins. You're brilliant."

"'Conformity equals coffins,'" I repeat with a smile. "*Ah.*" I'm not done with him yet, however. "Have you seen the commercial for Sanforized-Plus?"

"What the hell is 'Sanforized-Plus'?" Mitchell asks. "Pardon my French." He leans back on the bench and stretches his arms along the top. It's almost as if he's got his arm around me, but not quite.

"It's a fabric that doesn't wrinkle," I say. "The commercial is obnoxious, because it shows this long-haired guy who's barefoot and dirty and whose shirt is *totally* wrinkled."

"My kind of man," says Mitchell, in his neatly pressed button-down.

I give him a look. One side of his mouth quirks up.

"But the commercial is kind of clever, too, because the question the announcer asks is, 'Why do all nonconformists look alike?'"

"Why do all *nonconformists* look alike?" Mitchell says. "That's a contradiction in terms."

"Exactly," I say. Does he get it?

His eyes meet mine. It's intense. We study each other until it's almost *too* intense, like when you stare into the mirror and start to fall into your own pupils.

Then—not because he can't handle it, I don't think, but because it's time—he leans over and sniffs my hair.

"I do like your shampoo," he says.

"Lustre Crème," I quip. "'Never dries, it beautifies.'"

"Hmm." He regards me as if he likes what he sees. A moment passes, and he moves his arm from behind my shoulders and slaps his hands on his thighs. "So. Bliss-whose-hair-smells-like-apricots. Want to go to the Winter Dance with me?"

My insides soar, but I can't resist teasing him a bit more.

"I don't know," I say. "If it's a dance, there might be miniskirts. There might even be bobby socks."

"Is that a yes?"

I grin. "That's a yes. If you want, you can even iron your shirt."

It is time for Regular to reproduce and multiply. Liliana is amused by the idea and willing to indulge me, and I know the kittens will delight Her when they are born. My supplicant, who has a tender heart, will likewise be unable to resist their charm. These days she is foolishly enamored with a male of the species, but he is a mere boy and thus of no concern. I have observed no indications of other, more dangerous alliances.

As for Regular's impregnation:

Three blocks down lives a tomcat, a hulking yellow beast with a torn ear. Last spring he sired two litters of kittens with neighborhood females, if not more. But for Regular to mate with this tom, I would have to let her out. If I let her out, she may never return.

Of additional concern is the need
for a more private space. Mam already
hates Regular and wishes her harm. What
persecution might she inflict on a litter of
blind and helpless kittens?

I must acquire the key. I must ask—no,
__demand__—that my supplicant give it to me.

and yet you stall. why? i have told you:
she has it!

I know. I will! It's just . . . I'm just . . .

if she is worthy, she will want you to
have it. if you are worthy, you will have no
difficulty persuading her of this.

I'm trying my best—

you whine. we will speak again when you
possess the key.

Henrietta Swanson:
"She was voted young lady most likely
to become charming."

Sheriff Taylor:
"Well, say now. Becoming charming—
that is something to look forward to,
ain't it."

"a-tie Hill! Ka-tie Hill!"

The bleachers shake as everyone chants her name. I chant too. Katie makes it down the last row and onto the basketball court, and the gym erupts with stomps and hoots.

"It's like a Grateful Dead concert," I say to Thelma. I have to raise my voice. "I feel like people should be selling falafel and hawking shrooms."

"Hawking shrooms?" she says.

"Mushrooms," I explain.

"Why would people sell mushrooms at a concert?"

"Magic mushrooms, you goof."

She's not following. "Magic? What's magic about them?"

"Not magic like that. Magic like . . . you know." I trail my fingers in front of my face and make my expression rapt. "Ooh, look at the pretty colors!"

She purses her lips. "Bliss, don't be weird. Not today. Anyway, there's no such thing as magic."

I roll my eyes and focus back at the spectacle on the gym floor, where Katie Hill is getting her crown. Her jet-black hair gleams, and she's got a foxy figure that even her school uniform can't conceal.

"She's gorgeous," I say.

"Tell me about it," DeeDee says.

Beaming, Katie takes her seat next to the junior and senior Snow Princesses. All three are gorgeous. All three are foxy.

The guy beside DeeDee whoops and circles his fist in the air. "Righteous!" he calls.

DeeDee giggles. "*Boys*," she says.

"I know," I say, pretending to be oh-so-wise in the ways of the world. Now that Mitchell and I are . . . well, a couple, kind of . . . I've become the resident "boy" expert. I'm happy to oblige.

On the floor, Coach Nelson holds up his hands. "And now, ladies and gentlemen, the final member of the Snow Court."

"Why's it called the *Snow* Court?" I ask.

"Just because," DeeDee says.

"It's the theme," Jolene says. She grabs my right hand, and Thelma grabs my left. They really want it to be Sarah Lynn Lancaster.

"It is my great pleasure to announce this year's freshman Snow Princess—"

"I can't breathe," Thelma says, fanning herself with her spare hand. "I can't breathe!"

"—Sarah Lynn Lancaster! Sarah Lynn, come on down!"

Thelma, Jolene, and DeeDee squeal. The crowd chants, "*Sarah Lynn! Sarah Lynn!*"

In one of the center bleachers, Sarah Lynn stands, looking pleased, but embarrassed. Her friends push her along the aisle, and she jogs down the stairs and across the floor. She hides her face, then lets her hands fall away as Katie pulls her into a hug.

Everyone claps and cheers. Thelma and the girls jump to their feet, and Jolene pulls me up too. I put two fingers in my mouth and whistle, making Jolene laugh.

A few rows down, there's some sort of a disturbance—there's jostling and angry voices—but I don't look. I smack my palms together and keep focused on the pretty Snow Princesses, ignoring the sudden cramps in my stomach. DeeDee turns her head, then Thelma, and though I try to resist, my head pivots as if it's connected to a string that's just been yanked.

It's Sandy.

Of course it's Sandy.

Her expression is mulish, and she's pushing past a group of guys. They're mooing. A teacher at the end of the aisle rises, his mouth a warning.

Sandy tramps over to the teacher and speaks into his ear. He frowns, but nods and steps back. Sandy heads down the bleacher stairs.

A guy with zits on his forehead sticks his leg out.

She trips.

"Have a nice fall, pig!" he calls, and a second guy laughs and holds out his palm.

My gut clenches. I want to kill him.

Next to me, Jolene bites her lip. She knows what happened was bad, and wrong, but she won't meet my eyes. I want to kill her, too. Or cry. Or both.

"Excuse me," I say brusquely. On the other side of the bleacher, Sandy heaves herself up. With a red face and stiff posture, she clomps up the stairs toward the main level and the exit.

Jolene tries to hold me back. "Bliss . . ."

I shake my head. We've been through this before, so I shouldn't be disappointed, but I am. I jerk free and head angrily after Sandy.

On the gym floor, the captain of the football team presents Sarah Lynn with a long-stemmed rose. Sarah Lynn gets roses, Sandy gets tripped, and the whole world sits back and lets it happen.

FROM A MAGAZINE AD FOR LADY SUNBEAM
ELECTRIC SHAVERS

"Queen Size—to do
a delicate job quickly."

I spot Sandy outside of Hamilton Hall, sitting rigidly on a stone bench. Her gaze is fixed on some far-off point. I hesitate, then go over. It's my first time on this part of campus since visiting Agnes, and goose bumps tighten my skin. Will Liliana reach out to me, given that I'm so very close?

"Hey," I say to Sandy, sitting down next to her.

Her breathing accelerates so that I can see the rise and fall of her chest. "Did you see her expression when her name got called?" she says. "Like she was *so* surprised to be chosen. Like, 'Goodness gwacious—*me?*'"

"What, you think she was faking it?"

"I *know* she was faking it. I bet she practiced that face in the mirror all last night." She mimics Sarah Lynn, forming her mouth into an "O" and widening her eyes. She draws her hand to her cheek in a prissy manner, and I look away. I'm embarrassed for her.

"Fine," I say. "Who did *you* want to be picked?"

Her cheeks puff out with disbelief. "You think I care who the freshman Snow Princess is?"

"Apparently."

"No, no, and no again. I couldn't give a rat's ass who any of the Snow Princesses are, and if . . . if a bomb exploded during the Winter Dance and killed everyone there, you wouldn't see me crying."

"I'm going to be at the dance," I say. She might as well know. She's going to be mean about it, but I'm not going to hide it.

"Oh, God," she says. "With Mitchell?"

"Yes, with Mitchell." *And you won't ruin it for me,* I add to myself.

She huffs. "You call yourself a freethinker, and yet you're voluntarily choosing to participate in an archaic ritual that objectifies women and sustains the myth of happily-ever-after fairy-princess bullshit? Are you insane?"

"It's a *dance,* Sandy," I say. "I think maybe you're the one who's insane."

Her lips twist. I've pleased her. Such a funny girl to be pleased at being called insane.

We sit. I wonder if I can leave now that I've done my duty, and then I wonder at my own thought process. When did tending to Sandy become my "duty"? Last night on the phone, I agreed to spend the night at her house this weekend, a decision I already regret. But Sandy pushed and pushed until it was easier to say yes than to keep offering flimsy excuses.

I shift positions, intensely aware of the looming structure

behind us. I hold my psyche close, careful not to open myself to pale feelers wanting to woo and enchant me. Yet no one— or no thing—seems to want to communicate with me. Has Liliana truly gone dormant?

No. I do sense something. Curious fragments, more on the outside of my brain than the inside.

the key, you ninny, the key.

It's Liliana. But who is she talking to, if not me? Surely not Sandy, who is mired in her own strange mind.

"Were your parents ever beaten?" Sandy asks.

"What?"

"Because of being against the war and all. Sometimes demonstrators are beaten, aren't they?"

I look at her askance. "I guess. But no, not my parents."

"Were they clubbed? Did they ever get teargassed?"

"Sandy . . . you're being weird."

"Did people throw rocks at them?" Sandy asks. "People threw rocks at me once. In fifth grade."

I lean back on my hands. I'm not interested in hearing about fifth grade again. I also have a hard time believing kids threw rocks at her. I mean, come on.

give it to her. get it from her. give get GET

I shiver, because something's wrong, wrong even within the already-wrong context of hearing Liliana's voice again. There's too much pressure in my brain. Too much pulsing desire. The wind scrapes a tree branch against the side of Hamilton Hall, and I hunch my shoulders. Sandy turns and takes a long look at the looming stone façade behind us.

"That's where Liliana was locked away," she says.

I don't respond.

"You know," Sandy goes on, "before she did herself in."

I glance away. Of course I know, and she *knows* I know. An almost unbearable compulsion flaps against my rib cage, and I get the airy feeling of floating above myself. I need to leave, I *want* to leave . . . yet instead I blurt, "Did I ever tell you about the day I got lost?"

"You got lost?" Sandy says with sudden still alertness. "Where?"

I'm confused. Why am I telling her this? Sandy is the last person I should tell about this. But something is squeezing and squeezing . . . and there's blood on the flagstones . . . and as if I'm a puppet, I hitch my chin in the direction of the building.

"You got lost in Hamilton Hall?" Sandy says peculiarly.

"It sounds ridiculous. I know."

i will squeeze it out of you, don't make me squeeze it out of you

I press my thumb and forefinger against my eyebrows. My head hurts. "There's an entire wing on the third floor that's unused," I hear myself say.

Her intake of air is quick and sharp. "Go on."

"You go through this heavy door, and you're back in the past. Dark. Dusty. Old-fashioned wooden doors that lead to dorm rooms." The words gust out of me, relieving the pressure. "Liliana's room, like you said."

Sandy gets to her feet. "Show me."

Suddenly I'm cold, because I'm not going back there. I shouldn't have brought it up. Why *did* I bring it up?

There is smugness in the air. It comes from neither Sandy nor me.

What have I done?

"I've got to go," I say.

"Did you try door three-thirteen?" Sandy asks forcefully. "Did you . . . did you . . ."

I get to my feet. I've said too much.

She grabs my arm and pulls me toward the building. She's agitated. "I couldn't open it," she says. "Maybe you can."

"No!"

"Why not?"

"I don't know!" I'm panicky, and I try to hide it with a joke. "Because maybe Liliana's ghost is there, waiting for her next victim!" I make spooky hands that tremble too much. "Oooooo!"

"Don't talk about Liliana like that," Sandy says.

"Wh-what?"

"*She* was the victim," she says fiercely. "*She* was the one who was wronged."

"Uh-huh," I say. Forget the dead lamb, forget the small matter of binding Elizabeth to a cross, and sure, Liliana was wronged. "Hey. Look. The pep rally's done." From the gym, kids stream out. "I've got to get to English," I say, speaking rapidly. "I'm, uh, supposed to have five possible topics for my research paper, but I've only got two."

Sandy's gaze travels to the top story of Hamilton Hall. I ease toward the path, but her hand snakes out and grabs my wrist. Her grip is steel.

"I've got to go," I wheedle.

"I need the key," she says, still staring at the building. "Give it to me."

"I . . . Sandy . . ." My blood thrums. How does she know that there *is* a key, much less that it's in my possession?

She swivels her head to face me. Her eyes are as vacant as the dusty third-floor windows behind us.

"Sandy?" I say.

Nothing. It's as if she isn't really there—except she's still holding my wrist.

just give it to her and be shut of it

My head. My ribs. That *pressure*, like a wending, outstretched tentacle, probing and probing . . .

My hand, the one not locked in Sandy's grasp, slips into my satchel.

Sandy holds herself perfectly still.

I pull out the key, but not the dove. The dove is not for Sandy, and though the need pressing in on me is unbearable, I find enough strength—and no more—to manage this small rebellion.

Sandy's eyes flicker, and she snatches the key with the

swiftness of a cat pouncing on a songbird. I tug at my wrist. "Can I go now? I really have to get to class."

"Of course," she says, releasing me so abruptly that I stumble backward. She laughs, revealing the tips of her incisors. They're small and pointed.

ninny. stupid sot.

Don't be mean to me!

i spoke. i spoke! but did you listen?

I did! She gave it to me! You know!

and then you let her go.

But—

no, you're right. i grow, perhaps, too
impatient. you have the key; you have
the relic. yet there remains one essential
component to be acquired before our Holy
Communion.

And when we are joined, our power will be
without limits?

yes.

And I will be worshipped! And I will be
revered! And my bidding will be done, or I
shall mete out discipline as I see fit.

we shall be worshipped. never forget.

but only if you secure the offering.

Yes, Mother. I understand.
and it must be human.
Yes, Mother. I know I frustrate you,
I know I'm less than you hoped, but—
procure the Blood, or all is for naught.

"Well, I got a girl with a diamond ring,
I'll tell you, boys,
she knows how to shake that thing."

—Janis Joplin

n Friday, Mitchell takes me to the Varsity diner after school. He lends me his jacket, and we ride his motorcycle. I sit behind him, my arms around his waist, my thighs squeezing his legs.

It is unbelievably sexy.

He is unbelievably sexy.

His motorcycle—this purring, rumbling beast—is unbelievably sexy as well.

"I want a motorcycle," I say in the Varsity parking lot. Mitchell cuts the engine, and I climb off and remove my helmet. I shake out my hair.

"So get one," Mitchell says.

"Riiiiight. My grandmother would kill me. She'd kill me if she knew I even rode on the back of one." I hand Mitchell my helmet. "I told her we were taking the bus."

He laughs, and since nothing I said was all that funny, I decide it's just because he likes me. Which is lovely, since I like him too.

We go inside and sit in one of the red-checkered booths. I order a cheeseburger and fries; he orders a hot dog. When the waitress brings our food, she lays two paper Varsity hats on the table, the kind you puff into shape by pushing against the middle. We both put them on, and we resemble sailors. Or Varsity fry cooks.

Mitchell grins. "That's a good look for you," he says. "I approve."

I tilt my hat more jauntily. "Why, thank you."

"I like a girl who's not afraid of hat-head."

"Oh yeah? What about helmet-head?"

He winces. He makes a thumbs-down sign.

"Hey!" I swat him. "You're the one who made me wear it!"

He leans forward seriously. "Bliss. At work and at play, let safety lead the way."

"Of course," I say. "Silly me."

"Danger never takes a vacation."

"That's right. Expect the unexpected."

"And never, *never*—"

"Yes?"

He wags his finger. "Check a gas tank with a lighted flare."

A laugh snorts out. "Good to know," I say, popping a french fry into my mouth.

We talk about random stuff, like how Lacy McConnell got a cherry-red MG convertible for her birthday. Mitchell tells me that after midnight she and her friends go drag racing, two girls in the front and three or more in the back.

"Without helmets?" I say.

"I know," he says. "Shocking."

Sarah Lynn is friends with Lacy. In my mind's eye I see her perched on the back of the convertible, her face in the wind and her pale hair blowing out behind her. In the moonlight, it would probably look silver.

"I bet they have fun," I say.

He shrugs. "There's more to life than convertibles."

"And that would be . . . motorcycles?"

"Smart-ass."

"What, then?"

Between bites of hot dog, he tells me. Most of it we've touched on before: how kids at Crestview don't know how good they have it, how most of them don't even seem to realize a war is going on. It's a continuation of our "little boxes" conversation, only this time he pushes further, informing me that his dad has been missing in action since 1966.

I put down my cheeseburger. "Since sixty-six? Mitchell . . . that's three years."

He holds my gaze to indicate that, yes, he's done the math.

"Oh, Mitchell," I say. "That's awful. I'm so, so sorry." I want to ask more—Where *is* he? Where did he go missing?—but I'm smart enough not to. It's like when I can't find my purse, and Grandmother says, "Well, where did you leave it?" If I knew, it wouldn't be lost.

Only a dad is . . .

Yeah. Way different from a purse.

I let out a pent-up breath and tell Mitchell about my own dad being a deserter, and how I haven't heard from him or Mom in months.

"Don't they have phones in Canada?" he asks.

"I'm sure they do," I say.

"Then—do you think something happened to them?"

I raise my eyebrows. "My dad always said the enemy could be anyone, but I hardly think that applies to Canadians. He and Mom are probably off in the Canadian wilderness, roasting marshmallows and playing folk songs."

"While you're stuck conjugating verbs at a fancy-dancy prep school."

"Well . . . it's not *so* bad."

He smiles. He reaches across the table and takes my hands.

There's a jangling at the door. Still holding my hands, Mitchell glances up and calls, "Lawrence! Hey, bro!"

Lawrence smiles and ambles over. "Hey, Mitch."

Mitchell releases one of my hands to slap Lawrence's outstretched palm, but he keeps a firm grip on the other. Even in front of Lawrence he does this, which makes our couplehood public. Which makes me all kinds of happy.

"Lawrence, you know Bliss, right?" Mitchell says.

"Sure, sure," Lawrence says, and the way he looks at me without really looking at me tells me that he remembers that day in the stairwell. I wonder, suddenly, if Sarah Lynn remembers. Does she realize I'm the girl who saw them?

"How you kids doing?" Lawrence says.

"A-okay," Mitchell says. "Right, Bliss?"

"Um . . . ," I say. With Lawrence right in front of me, I notice several things that I haven't noted before. One: He is insanely handsome, even more handsome than I'd realized. Two: His palms are pink. Three: The only other black people in the Varsity are the fry cooks in their paper hats, back behind the counter.

This last fact didn't register until this very second. Have I gotten so used to life in the South that it seems normal for all the customers to be white and the help to be black?

"Bliss?" Mitchell says.

"Huh?" He and Lawrence are both apparently waiting for me to say something. "Oh. We're good." I sit up straight. "I'm good!"

Lawrence actually meets my eyes. He seems amused. "That's good."

"It's good to be good," Mitchell contributes.

I blush. I have the craziest urge to bring up Flying V, Daisy, and Clementine to prove I have black friends too.

"All right, stay cool," Lawrence tells us. "Time to get some grub."

"Later, bro," Mitchell says.

I wait until Lawrence is at the counter, then say, "He seems nice."

"He is," Mitchell says, his jaw tightening. "He's a great guy."

"Um . . . I agree. That's why I said he seems nice. I mean, I don't really know him, but—" I break off. I glance around the restaurant, then lean forward. "I think he and Sarah Lynn Lancaster might . . . you know, have a thing."

Surprise flickers in his eyes.

"You know who Sarah Lynn is, right?" I say.

"Of course." His expression grows guarded, and he lowers his voice. "But how do you know about them?"

"You know too?"

"Be quiet. Only because I'm his best friend—or more like his only friend."

"What do you mean? Lawrence has tons of friends." Quoting Thelma, I add, "Everyone adores Lawrence."

"Sure, at school. At football games. But do they bring him home for dinner? Do they borrow his Speed Stick in the locker room?" He lets go of my hand and shoves a fry into his mouth. "No way. He might have colored germs, you never know."

I miss Mitchell's hand. I feel like he's punishing me for something I didn't do. "That's ridiculous," I say. "And not everyone feels that way. Sarah Lynn, for example."

I think about how Sarah Lynn pushed Lawrence away, and frown. "Well . . . maybe, I mean. I don't really know."

Mitchell exhales. "Sarah Lynn's a good girl. But her dad's a bastard."

"How come?"

"How come? Because he was born and bred in this fine city, where 'niggers' are tolerated as long as they know their place. And their place is bowing and scraping, not dating their lily-white daughters."

I trace a scar on the table. It's not that I don't sympathize. It's just that we were having such fun before.

"You don't know that," I say.

"Bliss." He waits until I lift my eyes. "Her dad's a Klansman."

Shock pulls at my features.

Oh, I think numbly. *That would explain why she'd want to hide their relationship, I guess.*

Mitchell watches my face. "Uh-huh. I told Lawrence he's an idiot."

"But . . ." I recall how Lawrence's lips brushed Sarah Lynn's. I remember how Sarah Lynn looked at him in the hall, her gaze a warning, but also more.

"No girl's worth that kind of risk," he says, reading my mind. "No offense."

"None taken," I lie. *Sarah Lynn might be,* I think. I dip a french fry into my ketchup and push the ketchup around. *I might be.*

"I think your grandmother's here," Mitchell says, looking out the wide window. A white Cadillac pulls up, and I stand.

"Well, bye," I say stiffly.

"Stay," he says. "I'll give you a ride home."

I shake my head. "Like she wouldn't notice a motorcycle roaring up the drive? Anyway, I've got plans."

"You do? Doing what?"

I could keep it a mystery. It would serve him right. But I'm tired all of a sudden, and not in the mood for games. So I say, "I'm spending the night with a friend."

"Who?"

"Why? Are you going to stage a panty raid?" I say it with an utter lack of playfulness, and it throws him.

"Are you mad?" he says. He leans back in the booth. "I don't want the guy to get himself lynched. Is that so hard to understand?"

"Not at all," I reply.

"Lawrence doesn't have it easy. He's . . ."

I wait.

"He's different," he says. "Christ, I thought you of all people would understand."

I stop making designs in my ketchup. I release my french fry, and a splat of red splashes my white blouse. Great. But I leave it and say, "Sandy Lear. That's who I'm spending the night with."

His expression changes. "Sandy Lear? For real?"

"For real. So yeah, I get it about being different. I'm not quite as shallow as you think."

"What? Bliss, I *never* thought you were shallow." He gives me a long, charged look, and my resistance weakens.

"Sandy's an odd duck," Mitchell says, shaking his head. "But . . . so what, right? That's great that you're her friend."

I blink. Truthfully, I'm no longer sure I want to be her

friend. If I had an easy way of getting out of our sleepover, I would.

"That's what I like best about you," he says. "You don't care what other people think."

"I care what you think," I say.

"Well, of course." He rises to his feet and hugs me. But the way he sighs, when at last he pulls away, tells me he won't be cruising by Sandy's for a late-night flirtation. There will be no panty raids tonight.

Since giving me the key, my supplicant has grown distant. Why? Does she not realize what this means for me? What this means for her?

Apparently she does not. I am well versed in the signs of waning interest; to experience it again . . . the prospect of yet another betrayal . . .

But, no. Such betrayal will not come to pass, as tonight I will open her eyes to the power I can offer her. Ultimate power, no. That is the privilege of the divine. But as our human supplicant, she will reap the many rewards of our favor.

One ritual offering, and it is done. Not here, not now. But soon. And should she balk at what is asked of her, I shall remind her that I, too, have made sacrifices. I have faced abuse all these many years, and now

Liliana abuses me as well, with her ill temper and her hurtful words.

She doesn't mean it, though. She is . . . hungry, that is all. And once we are joined, none of it will matter.

I hear a car pulling into the driveway—my supplicant is here! And, oh, my heart races, because how long has it been since anyone other than Mam has set foot inside this room? Four years?

At least I don't have to worry about Mam herself. I gave her twice her usual dose of pain medication, and that, plus her whiskey, has more than adequately put her out.

he moment I step into Sandy's house, I want
to turn and leave. If she hadn't extended the
invitation before the pep rally, I wouldn't have
accepted. But here I am—and Mitchell thinks it's great.

I suppose I should make the best of it.

But her house smells, in an animal sort of way. And it's
incredibly messy, with stacks of magazines and books on
every available surface. Also, dirty dishes. And old yogurt
containers, lots of yogurt containers. It's gross, though as I
follow Sandy down the dank hall, I remind myself that it's not
as gross as some places. The pigeon coop on the commune, for
example, with its rivers of bird poo and clumps of feathers.
Nothing could be as gross as that pigeon coop.

"So . . . here's my room," Sandy says, pushing open a
flimsy particleboard door. She bites her lower lip, and I go in.

"Oh," I say. The animal smell is far stronger, and I sneeze
three times in a row. Clots of yellow fur drift lazily in the
stirred-up air.

"You . . . have a cat?" I venture.

Sandy beams, and I notice about a dozen cat figurines

on her dresser, plus twenty or so more arranged on her bookshelf. Porcelain ones, ones made of stone, a gleaming gold one with a jeweled collar. The gold one has a regal bearing and a haughty expression. It looks Egyptian.

"Ah," I say. "You have a lot of cats."

"But only one that's flesh and blood—at least, so far." Sandy walks to her bed, crouches, and rubs her fingers together. "Here, Regular. Here, girl."

"'Regular'?" I say.

"I got her when I was ten. She's my best friend in the world." She looks up. "Except for you, of course."

Her tone is oily and gives me the heebie-jeebies. I slip off my coat and drop it, as well as my overnight bag, on the floor, and dust puffs up from the carpet. From the looks of it, she hasn't vacuumed in eons. Where the carpet meets the wall, there are dust balls clustered like marbles.

"Regular, don't be shy," Sandy coaxes. She knee-walks closer to the bed, sticks her head beneath the dust ruffle, and reaches her arm in deep. Her butt sways as she fishes around. Regular meows.

"Gotcha!" Sandy cries, and Regular's meow jumps an octave higher.

Sandy backs out, still on her knees. She tugs at a bedraggled butterscotch cat who resists every step of the way.

"Sandy, just leave her," I say. "She obviously doesn't want to come out."

"She does so. She wants to meet you, don't you, Regular?"

With a yank that makes me wince, she unhooks Regular from the carpet. She lifts one of Regular's paws and makes her wave. "Say hi to Bliss, Regular." She raises her voice to a falsetto. "Hi, Bliss."

I give a pained smile.

"Aren't you going to say hi back?" Sandy says.

"Hi, Regular," I say.

Sandy thrusts Regular at me, and reluctantly I accept her. I can feel her heart racing.

"It's okay," I say soothingly. "You're okay."

Regular is a squirming mass of mange, and I'm afraid I'm going to drop her. So I lower myself to the floor—gross—and hold Regular in my lap. I keep my hands firmly on her, rubbing circles into her matted fur. Eventually she stops trying to escape, though her ears stay cocked back.

"You're good with her," Sandy notes.

I shrug. "I like animals—except for birds. Well, pigeons. I'm not such a pigeon fan." I keep petting, and a wheezy purr starts up in Regular's chest. I feel the jutting-out of her ribs.

"She's so skinny," I say. "Don't you feed her?"

"Ha, ha," Sandy says. "Of course I feed her."

"Seriously, Sandy, if you put her in a tub of water, she'd be nothing but bones." On the commune once, I saw a raccoon waddle into the creek all big and bushy, then waddle out a drowned rat, at least three times smaller than when his fur was fluffed out.

"Well, I'm not going to put her in a tub of water," Sandy says. "Why would I put her in a tub of water?"

"Relax," I say. "But for real, there might be something wrong with her. Do you think she has worms?"

"She doesn't have worms," Sandy says.

"Are you sure? Have you taken her to the vet?"

"Um, yeah. He said it was, um, a digestive disorder."

"Oh. Do you have medicine for her?"

"Yeah," she says. She bends down and grabs Regular. "Hey, watch this." She crosses the room and puts her in the closet. She closes the door.

"What are you doing?"

"Nothing."

"Sandy. You just put your cat in the closet."

"I know. She likes it."

Regular claws the wood and meows.

"She wants out," I say.

"Re-gu-lar!" Sandy calls, keeping her eyes on my face. "Where are you, sweetie?"

Regular thumps against the door.

"I hear you, but I can't find you! Are you lost?"

Regular yowls.

"Come on, Sandy. It's not funny." I get to my feet.

Sandy opens the closet door before I can get there, and Regular dashes out.

"Regular!" Sandy cries, scooping her up. "What were you doing in the closet, you bad cat?"

Regular purrs manically, her claws extending and retracting against Sandy's shirt.

"What if I didn't find you?" Sandy murmurs. "What if you were stuck in there forever?" She gazes at me, her face half hidden by Regular's body.

"You're sick," I say. And then I sniff suspiciously, because a horrible odor emanates from the open closet. It's worse and more particular than the cat smell already in the air.

"It's a game," Sandy says reproachfully. "She likes it, don't you, Regular?" She points Regular's triangular face at me and switches to her cat voice. "*Yes.*"

"Sandy, your closet smells awful." I move to shut the door.

"Don't!" She tosses Regular to the floor. "I'll get it."

This time she's too late. My hand's already on the doorknob, and I peer into the closet's dark interior, searching for the source of the stench. Against the back wall I spot a litter box. As my eyes adjust, I realize it's jam-packed with hard brown balls of poop—so jam-packed that not a speck of litter is visible. There's poop on the closet floor, too. Clumps and piles and scatterings of it.

I gag.

"I ran out of time to clean," Sandy says.

I press my hand to my mouth. As I stumble back, I feel something squish beneath my shoe, and though I don't want to look, I can't help myself. What I stepped on is a sausage-shaped turd, only it's so ancient and dry that it crumbles instead of smearing on my sole. I scan Sandy's room again, and I see what I missed before. Yes, her room is filthy. Yes, there is dust upon dust. But it's not all dust. Some of the dust is actually cat shit.

The pigeon coop has nothing on Sandy's bedroom.

"I've got to go," I manage. "I can't stay here."

Sandy grabs me. "No!"

I shake her off and reach down for my things. She clutches my bag just as I do.

"I'll clean up. I'll do better. I just haven't had anyone over in so long!"

"Sandy, no. I shouldn't have come in the first place."

"*Please!*" She's agitated, and I flash back to the day on the quad when she hit herself over and over. Even then, I think some part of me knew she was nuts. Why did I let myself believe otherwise?

"I can't." I jerk at my bag, but she doesn't let go. Panic mounts inside me, because Sandy is strong. What if she locks me in the closet and refuses to let me out?

I close my eyes. I struggle to find a still spot inside me, because who's being crazy now?

I release my bag, and Sandy flies back and lands with an ooomph on the floor. Regular howls and scats under the bed.

"Nice," I say. "You scared your cat."

Sandy swallows. She takes a deep breath. She is trying to calm herself, just as I'm trying to calm myself.

"I really don't want you to go," she says in a shaky voice.

"Will you hand me my bag, please?"

"I live in a shit hole," she says. "I know! My whole life is a shit hole!" Her eyes fill with tears, which pisses me off even—*dammit*—as it makes me feel sorry for her. She looks ridiculous sprawled there on the floor.

I look away, crossing my arms over my chest.

She pushes up on her hands and knees, then stands. She gives me my duffel bag.

"I could clean up now," she whispers. "You could sit outside. You could . . . read a book. And then I'd come get you."

The canvas strap of my bag is thick in my hand, a tangible reminder of reality. To go back home, I'd have to call Grandmother and ask her to come pick me up. Only tonight is Bridge night. She'll be out late.

I could call Mitchell, I suppose, but then I'd be the person who can't handle someone's differences. *Yeah, and why don't you come spend the night in turd land*, I say to him in my mind. But regardless, I'm not Mitchell's damsel in distress. I'm not anyone's damsel in distress.

Sandy bows her head. "Mam wants to drown her. That's why I keep her in my room. That's why there's so much . . . you know."

"Your mom wants to drown your cat?" I say skeptically.

"She's going to make me get rid of her. She says so every day. I just wish . . ."

Don't do it, I warn myself. *Don't take the bait.*

Sandy sniffles.

"You just wish what?" I say, despising myself.

"That she could have kittens. Just one litter."

"Why?" I glance around, gesturing at her cramped, foul room. "And where would you keep them? In here?"

"Just one litter. Well, maybe more. Why not, right? Nothing wrong with kittens, right?" She looks at me, and her desire is intense. "All I need is a safe place to keep them, somewhere Mam can't get to them."

"I'm not taking them, if that's what you're thinking," I say.

She regards me disdainfully, and hints of the old Sandy filter back. Less pathetic, more dismissive. "I don't want anyone to *take* them. I just want them to be safe, like I said."

She straightens her spine. "Anyway, I've got the perfect place—and not just for kittens, but for all sorts of wonderful things. *Wonderful* things! And don't try to worm it out of me, because you can't."

I have zero interest in worming anything from her.

Sandy waits. When she realizes I'm not going to pursue it, she says, "But maybe I'll show you one day." She lets out her man-giggle. "If you're a good girl . . . and if you do as I say."

I assume she's speaking of Hamilton Hall, of Liliana's old room. I push the thought from my brain, however, because I don't want her sensing that I've figured it out. I don't want her taking that as permission to speak of her "secret place" out loud.

"So are you going or staying?" Sandy asks.

I'm tight inside, and I'm as ticked off with myself as I am with Sandy. Maybe more so. Why do I put myself in these situations? Why am I such an easy mark? Maybe Thelma has it right and it is better just to be shallow and self-absorbed.

And yet, I don't want her growing so agitated that she . . . makes any rash decisions. "Fine, I'll go hang out in your backyard," I say, promising myself that this is the very last time. After this, no more mister nice guy. "But I'm taking my bag with me. And seriously, Sandy, you've got to use, like, cleaning supplies."

"Yes, ma'am."

"All the poop has to go."

She gives me a coy look. "Can't I save just one? For posterity?"

"Forget it, I'm out of here."

"Kidding! Kidding." She's already bustling around, picking up trash and bits of fluff. She shoos me out the door. "Go! I'll come get you when I'm done. And I swear, Bliss, it'll be the best sleepover ever."

"I promise I will never reveal any of the secrets of the Wildcats. I will not even tell anyone there is such a club as the Wildcats and, if I ever do, I will be struck down by the Curse of the Claw."

—Opie Taylor

I t's not the best sleepover ever. Even though it's my first sleepover ever, I know it's the worst and not the best. Sandy cleans up the turd piles, but the odor lingers. I doubt it will ever be fully gone. Plus, every time I glance toward the closet, I can't help but think of what used to be there. That's the problem with closed doors: Even if nothing's behind them, it's easy to imagine the worst.

Added to the fun is Regular herself, who stays in Sandy's room with us since she's not allowed anywhere else. At one point she meows at Sandy's door as if she wants to go out, but when I get up to let her, Sandy says the thing again about her mom throwing Regular into a river. This time I don't contradict her, but I do ask where her mom is, anyway. I haven't seen her all night.

"She got tired and went to bed," Sandy says.

I glance at my watch. "At seven thirty?"

"She has a bad back, all right? It takes a lot out of her to get around. It takes way more out of her than it does you or me, all right?"

I hold up my hands. "All right, all right."

Sandy goes to the closed door and snatches Regular. She plops down with her and gives her a good petting, which Regular endures with flattened-back ears and back-and-forth darts of her eyes. Eventually she purrs. Still, when I look at Regular, I don't think, *Now there's a cat that's meant to have kittens.* Instead I think, *Procreation is not for everyone.*

The worst part of the evening comes after dinner (fish sticks) and TV (*Bewitched*), when Sandy and I tromp back to her room and get ready for bed.

"So . . . should I sleep on the floor?" I ask hesitantly after I slip on a nightshirt that reaches past my knees. It's girly, with pink flowers. Grandmother bought it for me.

"Tell me you're kidding," Sandy says. She pauses in the middle of changing clothes. "You honestly think I'd invite you over and make you sleep on the floor?"

"Oh," I say. It's nice of her to let me have her bed, I guess, but I kind of want to ask if she put on fresh sheets. I also want her to go ahead and pull her nightgown on. She's standing there wearing neither shirt nor bra, which makes it seem as if she and her boobs are all three gazing at me.

I haven't been brought up a prude. I've seen plenty of naked people in my fourteen years, and I respect the human form and all that. But it's one thing to see a girl whip off her tie-dye at a Dead show and swing it around in a circle, yelling, "Woo-hooo!" It's quite another to be in a small, enclosed space with a too-bare Sandy, just the two of us.

I adjust my own nightgown, trying to use E.S.P. to get

her back on track, and it works, because she shoves her arms and head through the openings of her nightie and tugs it down. Then her hands slip up and under, *wiggle-wiggle-wiggle*, and off comes her underwear. It's exactly the kind of underwear I'd expect, large and pale and shapeless. She tosses them to the side.

I wait for her to go to her dresser and get fresh undies, but she doesn't. *First nightgown, then panties*, I coach her in my brain. *You can do it.*

Instead, she climbs into bed. I'm confused, because didn't she just say that I was going to get the bed? Then it sinks in: She expects us to sleep together in the bed, *and* she's one of those people who sleeps without underwear. Not so long ago, perhaps such a matter would have seemed trivial, but that time is gone. That *me* is gone, and the *me* I am now doesn't want to be here.

"Is there a problem?" Sandy asks.

I hunch my shoulders and climb gingerly into the bed, staying on the very, very far edge.

"Okey-dokey," Sandy says. She rolls over to turn off her lamp, and the room goes dark. I lie there, immobile. Then there's a near-silent padding, followed by a thump-pounce that rocks the mattress.

Regular treads across me, and her tail flicks my face.

"Chuckle buddy," Sandy coos, or maybe "suckle buddy," though neither endearment makes sense. Cats don't chuckle. Still, I'm glad for another body between me and Sandy.

Regular's squeaky purr starts up, and I allow myself to shift around on my pillow.

"Can I tell you something?" Sandy says in the shadows.

"Um . . . I'm pretty tired."

"It's about . . . friendship. And being true, and doing things for one another. That's what friends do, right? And sometimes it feels, well . . . like a sacrifice, maybe—but it's for a greater good, right?"

"Sandy, what are you talking about?" I say wearily.

"I thought I had a friend, once. A true friend. But she betrayed me."

"Yes, I know. I know all about Sarah Lynn, and I see no point in talking about her, because I already know you hate her."

She giggles, but it sounds forced. "There are things you don't know, though. Like . . . she and I have the same initials. Even our middle names. They both start with 'L'."

"You don't say."

"My middle name's Lurlene," she offers.

"Okay."

"We thought that was so great when we were in the fifth grade," Sandy goes on. "We thought it was a sign."

I gaze at the ceiling, which is beginning to gain definition. I really would prefer to sleep—or be gone from this bedroom altogether.

"And for the record, I made the first move. She was new and had no friends. I was nice to her."

Out of the corner of my eye, I see Sandy turn to face me.

"She spent the night, like, every weekend. In this very bed. In the very spot where you are now."

I imagine a ten-year-old Sarah Lynn lying right here with her hands clasped over her chest. Maybe gazing up at the ceiling, just like me?

"We used to play a game," Sandy says, her voice changing. "A private game. Just for us."

"Better keep it private, then," I say, my blood pressure taking a sudden plunge. I've already told her I don't want to talk about Sarah Lynn. I certainly don't want to hear about any . . . private games between the two of them. My chest goes up and down with shallow breaths.

"We would draw designs on each other's skin, with our fingers." Her voice dips. "We'd lick them first."

"Your . . . fingers?"

"I'd lift her nightgown and tell her to hold still, but she never could. She said it tickled."

I make a noise, but I'm not sure it's audible.

"But she loved it! She loved being tickled!"

"Sandy, I'm *really* tired. I think we should go to sleep."

"Do you know what she told Lacy and Heather and Melissa?" she says, her voice breaking. "Once she decided she didn't want to be friends anymore, because I wasn't *good* enough? Because I wasn't pretty enough and peppy enough and *stupid* enough?"

Sandy's words quaver, but Regular keeps purring. If anything, her purring grows stronger.

"She told them"—she gulps—"She told them . . ."

I turn my head, and our eyes lock. Hers have circles of brightness in them despite the dim light.

"She told them I was unnatural, that's what she said!"

You are, I think. And, *Oh, Sandy.* My heart breaks for her even as it puts up a wall to keep her out.

"But who cares?" she says, sniffling. "'Cause now I have you, right? And you've been a super-good influence on me. I mean that. And . . . well, I was wondering . . ."

My pulse spikes. *No, you may not draw on my stomach.*

". . . if you might like to know something special about me." She says it nervously, but with white-hot desire thrumming below the surface. It makes *me* nervous. It makes me *very* nervous.

God, where do I go with this?

"Um, I'm kind of feeling . . ." I breathe out a puff of air. "I just, um . . . *phew.* You are special, Sandy. I already know that." I yawn. "I'm just really, really, incredibly—"

"I have power," she interrupts fervidly. "True power. You can have it too."

I look at her. Moonlight shines through the slats in her blinds, and her face is slivered dark, then white, then dark. I'm in this room—in this *bed*—with a person whose grasp on sanity is no longer solid, if it ever was, and my senses kick into overdrive. I need to be careful.

"Do you believe me?" Sandy says.

"Y-y-yes," I say, because I think it's better not to contradict her.

"I'll show you." She's getting worked up. "You see, I've found a way to communicate with Liliana, Mother of All. She speaks to me—she speaks through me! Shall I call Her to us?"

"No!" I say, experiencing a surge of fear so deep that my insides lock up, especially my lungs. I have a hard time breathing.

"Pretty please with a cherry on top?"

"Um, I just don't think it's a—"

"*Please.*" This time it's more of a groan.

"Sandy . . . *no!*"

She stares at me reproachfully. Seconds trudge by, and her reproach changes to resentment. I can't seem to pull my gaze away, and so I see in her eyes the very moment her resentment turns to hostility, as if I've let her down and must be punished. I'm suddenly scared of what she might do.

"Maybe another time?" I say. I purposefully slow my breathing, and I don't break our eye contact, hard as it is not to look away. Beneath the covers, my toes are clenched snails.

She blinks.

"You've got to realize, you're kind of springing this on me out of the blue." I laugh with what I hope is the right mix of confusion and awe. "I need to get my head around it, you know?"

She wants to believe me. Her eyes are shining beacons.

"You are part of it," she whispers. "What you could offer, it will make everything . . . come together."

"Yeah, sure," I say, nodding. "I get that. Just . . . be gentle with me, okay?"

By chance I've landed on the right thing to say, because a smile stretches across Sandy's face. "Okay," she says happily. "I'll be your teacher, and you'll be my student. We can't take too long, though, or Liliana will grow impatient."

"I understand."

"I knew you would say yes. I knew it." She sighs. "I feel really good about this. Do you?"

"Why wouldn't I?" I say. I feel absolutely, gut-wrenchingly nauseated about this. Sandy and Liliana are a bad mix, a very bad mix.

She laughs. She adjusts the covers and scooches to get comfortable, and then bam, she falls asleep. Within minutes she's snoring.

For me, it takes longer. If Liliana is in touch with Sandy—and I have no reason to believe she's not—what is she telling her? Is Sandy to be the next Nanette? The next Elizabeth, strapped to a roughhewn cross? And what did Sandy mean when she spoke of what I could offer?

I am offering nothing, not one bloody thing. On that I stake my life.

I shift my gaze back to the ceiling and watch the movement of the shadows. I think about how strange life can be. Being here in Sandy's bed—this is where I am right now. I don't want to be, but I am.

Just get to the morning, I tell myself. *Just get through the next eight* hours, and a new day will begin. From the moment I leave this house, I'll have as little to do with Sandy as humanly possible.

Sleep lures me in despite my best intentions, and as my thoughts go drifty, a long-ago memory is dislodged. When I was seven, Mom took me with her to a concert, and afterward, we crashed at one of her friends' apartments. The sleeping bag her friend pulled out for me smelled like pee, and I wanted to go home. Mom told me to lie down and quit complaining. I woke up the next morning covered with bites, and when Mom pulled me out of the sleeping bag, she saw that it was teeming with spiders. In the lining she found the remains of an egg sack, sticky and white as a marshmallow.

When at last I fall asleep in Sandy's bed, I dream of spiders with pinhead bodies and spindly legs. They scuttle over me . . . and then they change in their dreamlike way. Spider legs turn to cat claws, cat claws turn to human fingers. Human fingers whispering—*shhhh*—over my skin.

"These children that come at you with knives—they are your children. You taught them. I didn't teach them. I just tried to help them stand up."

—Charles Manson

The Tate-LaBianca murder trial continues to keep people buzzing, as each day brings new and ghastly details. Today, the morning news anchor reported that Charles Manson showed up in court with an "X" carved into his forehead. Several hours later, the three female defendants—Patricia Krenwinkel, Sadie Atkins, and Leslie Van Houten—were led in front of the judge, each with an "X" carved into her forehead.

But they hadn't been in communication with Charles Manson, or, supposedly, one another. The three females were housed in different cells, and Charles Manson was in a separate facility altogether. So how did they all come to carve identical "Xs"?

"Communist hippie freaks," Thelma says as we walk to class. Her hair in its high ponytail bounces.

"Thelma," I say. "Do you even know what a communist is?"

"Of *course*," she says, like I'm an idiot.

I wait.

"A communist is someone who doesn't believe in America. Like Charles Manson!"

I roll my eyes, thinking that Thelma is Thelma is Thelma. Then she surprises me by growing uncharacteristically subdued.

"They said that one girl, Sadie Atkins—the one who's so young?"

I nod. I've seen bits of the coverage when Grandmother was otherwise engaged, and Sadie's the one who sits in the front of the courtroom with her hands clasped in her lap, as if she's in church. She's accused of slaughtering five people.

"They say she watched the news the day after the murders," Thelma said. "In a trailer in Death Valley, where the Family lived? Another of the Family members came forward and talked to the cops, and he said that Sadie laughed as the reporter described the slayings."

Thelma's expression is bewildered. "How could anyone do that? How could anyone kill those people . . . and then *laugh?*"

"I don't know," I say. I don't know much at all, it seems, and the extent of my ignorance has been troubling me. Not about Sadie Atkins; about Sandy Lear. And Liliana, of course. I don't want to think about them, but I can't help it. And what if it's my responsibility to stop them? But . . . from *what?*

Thelma keeps walking, pensive. Then she cups her hand over her mouth and blows. "Do you have any gum?" she asks. "I feel like my breath is stinky."

All day long, I think about the Sandy problem and what, if anything, I should do. That afternoon, instead of going straight home, I catch a bus to Peachtree Street and get off at the stop closest to the Eternal Fountains Nursing Home.

I need to talk to Agnes Nutter.

"Bliss," Agnes says when I step into her room. "Why, hello, pet. I thought you might stop by one of these days."

"You did?" I say.

"Sit," she says, patting her bed. The effort makes her wheeze. And am I mistaken, or has she shrunk since the first time I met her? Her eyes are olives deep in her face, and her body is tiny beneath the covers. Her birthmark, on the other hand, seems to have grown.

I perch carefully on the edge of the mattress, taking care not to jostle her. Her bones look as fragile as a bird's.

She takes a rattling breath. "Gracious. I'm not as . . . young . . . as I . . . used to be. Now, what can I do for you?"

"I don't know," I say, which is the truth.

Agnes waits. The lesion above her lip appears to pulse.

"It's Sandy," I say at last. "I'm scared for her."

"Ah," she says. She doesn't seem the least bit surprised. "Scared for her—or scared of her?"

I blush. I don't know why, but I do.

"Do you know how old I am, pet?" Agnes asks.

Her question catches me off guard. "Um . . . eighty?"

She chuckles. "One hundred and one!"

My eyebrows shoot up.

"I'm right near done, though. My time's almost up."

"You . . . you don't know that," I say.

"Oh, I do. But don't feel bad. It should have happened long ago."

My fingers twitch, pattering against my skirt like spiders. When I notice, I stop.

"Um . . . does this have anything to do with Sandy?" I ask.

"Sweet thing, Sandy took the relic," Agnes says.

As soon as she says it, it clicks with dreadful certainty in my mind. Of course she did, just as she took Elsie's twenty dollars—I didn't notice a thing. And it's the relic, that horrible collection of flesh and hair, that's made it so that Sandy can hear Liliana. I remember Sandy's feverish proclamation as we lay together in her bed: *I have true power.*

"Oh, Agnes," I say faintly. "I think . . . I think this isn't good."

"Ever since the day you two visited, my health has declined," Agnes muses. "It's been quite rapid. The doctors don't understand, but I do. After all, I gave her offerings. I kept her safe. In return, she fed me life."

My mouth goes dry. "The 'she' you're talking about . . . ?"

"Liliana. Yes."

I wrap my arms around my chest. This is really, really not good.

"Before you, I'd shown the relic to no one. But then you came—and I felt compelled to bring it out. I think now that it was Liliana, guiding me one last time." She cocks her head. "She sensed your power, you see."

"But Sandy ended up with the relic," I say. "Not me. And I think, um, that she and Liliana are kind of connected now." I don't mention the key. I'm too throbbingly, skittishly ashamed to speak out loud of how foolish I was.

"Then Sandy is standing in the need of prayer," Agnes says flatly. "Liliana will use her, just as she used me. And Sandy will let her, just as I did." Her dark eyes lock on mine. "Liliana might have been drawn by your power, but Sandy's weakness will serve her even better."

"I don't understand," I say.

Agnes's frail chest rises under her sheet. Her eyes go distant.

Don't drift away on me, Agnes, I say silently. I shift on the bed—just slightly—and the movement brings her back.

"Liliana's needs were deep," Agnes tells me. "Or rather, *are* deep, and until recently, I've existed purely to fill them." Agnes takes my fingers. "Do you know how wonderful it feels to no longer serve her? I would never have known it, never have chosen it. But, oh Bliss, it's lovely to be free of her."

"I'm glad," I say.

"Sandy, too, has a deep need," she says.

"I know," I say. "That's what I'm worried about, I guess. Should I try to stop her or something?"

"Stop her from what?" Agnes says. "Being needy?"

We look at each other. We both know the impossibility of that proposition.

Agnes coughs and pulls her hand to her mouth. When she brings it away, I see spittle tinged with red.

"Agnes, are you okay?" I ask.

She fumbles for a tissue and wipes her mouth. "Stay clear of her," she tells me in a weak voice. "Don't get . . ."

"Should I call someone? Do you need a nurse?"

"Ensnared," she whispers. "Go on, now. Let me rest."

"Now is the time for all good men
to come to the aid of their neighbor!
Repeat! Now is the time for all good men
to come to the aid of their neighbor!"

—Deputy Sheriff Barney Fife

'm glad to be warned away from Sandy. I'm glad
to have that dictate: Stay clear. And stay clear I do.
Over the next several days, I sequester myself in the
library and devote myself to my studies. I conjugate French
verbs. I solve math problems. I settle on a thesis for my
research paper.

On Wednesday, I find Sarah Lynn Lancaster at the library
table I've grown to think of as my own.

"Oh," I say stupidly. Clutching my satchel full of books,
I turn to leave.

"No, wait," Sarah Lynn says. "Were you planning to sit
here?"

"Um, yeah. I have to work on my English paper. But that's
okay, I'll find another spot."

"Ms. Phillips?" Sarah Lynn says.

Ms. Phillips is my English teacher. I nod.

"I'm working on my paper too." She grins. "Join me.
Sometimes I work better just knowing that someone else is
stuck doing the same thing I am, you know?"

This is the first time I've seen Sarah Lynn since my

sleepover at Sandy's. Sarah Lynn and I, we slept on the same spot in Sandy's bed. I feel an unexpected kinship with her.

I smile tentatively and slide into the chair across from hers. I jot down several ideas in my notebook, then stop, realizing that my pencil is the only one making any noise. I glance up at her, and she startles and leans over her piece of paper.

We scribble away for several minutes before once again I realize that Sarah Lynn's pencil is limp in her hand. This time when I glance at her, she wrinkles her nose in that way she does.

"I'm distracting you," she says. "Sorry. I'm just having a hard time focusing, you know?"

"Yeah, that happens to me, too," I say. *Boy, does it.*

"Did you watch the trial yesterday?" Sarah Lynn asks.

"No," I say. "Did something new happen?"

She draws a strand of her honey-colored hair between her lips. "Not really, just more of the same. I feel so bad for Sharon Tate, don't you?"

I put down my pencil. I nod.

"And how awful for her husband," she goes on. "To lose not only his wife, but his unborn baby."

"I know." It *is* awful, every bit of it.

"And the second night, with the LaBiancas . . ." Sarah Lynn pauses. "They were somebody's *grandparents.* That's how old they were."

"I hate thinking about that," I say.

"I think about how scared they must have been when Charles Manson tied them up, and I wonder . . ."

The silence stretches out. Sarah Lynn's eyes are dark with pain.

"If they knew they were going to die?" I finally say.

She nods. "Or if maybe Mr. LaBianca said to his wife, 'Just do what he says. It'll be okay.' Because Charles Manson only tied up their hands, you know. He tied up their hands and put pillowcases over their heads, and he told them nothing would happen to them if they just sat still and didn't make any noise."

"And then he sent the other members of his Family back in to finish them off," I say helplessly.

"But not until twenty minutes later! They could have gotten away!"

"I know. But they were trying to be good and follow Charles Manson's instructions."

We gaze at each other. *Yeah, and look how far it got them,* is our shared, unspoken thought.

"Did you know that Charles Manson told them to steal Rosemary LaBianca's wallet?" Sarah Lynn says. "But it wasn't for the money. He just wanted one of his followers to plant it in a gas station restroom in the black part of town."

"Why?"

"So that a black person would find it and use the credit cards and get blamed for the murder."

Black part of town, black person . . .

I think about Lawrence, and I assume Sarah Lynn's thinking about him too. Does she remember that day in the stairwell, when I saw the two of them together? Surely she must.

"Did Charles Manson especially want a black person to find it?" I ask. "Or would anyone have done?"

"No, he wanted it to be a black person," Sarah Lynn says bitterly. "He had this whole plan: White people would blame black people for the murders, and then the black people would get angry and exact revenge. Charles Manson wanted the blacks to kill every single white person in the world."

"But he's white himself."

"Yeah, only he and his Family would be holed up in some cave out in Death Valley," she says. "And once all the other white people were dead, Charles Manson would lead his followers back out into the sunlight and they'd rule the world."

"But Charles Manson is white. Why would he think black people would let him be their leader?"

"Because he's a racist jerk," Sarah Lynn says. She tilts her head. "To quote his right-hand man: 'So Blackie will say, "I did my thing, I killed them all." And Charlie will scratch Blackie's fuzzy head and kick him in the butt and tell him to go pick cotton and go be a good nigger.'"

Sarah Lynn looks down, and if I'm not mistaken, she's fighting tears. "Or something like that."

Blackie, I think. Blacks, coloreds, Negroes, niggers. Little Nigra girls.

"Oh, gosh," she says. "Let's talk about something else, okay?"

Yes, I think, but first I say, "Only an idiot would think something like that."

She lifts her head. Her eyelashes are long and generous. "My daddy thinks that. He thinks it was better before, when black people . . . knew their place."

"Oh," I say.

"I don't think that!" She blushes, only it's more intense than blushing. "I think *white* people need to know their place, and not pass judgment on others all the time!"

"Girls?" the librarian says, appearing at our table and resting her hand on the back of my chair. "Is everything all right?"

"Yes, of course," Sarah Lynn tells her. "Sorry, Mrs. Lambert."

Mrs. Lambert attempts to maintain her disapproval, but like everyone else, she's charmed by Sarah Lynn.

"Try to keep it down," she says.

"We will. Like I said, we're really sorry."

As soon as Mrs. Lambert's out of earshot, Sarah Lynn exhales shakily.

"I shouldn't have laid that on you," she says. "But . . . he's my daddy, you know?"

I think of my own dad, eating wild berries somewhere in the wilds of Canada.

"Yeah," I say. "I know."

"When you make a solemn promise
to a friend, it ain't right to go back on it.
No. Never let your friend down, never
break a trust, and when you give your
word, never go back on it."

—Sheriff Andy Taylor

n Thursday, Sandy finds me despite my best efforts to stay out of her path.

"Have you thought about what I told you?" Sandy asks.

I look at her, then look away. My pulse goes jittery.

"*Have* you?"

"Um, I haven't really had time," I say.

"What, too busy with all your social engagements?"

I let her sarcasm slide, because as a matter of fact, yes. I have been busy with social engagements. Yesterday Mitchell offered me a ride home on his motorcycle, and I accepted. He pulled up five houses down from Grandmother's and walked me the rest of the way. He rubbed my shoulders to warm me from the chilly ride.

Sandy snaps her fingers in front of my face. "Hey! Anyone home?"

"Quit it," I say tensely. I push away her hand and dart into my classroom.

On Friday, she finds me in the cafeteria and asks again if I've considered her offer.

"Because I've been thinking," she says in a let's-tell-secrets tone. Her voice dips to a dusky whisper. "The perfect time to perform the ceremony . . . well, why not do it on the night of the Winter Dance?"

Ceremony? "I don't think so, Sandy," I say, just barely able to keep the contents of my stomach where they belong. I should just say *no* and be done with it—and I would, if she didn't seem so unstable.

"But why not?" she says. She reaches for one of my fries, but in her agitation, she knocks over the plastic salt shaker. "You'd be all dressed up. You'd be so pretty. I could dress up and be pretty too."

"I just don't think the dance is the right time," I say, hating myself for my cowardice. Strangely, my foot moves below the table to touch the fabric of my satchel, where the wooden dove still lies. The key—before I lost it—disturbed me, and yet I kept it close. The dove, on the other hand, comforts me, and so I keep it close.

"You big silly," Sandy says. She smiles and rolls her eyes.

I frown. "Why am I silly?"

"Because of course the dance is the right time. The dance is supposed to be magical, right?"

"Yes, but *romance* magic," I say. "Enchantment-in-a-winter-wonderland magic."

"Exactly," Sandy says. She wets the tip of her finger and drags it over the spill of salt. She brings her finger to her mouth, sucks it, then slowly draws it out. She gazes at me until I look away.

She half-laughs. "You're nervous. I understand." She pushes back her chair. "But don't keep me waiting forever. After all, a girl can't make magic if she doesn't have anyone to make magic with."

My stomach cramps. I stare doggedly at my half-eaten hamburger until I'm sure she's gone.

Liliana grows increasingly irritable. She is displeased with me as well as my supplicant. She is ready for the ceremony and does not want to wait. If the offering must be obtained by force, then let the offering be obtained by force. That is Her position.

I, too, am vexed by my supplicant, but I plead on her behalf. Far better she come to Us willingly . . . especially as Liliana has informed me that contrary to my assumptions, the one offering will not suffice for all of time. Multiple offerings will be required. Infinite offerings. For now, I use this argument to my advantage—after all, wouldn't it be easier to have a ready source than to be constantly on the hunt?

but i enjoy the hunt.

Oh. Yes, of course.

one girl will do for now. later, we shall have more. but hear this: do not ever think you are bending my will to yours. do you understand? that would make you foolish, and you're not foolish, are you, fool?

Don't call me that, please.

then make it be so.

he next week, I return to the library. I look for Sarah Lynn, and I'm disappointed when I don't see her. But on Thursday, after our last class has let out, she appears.

"Hey," Sarah Lynn says. Am I making it up, or does she look pleased? "Can I sit with you, or am I too much of a nuisance? I feel terrible about last time, how I just kept going on and on and didn't let you get a thing done."

"Oh, that's okay," I say. She stands there, and I realize she's waiting for an actual invitation. "Sit. Of course. We can work on our papers together."

She sits, and we work. I'm actually fairly productive, and she must be too, because at the end of the hour, she says, "Listen, want to trade essays once we're done?"

"Um . . . sure," I say.

"You want to come home with me from school on Friday? We could critique each other's essays, and you could stay for dinner, maybe?" Sarah Lynn looks at me, and everything about her—her hair, her flawless complexion, her perfectly applied lipstick—reflects her golden-girl status. She's accustomed to getting what she wants, and before I spent any real time with her, I misinterpreted that as arrogance. A sense of entitlement.

There's something else beneath that, though. If I had to name it, I'd say it was hope.

"I'd like that," I tell her, and my chest expands with a sudden happy certainty. *Of course,* I think. *I've been so blind.*

She smiles. "Me too."

Stayed late today in the library, because I find, unexpectedly, that being in my room is sometimes . . . claustrophobic. Indeed, I write this entry on a bench across from my house, as my mind is clearer when I am away from the relic.

Not that I shy from my fate and my honor! Never. But I do like a moment to myself . . . a moment of distraction . . .

Regular's planned impregnation is such a distraction, as Liliana is tolerant of this pursuit for reasons of her own. The blood of a feline, while not on par with human blood, nonetheless has its value—or so I am told. A litter of kittens is more valuable than a single cat.

So it was that I found myself in the resource room, researching animal husbandry. I learned that it's common practice for veterinarians to extract semen from boars for the purpose of inseminating female pigs. The veterinarian sexually stimulates the boar with his hands and collects the sample in a tube. The semen is then inserted into the sow using a turkey baster or syringe.

Exhilarated by this finding, and distracted by the tiresome librarian who insisted the journal stay in the resource room, I almost failed to notice my supplicant as she exited the library before me, with none other than the little whore Sarah Lynn Lancaster.

They were laughing. Before they parted, Sarah Lynn pushed my supplicant's shoulder playfully. But just now, when I telephoned my supplicant, she made no mention of the encounter. In fact, she implied that she worked diligently on her paper for the entire hour, speaking to no one.

I'm troubled—but perhaps she has her reasons for lying. I hope this is the case, for if not, punishment will be swift and severe.

n Friday morning, I put on eyeliner and a teeny bit of blush. Rosie stops by my bedroom to deliver laundry and does a double-take.

"Look at you," she says.

My cheeks heat up, but I smile. "Yeah, you know. The 'new me' and all that." Am I a new me? It certainly feels that way.

In the kitchen, Grandmother grills me on the details of my study date with Sarah Lynn.

"I'll pick you up at eight, then?" she asks.

"Um, sure," I say, figuring we'll be done with dinner by eight. Sarah Lynn *did* say dinner, didn't she? Suddenly I doubt myself.

"You realize I'll have to leave my mahjong group early."

"I know. I'm sorry. Do you want me to . . . try and figure something else out?"

She sighs. "No, I suppose not."

I breathe a sigh of relief, glad Grandmother approves of the match enough to cut out early from mahjong. Indeed, when I told her Sarah Lynn's last name, she was clearly impressed.

At school, I'm bubblier than usual. "Bubbly" comes naturally to me. I like people. But I'm especially vibrant today, and both Thelma and Mitchell notice.

"You sure are smiling a lot," Thelma says during lunch.

"I am?" I say.

"Uh-huh," she says. A particular "Thelma" expression crosses her face, one that sometimes annoys me and sometimes breaks my heart. It's a mix of longing and something akin to dim-wittedness—only not exactly, because Thelma's not dumb. She does, however, see the world through one specific lens, and when things don't fit with what she's expecting, she doesn't know what to do.

"Did Mitchell give you his school pin?" she asks.

I laugh. "Mitchell doesn't have a school pin."

"Then what is it? What happened?"

"Nothing, I'm just happy," I tell her.

Mitchell himself finds me after lunch, coming up behind me at my locker and putting his hands over my eyes.

"Guess who?" he says. I twist around so that we're face-to-face and slip my arms around him.

"Who?" I say. I let my fingers dip into his back pocket, and the corner of his mouth goes up.

"You're in a good mood today," he comments.

"Why yes, I am."

Mrs. Watkins, Dr. Evans's secretary, walks by and tuts loudly. "Twelve inches," she says, and Mitchell reluctantly steps back to create the required foot of space between us.

"I like your good mood," he says in a low voice.

"Does that mean you're going to give me your school pin?" I ask.

"I don't have a school pin," he replies. His eyes widen in alarm, and it's so comical—and so *boy*—that I laugh.

"Alas," I say. "Guess I'll forgive you this time."

The one person I don't share my good mood with is Sandy, and when I see her barreling toward me at the end of fifth period, I duck into the stairwell and take the long way to my next class. She calls out, but I pretend I don't hear.

At 3:35, I meet Sarah Lynn at the front parking lot. I've been looking forward to this moment all day, but now that it's arrived, perspiration pops out under my arms. I have the crazy fear that I made it all up and she didn't invite me over after all.

But she smiles when she sees me and says, "Good, you're here. My mom just pulled up."

"Okay," I say. I flush at my nerves. "Um, yeah."

I follow her to a sleek black Buick Riviera and climb into the backseat. Her mother smiles at me, and I smile back. As she pulls out of the parking lot, she asks polite questions, like am I enjoying Crestview and do I feel settled in. I'm flattered, because it means Sarah Lynn's told her a little about me, such as the fact that I'm new this year. I wonder what else Sarah Lynn told her, if anything, and I miss the next question. Something about Atlanta—do I like it here?

I reply enthusiastically, and Sarah Lynn turns around and gives me an amused look.

"What?" I say, replaying the conversation in my head. *Ohhh*—her mom didn't asked if I liked Atlanta; she asked *how* I liked Atlanta. As in, "So how do you like Atlanta, Bliss?" And I, with my enviable conversational skills, had caroled, "Absolutely!"

I giggle, and Sarah Lynn giggles too. Mrs. Lancaster's glance, which I catch in the rearview mirror, is perplexed, and this makes us giggle even more.

The Lancasters' house turns out to be an honest-to-goodness mansion, with a long, winding driveway, Greek pillars, and a balcony stretching along the second story. It's like a plantation house from *Gone with the Wind*. I wonder if the Lancasters had slaves, long ago in the not-distant-enough past.

We enter through the back door, and Mrs. Lancaster drops her keys on the kitchen counter.

"Sarah Lynn, tell your father I'd like to go to the Colonnade for dinner tonight," she says. "All right, sweetie?"

"Okay," Sarah Lynn says.

"Mamie made some chicken and biscuits for you girls. You'll find two plates in the refrigerator."

"Okay," Sarah Lynn says again.

Mrs. Lancaster smiles remotely, then clips across the tiled floor and disappears to another part of the house.

"Want some chocolate milk?" Sarah Lynn asks.

"Um, sure," I say.

She pours milk into tall glasses and gets out a container of Ghirardelli chocolate shavings. I've eaten Ghirardelli chocolate before, but only once. I was in San Francisco with my parents for a protest march, and Dad splurged on a four-piece box for us to share. We split the fourth piece three ways.

"Here," Sarah Lynn says after dumping two heaping spoonfuls into my glass. She passes me my milk, along with a silver spoon unlike any I've seen. It's a combination spoon-straw, with a long, hollow handle. It clinks against the glass as I stir, and when I take my first sip, the cool metal feels exotic against my tongue.

"Let's drink it on the porch," Sarah Lynn says, leading the way. She walks with an easy self-assurance. She's self-assured at school too, but here, her confidence is more relaxed, less Snow Princess perfect.

The porch is enclosed, with wood-paneled walls and wide windows overlooking a spacious yard. There's a bookshelf in the corner filled with paperbacks, and on the top sits a large gourd painted to look like a whale. A patchwork quilt is draped over a spindle-legged chair. The décor has the feel of a mountain getaway, not that I've ever been to a mountain getaway.

Sarah Lynn takes a long sip of her chocolate milk, then sets her glass on a rickety side table and kicks off her shoes. She flops onto a hammock and says, "Ahhhhh." It's not one of those cheap nylon hammocks that a couple of people on the commune slept in, but a thick rope hammock suspended from a green metal frame. Sarah Lynn pulls in her elbows and moves to one side, balancing carefully so the hammock doesn't flip.

"Here," she says, patting the space she's made. "Put your head by my feet and we can both fit."

I hesitate, then place my glass by Sarah Lynn's and slip off my shoes. I ease onto the hammock. When I'm situated, Sarah Lynn pushes the wall with her foot so that the hammock swings back and forth.

"In the summer I'm out here every day," she says. "Sometimes I even sleep here. It's my own private place."

"Mmm," I say. The cords of the hammock cradle my body.

"I'm *so* glad it's the weekend," she goes on. "I get so sick of it all, you know?"

"Of what?"

"Of school," she says. She laughs a little, like *what else?*

"You don't like school?" To me, this seems incomprehensible. I like school, and I'm just *me*. Sarah Lynn is . . . Sarah Lynn.

She sighs. "Melissa's all mad because she says I treat my guy friends better than my girl friends, and Heather says she doesn't want to be in the middle of it, but she gives Melissa these *looks*, and it's obvious whose side she's on. And *Lacy*—"

She breaks off. "Oh, gosh. I invite you over and bore you to death with my stupid life. Nice, Sarah Lynn."

"No, it's okay." I don't mind in the least that she's boring me with her stupid life—which anyway, she's not. It's as if we got out here on her porch and were transported to an alternate universe: a universe where Sarah Lynn Lancaster confides in me like it's the most natural thing in the world, and where I open my heart and welcome the gift of natural friendship.

"What were you going to say about Lacy?" I ask. "Did something happen with her too?"

"Nothing *happened*," Sarah Lynn says. "It's just . . . this is going to sound incredibly dumb."

"No, it won't. What?"

She stalls, but I wait her out.

"She's mad at me for getting chosen as Snow Princess," she confesses.

"What do you mean?"

"I don't know. Maybe she's jealous?" She quickly retracts her statement. "Or maybe not. Like I said, I don't know."

"But it's not like you asked to be picked," I say. "She shouldn't blame you for it."

Sarah Lynn loops her toes beneath a cord of rope. Since her feet are by my head, I can't help but notice their narrow elegance.

"I wish I hadn't been picked," she confesses. "That sounds like one of those things people just say, but it's true. I don't want everyone staring at me. I don't want to buy a dress. And I don't want to deal with my parents, especially my daddy."

"How come? Isn't he proud of you?"

"I guess."

"I'm sure he is," I say, wanting to convince her. "How could he not be?"

"You know what, just forget it."

I feel bad, like I've failed her.

Sarah Lynn frees her toe from the hammock, extends her leg, and pushes off the wall to get us swinging again. Her foot returns to curl among the hammock loops, like a kitten on its bed.

Well, no. Not like a kitten.

"It's just that he's already laying down all these rules," Sarah Lynn says unhappily. "Like what kind of dress I can wear and how late I can stay out and who I can—"

She breaks off abruptly, but I know where the sentence was going.

Who you can go with, I fill in silently. *Who you can dance with. Who you can love.*

"I know I sound like a spoiled brat," she says. "It's just . . . sometimes I feel so trapped."

We sway, and it's like being hypnotized: back and forth, back and forth. I stare at the ceiling, which seems to sway with us.

I wish she'd go ahead and bring up Lawrence, or that I was brave enough to do it myself. I wish I could make everything be okay.

FROM AFRICAN AMERICAN FOLK VERSE,
RECOUNTING AN IMAGINED CONVERSATION
BETWEEN A BLACK MAN AND A WHITE MAN,
AS THE BLACK MAN LOOKS LONGINGLY AT
A BEAUTIFUL WHITE WOMAN

Black Man: Oh, Lord, will I ever . . . ?

White Man: No, nigger, never!

Black Man: As long as there's life,
there's hope.

White Man: And as long as there's trees,
there's rope.

ater, we go upstairs so Sarah Lynn can change out of her school clothes. Her room is pretty much as I expected: pink floral curtains and a pink comforter for her bed; pillow shams with white ruffles; lots of stuffed animals. It's nice. It's clean. Not a cat in sight.

She opens a drawer and tosses me a shirt, which I catch by pure luck. She selects a shirt for herself, then opens the next drawer and pulls out two pairs of jeans. "Which do you want, butterflies or bell-bottoms?"

I'm caught unawares. "You don't have to lend me anything," I say.

"You want to keep your school uniform on? Bliss, it's the weekend."

She makes a good point.

"Um, butterflies," I say.

"Butterflies it is." She passes me the jeans, which have lavender butterflies embroidered onto the back pockets. I slip out of my skirt and wiggle into them.

"They look good," she says, and I turn to see that she's fully dressed. I change into the shirt she gave me, and it does feel nice to be out of my Crestview attire. It feels like we're just us, instead of the people we are in school. Even though I'm in her clothes.

"Listen," she says. "About the Snow Princess stuff . . ."

"Yeah?"

"I really do know how lucky I am. I hope I didn't come across as ungrateful."

"Oh, don't worry."

"Can you imagine what people would say if they heard me complaining? 'Poor little Sarah Lynn doesn't want to be a Snow Princess. Boo-hoo.'"

"They wouldn't say that," I say.

Her smile is rueful. "What about you? Will you be there?"

"At the dance? Why, yes, I will." I straighten my shoulders. "I'm going with Mitchell Truman."

"For real?"

"What do you mean, for real? Yes, for real!"

Sarah Lynn giggles. "Oh my gosh, I did *not* mean for it to come out that way."

"Uh-huh, sure."

"I didn't. Honest. I think Mitchell's awfully cute."

"That's because he *is* awfully cute."

"And he rides a motorcycle."

"He does at that."

She touches my arm. "I'm glad you're going to be there," she says. "And seriously, thanks for listening to all my crap. I can't talk to Melissa or Heather about it, and I definitely can't talk to Lacy. But it's different with you."

Happiness makes me grow warm. "Yeah?"

"Yeah." She's solemn for a second. Then she smiles and says, "Come on. We better get *some* work done at least."

FROM THE INVESTIGATION INTO THE LYNCHING
OF SAMUEL HOSE, WHO WAS TORTURED
AND THEN BURNED TO DEATH AFTER BEING ACCUSED
OF RAPING A WHITE WOMAN

"A Negro's life is a very cheap thing
in Georgia."

—Detective Louis P. Le Vin

I meet Mr. Lancaster before the evening is over. He's a big, burly man with big sideburns of the sort called "muttonchops," and sure enough, it looks as if slabs of meat have been slapped onto each side of his face. Meat with the fur still attached.

He has an affable charm, and I wonder if perhaps he's not as bad as some people say after all. His blue dress shirt matches his eyes—I see now where Sarah Lynn got her blue eyes—and he's comfortable in his body the way powerful men tend to be.

"Your mother say anything about dinner?" he asks Sarah Lynn after she has introduced us.

"Um, she wants you to take her to the Colonnade," Sarah Lynn says.

"That I can do," he says. "Are you two coming with us?"

"Mamie made us chicken," Sarah Lynn says. "We're going to stay and work on our essays."

"My smart girl," he says, mussing her hair. She ducks from his touch, and he chuckles. He turns to me and says, "She gets embarrassed, but a daddy's got to brag on his girl, isn't that right?"

"Yessir," I say.

He loosens his tie. "A man who can't take pride in his daughter, why that's a man I feel sorry for. Just today, I heard that Tom Dewitty's girl is up and marrying a Negro. Don't that just take the rag off the bush?"

Sarah Lynn's eyes dart to me. I don't know what to do with my expression.

"Little black nigger babies, that's what Tom's got coming," Mr. Lancaster says, striding to the refrigerator. "Little black nigger babies for grandbabies."

"*Daddy*," Sarah Lynn says, mortified.

"If I were Tom, I'd handle it different, I tell you what. A shotgun and a shovel would take care of it real quick, and not a man in Georgia would fault him for it." He opens the refrigerator door. "You two want a Co' Cola?"

Neither of us answers. Splotches of color blaze on Sarah Lynn's cheekbones.

Three Coke bottles clank as Mr. Lancaster brings them over. He sets one in front of me and another in front of Sarah Lynn, then uses a bottle opener to flip the caps off. He opens his last and takes a long swig.

"Reckon I better let y'all get back to your studying," he says. He winks at me before leaving the room. "Mighty nice to meet you, Bliss. Come back anytime."

Regular is in heat. I smell it on her. She rubs her hindquarters against me and mews incessantly. Her tail quivers.

There is a rising tide within me as well. I'm hot, feverishly hot, and I rarely need to sleep. Of course, Liliana's restlessness feeds my own and keeps me busy. I tell her "soon" and placate her with trinkets: barrettes and ribbons and Alice Sommersby's shiny gold teddy bear. She gets pleasure from the trappings of girlhood, since her own girlhood was stolen so cruelly.

onday at school, Thelma invites me to be on the freshman float committee.

"What's the freshman float committee?" I ask.

"It's the committee that makes the float," she says in the tone she reserves for moments of Bliss-stupidity. "For the Winter Dance?"

"Ohhh. Right. What's a float?"

"It's only what we've been slaving away on every lunch period for the last week! What did you think we've been doing?"

"Uh . . ."

She huffs. "The Winter Dance is on the first Friday of December. It's *always* on the first Friday of December, and that's only four days away. The float's almost done, but we need all the help we can for the final touches."

I'm still not getting the whole "float" thing, but I say, "Okay, sure." It has to do with the dance, and that's good enough for me. Plus, there's no way Sandy will be part of the float committee, whatever it is.

"Great!" Thelma says. "Meet us in the gym after fourth period."

But at noon, as I head down the hill that leads to the gymnasium, I hear rapid footfalls and heavy breathing, and a winded Sandy appears by my side. A nasty welt runs down the left side of her face, a dark line slicing her from eyebrow to cheekbone. Her eyelid is puffy, and on the white of her eye, below the iris, is a gummy red clot. It reminds me of an egg, how every so often the yolk is flecked with blood.

"Cripes," I say. "What happened to you?"

"What happened to *me*?" Sandy says. "What happened to *you*?! You haven't answered my calls, and all last week you never ate in the cafeteria. You didn't show up today, either!"

It's not my job to eat with you, I want to say. Instead, I dodge the question.

"Did Regular scratch you?" I ask.

"Regular? No." She smiles a funny little smile. "Well, yes. Okay, she did. But *this* is the scratch Regular gave me." She holds out her forearm, where there's another, equally violent gash. "This one"—she gestures at her swimmy eye, then blinks—"well, it just kind of happened. But it wasn't Regular."

"It looks bad," I say. "Like, you-need-to-see-a-doctor bad. You might have a burst capillary."

"Yeah, yeah, sure, sure," she says. "So are you going to tell me what's going on?"

"Nothing's going on," I say. "I'm helping out with the freshman float, that's all. What *is* a float, anyway?"

The distraction works, and for a moment, Sandy forgets to nag me. "It's . . . a big display," she explains, "and for the

Winter Dance, they're always made to be thrones. Every grade makes one—freshmen, sophomores, juniors, and seniors—and the Snow Princesses sit on top."

"And then what?"

"What do you mean, and then what? And then nothing."

"They just sit there?"

"Pretty much."

"So what's the point?"

She laughs. "Exactly."

I laugh too, though right away I stop. "Anyway, we're meeting at twelve, and it's already five after. So I better go."

She grabs my arm. "Wait," she says. "We need to nail down our plans. I know you're going to the dance with your *boyfriend*, but you and I could meet before. Or after, if that's better. But I think before, so we don't feel rushed."

So we don't feel rushed? Just what is it she imagines us doing? No—don't even think about it.

I've got to stop avoiding the issue. I've got to tell her it's not going to happen, not at the dance or any other time.

"I . . ." I gulp. "Sandy, I really don't think—"

"It should be a perfect night," she says, deliberately cutting me off. Her eyes are flat and hard. "I would hate for it not to be."

Is she threatening me? I think she's threatening me. It scares the daylights out of me, and I jerk free and escape to the gym.

FROM *THE ANDY GRIFFITH SHOW*

"Somewhere wandering loose around
Mayberry is a loaded goat."

—Sheriff Andy Taylor

he banner for the freshman float reads FLUSH THE UPPERCLASSMEN, and the girls on the committee are building a giant toilet that sends out sprays of confetti when the handle is pushed. Sarah Lynn, as freshman Snow Princess, will perch on the toilet and wave, and every so often she'll fling rolls of actual toilet paper into the wildly cheering crowd.

"Is that golden, or what?" Thelma crows.

"What does a toilet have to do with winter?" I ask.

She blinks. "I don't get what you're asking."

"Well . . . it's for the dance, right? And the theme is 'snow'?"

She puts her hands on my shoulders. She's very stern. "We don't have time for Being a Teenager 101, not today. So I'm only going to say this once: We have to make a throne, but instead of some boring throne, we're making a toilet. Because a toilet *is* a throne. Got it?"

Actually, that's pretty clever. Funny, too. Omigosh, Thelma made a funny.

"Got it," I say.

She drags me to the base of the float, where DeeDee and

Jolene are smoothing strips of papier-mâché over chicken wire. "Good," she says. "Now get busy."

Jolene pushes her hair out of her face. She smiles at me, and I smile back and kneel beside her. I dip a strip of newspaper into a pan of paste.

"Like this?" I say, patting the strip over a patch of exposed wire.

"Perfect," she says.

"If we can finish this part today, then tomorrow we can paint it, and that'll give it time to dry before we add the final touches," DeeDee says.

I glop and slop, and as I do, I take in the details of this work of art we're creating. It's the size of a sofa, and it's constructed from plywood and chicken wire. The float committee has plastered papier-mâché over about three-fourths of it. I can imagine it painted a bright, glossy white, being pulled majestically across the football field.

Thelma squeals, and I lift my head. A splodge of paste drizzles down her neck.

"Oh, DeeDee, you are in trouble," she says.

DeeDee smirks, and Thelma flings a wet strip of paper. It slaps onto DeeDee's chest.

"Hey!" DeeDee cries.

"We are so out of here," Jolene says. She stands and pulls me to my feet.

"The darker side of female bonding," I say, giggling. "What's next? Itching powder? Pillow fights?"

Jolene leads me to the end of the float, where there's another pan of paste. We kneel and start plastering, and as we work, we chat. Jolene has Ms. Phillips for English too, so we talk about how sometimes she's too strict and sometimes not strict enough, like when the football players act stupid and Ms. Phillips just laughs.

It's fun, and the next day I go again. I know Thelma appreciates my help, because the sophomore, junior, and senior floats are all further along than ours. The juniors' throne is especially impressive, done in the medieval style of King Arthur's court.

"Do you think we'll get it done in time?" I ask, near the end of our lunch period.

"We better," Jolene says. "Thelma and I stayed late yesterday afternoon, didn't we, Thelma?"

"All for the cause," Thelma says. She gestures with her chin. "Go check out the tank. It's totally far-out."

I stand up, careful not to upset the pan, and walk to the back of the float. It's painted the same color as the seat, and I can no longer tell that it's just plywood and chicken wire. On the top, near the edge, is an oversize silver handle. Maybe aluminum foil?

I return to Thelma and Jolene. "It looks great."

"We had to give up the idea of spraying out confetti," Thelma says. "Too complicated. But she can still toss rolls of toilet paper."

"Hmm," I say, considering. "What about putting a plunger

on the float? It could be, like, a royal scepter or whatever you call it. Sarah Lynn could hold it."

Thelma lights up. "Yeah! We could make a giant one out of a broomstick and, I don't know, a plastic bowl or something." She hops to her feet and pulls Jolene and DeeDee up too. "Let's go find a janitor and see if he's got anything."

"What about me?" I ask.

"Paint!" she calls over her shoulder.

I blink. Then I squat and pick up Jolene's abandoned brush. As I dip it into the can, someone clears her throat.

"You're going to make me hold a plunger? Gee, thanks."

I turn and see Sarah Lynn. Heather and Melissa aren't far behind, clanging down the metal bleachers to reach the floor of the gym.

"Hey, anything for the cause," I say, stealing Thelma's line. I smile. "What's up?"

"I wanted to see how the float was coming. I would have helped build it, but they're keeping us busy with all these stupid practices."

"You have to practice to be a Snow Princess?"

"I know," she says, rolling her eyes. "How hard can it be to sit on a giant throne? And then, right before the Snow Queen is announced, we all have to stand up *at the exact same time*. I guess they're worried we'll mess up, and wouldn't that be a tragedy?"

"Guess that's the price you pay for being so fabulous," I say. "Alas."

She shoves me, and I tip over.

"Hey!" I protest, giggling.

She scopes out the giant toilet. "The float looks terrific. Y'all have really worked hard."

"Today's only my second day," I say. "Thelma and the others, though, for sure."

She glances around the gym, then squats so that she and I are at the same level. She swallows nervously. "Um, hey. I have a favor to ask you."

"You do?"

"It's about . . . the dance. And who's going to be my escort."

My heart beats faster. I have an inkling where this is headed.

"A few guys asked me, but I told them all no, and now I'm stuck. Because who I *really* want to go with is . . ."

She can't seem to speak his name, so I do it for her.

"Lawrence," I say.

She nods. She's grown pale, though. I get the sense that she wants to trust me, yet it's an awfully new thing for her.

"I saw you guys once, in the stairwell," I say.

"I know. I pushed him away—I was such a jerk."

"You were scared," I say.

She tries to smile. Her eyes show her shame.

I lightly touch her forearm. "Sarah Lynn, it's okay. I think it's great about you two. I do."

"You don't know how much that means to me," she says shakily.

"Oh, maybe I do. So what's the favor?"

"Well . . . do you think . . ." She wraps her arms around her ribs. "Never mind, it's crazy."

"What is? Just say it."

She blows out a breath of air, then says the next bit in a dash. "I was wondering if we could switch dates."

I laugh, because I suspected this was coming. "You want to borrow Mitchell," I say.

My response encourages her.

"Just until we get to the dance," she says. "Mitchell could pick me up at my house and shake my daddy's hand, and you and Lawrence could meet us here. Or Lawrence would be happy to pick you up at your grandmother's house. Whatever you want."

While Grandmother doesn't have a white cloak and hood stashed in her closet, I don't think she's ready for me to have a date with a black boy.

"No," I say. "Meeting here is better."

"You mean you'll do it?"

"Well, I need to check with Mitchell first."

"Lawrence already did. He's in if you are."

"Okay, then," I say. "There's your answer."

"Really?"

"Really."

I'm engulfed in a hug so exuberant it makes me stumble. When Sarah Lynn releases me, she's beaming.

"You're the best," she says. "And no one will have to

know, I swear, because at the dance, it'll just be like we're mingling. People don't only dance with their own dates, right?"

"Right," I say.

"The only time it'll really matter is during the crowning of the Snow Queen, because Mitchell will have to be by my side. That won't hurt your feelings, will it?"

"No." I bite my lip, because I've just thought of something. "But . . . my friends will notice. I mean, I agree with you about the dance itself—nobody's going to keep track. But my friends will think it's weird if Mitchell's out there as your escort."

Sarah Lynn's face falls. In her eyes, I see her dreams swirling down the giant toilet.

"We could tell them," I suggest hesitantly.

"Who all knows that Mitchell's your date?" she asks.

"Thelma, DeeDee, and Jolene." And Sandy, but she won't be at the dance. "I think they could keep the secret, though. I really do."

"Even Thelma?"

"If I tell her how important it is. Thelma loves being important."

Sarah Lynn is torn. She really wants this to happen.

"Heads up," I say, jerking my chin at Melissa and Heather, who are strolling across the gym.

"Sarah Lynn!" Melissa calls. "What's taking you so long?"

"Just a sec!" Sarah Lynn says. She turns to me and speaks fast and low. "All right, let's do it."

"Yeah?"

"Yeah."

She grins, and I can tell she's petrified and happy, both. Then she lopes over to Melissa and Heather, neither of whom say hello or even look at me. But I don't care. Jolene, DeeDee, and Thelma materialize, and I realize they've been hanging back on purpose, giving me and Sarah Lynn space. Their expressions are bewildered.

"Did Sarah Lynn just hug you?" Jolene asks.

"Um . . . yeah?"

"Why?" DeeDee demands.

"I'll tell you soon. Not here."

Thelma gazes across the gym at Sarah Lynn, and then she looks at me as if she's no longer sure who I am. I smile to show her I'm the same old me, but I don't think either of us believes it.

"I can't judge any of you. I have no
malice against you and no ribbons for
you. But I think that it is high time that
you all start looking at yourselves, and
judging the lie that you live in."

—Charles Manson

I return to work on the float after my last class gets out. I stay late with the girls, and we get the entire toilet painted.

"It's looking good," Thelma says.

"*Real* good," DeeDee says seductively, flipping her red hair as if she's a vampy lounge singer. It cracks us up, because by now we're giddy and punch drunk. We're also sweaty and paint-speckled and proud, because although we still have lots to do, we're in fine shape for Friday.

I'm one of the last to leave, and I go sit outside the gym to wait for Grandmother. I rest my back against the wall and draw my knees up. I tilt my face to the setting sun.

"Hey, Toilet Girl," someone says, and I open my eyes to see Mitchell smiling down at me.

"Toilet Girl?" I say. "That's what I am to you?"

"Well, if the name fits . . ."

I swat him, and he grins. He sits at my feet and rests his head on my knees.

"You cool with helping out Lawrence and Sarah Lynn?" he asks.

My hand moves to his hair, which is soft. "Yeah. Absolutely."

"We'll be together once we're at the dance," he says.

"We better be."

He nudges my hand with his head, angling for more petting. I oblige, and he makes a contented rumbly sound.

"You have pretty eyelashes," I tell him.

"Hmm," he says. "You have pretty everything." He stretches forward, propping himself up with his arm, and brushes his lips against mine.

Our first kiss. In front of the gym. With Grandmother about to pull up any minute.

Oh, this wonderful boy.

He pulls back, and I feel like a lovely, warm noodle—loopy and yielding. I can't stop smiling.

"I've been wanting to do that for a long time," he says.

"I'm glad you did."

"I'm glad you're glad."

"And I'm glad you're glad I'm glad," I say, giggling. I stroke his cheek. "Only . . . and I hate to bring it up, I do . . ."

His eyebrows pull together, and I almost feel bad for teasing him.

"What?" he says worriedly.

"Well . . . does this mean you're a toilet licker?"

He pushes me hard enough that I fall over. "You're comparing my kiss to licking a toilet?"

"Not at all," I say, laughing as he pulls me upright. "You did good. *Real good.*"

Regular and I fast, from now until it's done. As She hungered, so do we—until She is restored.

veryone has dance fever. Streamers appear on lockers, banners stretch across classrooms, and the Decorating Committee goes hog wild transforming the gym into a winter wonderland. The four class thrones reside in the corners, connected by a forest of shiny aluminum trees. Silver icicles dangle on the branches. A long refreshment table appears, draped with a rich red cloth. Delicate paper snowflakes are strung from the ceiling.

The members of the Decorating Committee are in a frenzy trying to make everything perfect, and one girl almost comes to blows with Thelma when Thelma refuses to loan out her staple gun.

"Get your own!" Thelma says, clutching hers to her chest.

"I just need it for a second," the Decorating Committee girl says. "Just for one second!"

"No!"

The girl grabs it, and Thelma gives a mighty yank. They both go sprawling.

Even Sandy seems to burn with unusual zeal. When I

glimpse her in the halls, her face ravaged by that terrible scratch, the expression in her eyes makes me think she's lost in her own world. I don't know what's going on with her—and I don't want to know. Thursday morning I spot her by my locker, scanning the halls with those blazing eyes, and I hide in an empty classroom until she's gone. That afternoon she calls to me as I'm hurrying to the gym, but instead of stopping, I give her an overly friendly wave.

"Oh, hey there!" I call, as if that's all she's after.

"Hold up!" she says, huffing toward me.

"Hmm?" I furrow my brow as if I can't make out her words. "I've got to run—but listen, I'll be working on the float all afternoon. Come talk to me there!"

I know she won't, or I wouldn't have made the offer.

But on Friday, the day of the dance, she tracks me down out on the quad with the girls. DeeDee has just informed me that I'm supposed to wear an actual floor-length gown, and I'm freaking. Why didn't anyone teach me about winter dances on the commune? Why didn't Mom ever hawk her hemp weavings for a shiny frock, size four?

I don't notice Sandy till she's almost on top of me, and by then, it's too late to flee.

"Finally!" she says, breathing heavily. Her cut has scabbed over, but the skin around it is red and swollen. She glances at the girls and pulls me a few feet away. "I feel like it's been forever since I've seen you. You're not avoiding me, are you?"

"Ha, ha," I say weakly. I don't want to talk about this. I want to talk about dresses.

Sandy eyeballs DeeDee, who's openly staring, then drops her voice. "I have *so* much to tell you. So many good things are happening—and just think, you're going to be a part of it!"

Her assumption makes my stomach twist, but I need very much for her not to notice. So I give her what I hope is a blank look, polite but uncomprehending.

"Don't play games with me," she says. "You ran away last time we talked. You think I didn't notice?" Then she goes pale, the color draining so rapidly from her flesh that I think she might faint.

"Sandy? Are you okay?"

"Head rush. Whoa." She sways a little.

"I think you should sit down," I tell her. "No, actually I think you should go see the nurse—like, right away."

"I'm fine. Low blood sugar, that's all. I'm . . . on a diet."

"You are?"

"Not important. What's *important*"—she leans in so that I can feel her hot breath on my ear—"is that you're present for the assimilation."

"The assimilation?" This time I'm telling the truth when I say, "Sandy, I honestly have no idea what you're talking about."

"Bliss?" Jolene calls. "Are you ready to go?"

"I'm coming," I say, but Sandy steps into my path.

"Tonight at nine, because nine is the auspicious number of the cat."

"Wh-what?"

"Just tell me you'll be there," she says impatiently.

My heart pounds. Sandy's eyes are glassy, and I'm not positive she's in there. *The auspicious number of the cat?*

"I'm going to class now," I say.

"Wait—I have more to tell you. I'll bring Regular tonight too, because I found a new home for her. Isn't that great?"

"Um, sure," I manage.

"Don't you want to know where?" She doesn't wait for me to respond, but says triumphantly, "Here."

"Here?" I repeat. I'm getting that light-headed feeling. "What do you mean, here?"

"The room you gave me the key to. I've made it really special."

"No," I say numbly.

"You'll come at nine," she says, gazing at me with a not-there look that tells me I'm right to be scared. Her hand rises and comes toward me. I realize she's going to stroke my cheek, and I step back. In a heartbeat, her fingers grasp my wrist.

"No more running," she says in a voice I didn't know she possessed. "Remember?"

"S-sorry," I stammer.

"Bliss?" Jolene says with growing concern.

Rapture takes over Sandy's features. "And do you know why we'll hold the ceremony there? Because, Bliss . . . *it remembers Her.*"

No, I think desperately. It's the day of my first dance. I should be chattering about makeup and shoes and accessories, not ceremonies involving dead girls.

I'm trembling, but I lift my chin. "Sandy, I'm not meeting you tonight," I say. "I'm not going to . . . that room. Not tonight, not ever."

Her eyebrows come together. I think she's still lost in another world. "What?"

"I'm done," I say. "I don't want to play anymore."

"You don't want to *play* anymore?"

Uh-oh. Now she's coming back to reality.

"That's what I said," I say, trying to act braver than I am.

"But . . . you gave me the key," she protests. "You're part of the plan!"

"There is no plan, Sandy."

"Yes, there *is!*" She takes quick breaths and pushes her words out so that it sounds as if she's bleating. "I've got the key. I've got the relic. You're to provide the offering . . . and everything will change! Everything will be perfect!"

"No, Sandy," I say, and I dig deep to get through to her. "Nothing is going to change, because Sarah Lynn was right. You *are* unnatural. Now, leave me alone."

There, I think. It's out, and I couldn't have dug any deeper. Indeed, perhaps I dug too deep, because Sandy's expression alarms me. Her mouth hangs open, and her brow is furrowed. But her one good eye seems possessed by a different owner, and it burns with malice.

I turn and walk shakily back to the others, scared to the bone that it's not over yet.

No. She's wrong. Tonight at nine I will restore the relic, and Liliana and I will be joined. A girl will be reborn.

Me. I will be reborn! And my name will no longer be Sandra, but Lurlene, which starts with L and is seven letters long. <u>This</u> is the truth. <u>This</u> is the light. <u>This</u> is the way.

My supplicant will come, and she will see. She is blinded by the glamour of the other, but glamour is as fleeting as confetti: It twinkles and gleams, only to wink out the moment it hits the floor.

She will not choose that whore. She will choose me.

and if she doesn't?

She will!

you try my patience. if she doesn't?

Then I will do what must be done.

yes, and Our baptism shall be in blood.

hen I get home, I ban Sandy from my thoughts and fix my mind resolutely on the challenge of coming up with acceptable Winter Dance attire. It's far too late for fabulous; "not completely hideous" is the best I can hope for. I'm supposed to meet Lawrence at the gym at seven, and I have to figure something out. I have to figure it out now.

I rush into my room, and there on the bed is the most beautiful gown I've ever seen. It's made of the softest, pearliest gray velvet, with a fitted bodice and a scooped neck. The skirt is floor-length and narrow, but not so narrow that it won't flare when twirled. Gingerly, I approach it. I touch its plush folds.

"It was your mother's," Grandmother says.

I turn to see her in the doorway. Her expression is sad, and perhaps for the first time ever, I sense no implied criticism.

"Try it on," she says.

I do, and she helps me zip it up. Then I walk nervously to the full-length mirror. When I see my reflection, I suck in my breath.

The bodice clings perfectly, and the neckline dips low,

showing off the pale tops of my breasts. At my waist, the velvet cinches in, then swoops gracefully from my hips. I never would have thought to clothe myself in gray, but the color complements my fair skin. My dark hair gleams, and my eyes look as inky and deep as Agnes's—

No. I will think of Agnes later. I will think of Sandy later. I will think of myself now. I am allowed to think of myself.

"It's a bit mature," Grandmother says. "But it suits you."

I turn from the mirror and fly into her arms. She pats me, alarmed.

"Thank you thank you thank you," I gush. "You're the best grandmother ever."

"Well, I don't know about that," she says. When I release her, her cheeks are pink.

She brushes nonexistent lint from the dress and tugs the shoulder straps to raise the neckline. "Do your makeup," she commands. "Do your hair. And then I'll take you to this dance of yours."

"Mayberry'll shine tonight, Mayberry'll shine. When the moon comes up and the sun goes down, Mayberry'll shine."

—Mayberry Founders' Day song

randmother drops me off outside the main entrance to the gym, tutting about the unseemliness of arriving at a dance on one's own. In her day, no young lady would go anywhere without an escort—most certainly not a dance.

"It's fine, Grandmother," I tell her. "Lots of kids are going in groups. See?" I point at three girls spilling from a wood-paneled station wagon. I open the door of Grandmother's Cadillac and call out to them. "Jolene! Thelma! Hi!"

"Well, in my day it would have been a scandal," Grandmother says.

"I know, I know." I lean over and kiss her cheek, pushing down the irrational fear that this will be the last time I get to kiss her cheek. *Stop it*, I tell myself. To Grandmother, I say, "Bye!"

Thelma and the others squeal when they see me, and I squeal too. It feels good to squeal. It feels good to release some energy.

"Oh my gosh, you look *gorgeous*," DeeDee says.

"You too!" I say. She's wearing a green dress, and her hair is in a bun.

"We all look gorgeous!" Thelma says, and I laugh, because it's true.

Jolene nods toward someone standing in the shadows a couple of yards from the gym entrance. It's Lawrence. I've told the girls about the great date switch, and they swore up and down that they'd take the secret to their graves. Even though they disapprove, they think what Sarah Lynn is doing is incredibly romantic.

"You better go," Jolene whispers. "See you inside?"

"Yeah," I say, and I shyly approach Lawrence, who's wearing a white evening jacket. He looks like a prince, just not my prince.

"Hello," I say.

"Hello," he replies. His Adam's apple jerks. "I wanted to say . . . I wanted to tell you—"

"It's fine," I interrupt. "I'm happy to help. Really."

He smiles, and just like that I'm no longer intimidated by this handsome, gallant stranger. He nods at my dress and says, "We're a chessboard."

"We are?" I glance down and figure it out: my gray dress and his white jacket; my white skin and his black skin. "Oh, we are."

His eyes are full of humor, and I like that Lawrence can joke about it, especially given the situation. I can see why Sarah Lynn likes him.

He offers his arm. "Shall we?"

I look over my shoulder to make sure Grandmother's Caddy is gone, and then I link my arm through his. "We shall."

We walk into the gym, and a boy standing by the door hands us each a creamy program with the words *Winter Dance, 1969* embossed in blue. Below, the names of the Snow Princesses are listed, as well as the names of each girl's escort. *Sarah Lynn Lancaster*, it says at the bottom, and beside it, *escorted by Mitchell Truman*.

Lawrence and I share a look. I don't know about him, but while I enjoy the thrill of our collusion, I can't help feeling a pang at seeing their names linked. Mitchell is my escort. I'm his princess, not Sarah Lynn.

But when we carefully descend the bleacher stairs to the basketball court, my pettiness drops away and amazement takes its place. The gym has been transformed into a wonderland, and while I witnessed much of what the Decorating Committee did over the last week, the final effect exceeds what I expected.

The basketball nets have been retracted, and foil stars dangle from the ceiling. Aluminum trees form a glistening forest against the walls, and a makeshift platform has been erected for the band, which is playing "Yesterday." Couples sway on the dance floor while soft dots of light swoop and dip over them.

Tears come to my eyes. Everybody looks so lovely. Everybody looks so happy.

"There's Sarah Lynn," Lawrence says. I follow his gaze, and yes, there she is, more exquisite than ever as she chats with Mitchell beside the giant toilet. She wears an elegant high-necked dress with buttons, and her honey-colored hair falls in waves around her face. She's already donned the glittering tiara that comes with the title of Snow Princesses.

"She's so beautiful," Lawrence says, as if he can't help himself. If I weren't already aware of his feelings for her, I would be now. His voice has dropped, and he's no longer a boy making friendly conversation with someone he hardly knows, but a young man gazing at his true love.

"She is," I say. "Let's go over." I want to hear how everything went at Sarah Lynn's house, and if Mr. Lancaster approved of Sarah Lynn's date. But more than that, I want to reclaim him as my own date. I, too, want to make true love grow.

We weave through the crowd, and when Sarah Lynn spots us, she squeezes Mitchell's hand and drags him over. The moment the two of them reach us, Sarah Lynn lets go of Mitchell and slips her arms around Lawrence's waist.

"You are so beautiful," Lawrence says thickly, pulling her close. "You will never be more beautiful than you are right now."

"Well, that's kind of morbid," I say before I can stop myself.

Sarah Lynn lifts her head. "Morbid? How is it morbid?"

"Uh . . ." A laugh chokes out, because I didn't mean anything by it. I'm not about to explain my ghoulish train of thought, either. "It's not. Just, it's like someone saying, 'It's all downhill from here. You've peaked, and now it's over.'"

She and Lawrence gaze at me blankly. I decide it's time to move on.

"Sorry," I say. "And you do look lovely. You smell really good too." She does, like lilacs.

"It's my new perfume," she says, smiling up at Lawrence. "My boyfriend bought it for me."

Lawrence squeezes her waist.

"That's sweet," I say. "But don't you think maybe you should, uh"—I gesture how close they're standing—"be a little less obvious?"

They quickly pull apart. I feel bad, but I'm just looking out for them. On the dance floor it makes sense for a boy to touch his partner, even if his partner isn't his date. If the guy and girl are just chatting, I would think it might look suspicious.

Or maybe I'm just paranoid.

Mitchell steps toward me, loosening his tie. The hollow of his throat is smooth and strong.

"You look beautiful too," he tells me.

"I do?"

His eyes are liquid and catch the light. I'm not so worried about Sarah Lynn and Lawrence anymore.

"Let's dance," he says.

I smile. "Okay."

As we head for the dance floor, we pass Thelma, Jolene, and DeeDee, who are swaying and tapping their feet on the sidelines. Their expressions are dreamy.

Thelma sees me and touches my arm. I stop.

"You're so lucky," she says. "You know that, right?"

I hesitate.

Mitchell pulls me forward. He takes me in his arms, and the world melts away, leaving only warmth and music and skin and sweetness.

FROM THE LAST WITNESS EXAMINATION CONDUCTED
BY VINCENT BUGLIOSI, PROSECUTING ATTORNEY IN THE
TATE-LABIANCA MURDER TRIALS

"Did Susan Atkins say whether she
in fact killed Sharon Tate?"

"Yes, she did."

"What did she say?"

"She said, 'I killed her.'"

"Did Miss Atkins say anything
about blood at that point?"

"Yes, she did."

"What did she say?"

"She said that she had blood in her hand
and she looked at her hand and she took
her hand and she put it up to her mouth
and she said, 'To taste death and yet give
life, wow, what a trick.'"

—summary of testimony given about Susan (Sadie) Atkins,
member of Charles Manson's Family

hen the band takes their break, Mitchell says he'll find us a table so we can sit for a bit. I volunteer to get us some punch, because I'm just that liberated a gal. Mitchell chuckles when I say that, which makes me happy, and I float all the way to the refreshment table. I'm still floating when someone sidles up behind me and says, "Sorry I'm late."

I know that voice, and I startle, splashing red juice down the front of my gown.

"Sandy!" I wail. "Look what you did!"

She giggles, and it sounds deranged. I turn around, and she looks deranged, too. She's wearing a tight yellow dress that pulls across the chest, and her arms stick out from her sides as if the fabric won't allow her to let them hang free. Her hair is pulled back with a yellow headband, and I note with the part of my brain that hasn't locked up that it's the same yellow headband she was wearing the first time we met.

But her eye . . . her eye is hideous. It's swollen shut, with pus oozing from the slit. The scabbed-over scratch running from her eyebrow to her cheekbone is equally grotesque.

The mirrored ball hanging from the ceiling illuminates the scar as it rotates, turning it first black, then maroon, then black again.

She jerks her chin at my dress, where the punch blooms like a bloodstain on the gray velvet. "Look," she says. "It's the exact color of Agnes's birthmark. Well . . . maybe a little darker."

"You ruined it," I say. I'm still in shock, and the dress is growing clammy against my skin. I grab a napkin and start dabbing, and at the same time steal a glance at the large gymnasium clock above the retracted basketball hoops. It's only eight o'clock. "Why are you here, Sandy?"

"I'm not allowed to come to my own school dance?" she says. "And my name's not Sandy anymore. I've changed it to Lurlene."

"You've . . . what?"

She smiles. "But you can call me Lurl. Lurl the Pearl."

"Sandy . . ." I laugh, but it's not a real laugh, and it comes out of its own accord. I try to control my fear. "I'm not calling you that."

"Hmm," Sandy says, seemingly unconcerned. "Regular was naughty. She escaped from her cat carrier, that bad cat. But don't worry. I got her back."

"You brought Regular to the dance?"

"Do you *see* Regular here at the dance?" Sandy asks. She widens her plump arms as if perhaps I want to search her.

"But . . . Sandy . . ."

"Lurl," she says.

"I don't have time for this." I hear the desperation in my voice, since what I'm really saying is, *Please don't mention the ceremony. Please don't let it be true. Please go away and never come back.*

She crooks her finger, beckoning me forward.

"No," I say. I scan the gym and spot Mitchell talking to a guy from the football team. Why isn't he coming to find out what's taking me so long?

Sandy closes the distance between us and whispers, "I have the relic. I have the key."

The gym tilts.

"You need to come with me to you-know-where."

"But . . . it's not nine o'clock," I say stupidly.

"I decided eight was better," she says, as if all the logic and reason in the world is behind her.

"Sandy?" My voice wobbles.

"And just in case you're feeling like you don't want to, I have a little extra incentive." She giggles. "Come with me—right now—or I let the pigeon out of the coop."

"What pigeon?" I say. "What coop?" For a second I wonder, *Is she talking about the pigeon coop on the commune?*

"It's an expression, you numskull," she says, and her too-familiar tone says, *You are such a dum-dum, but that's okay, because you're my dum-dum.* "It means to tell a secret."

"What secret?"

She looks at me coquettishly. Then she turns her head

to the right, gazing across the gym at Sarah Lynn. Sarah Lynn is smiling up at Lawrence, who's standing close and entertaining her with some story. Down lower, almost hidden by the sleeve of Lawrence's jacket, I can see that their pinkies are entwined. It's not something the casual observer would notice, but Sandy isn't a casual observer.

"Hmm," she says, tilting her head and placing her finger on her cheek. "Let's see if I've got this right. Sarah Lynn's escort is Mitchell—it's listed right there on the program—but she's spending all her time with Lawrence." She widens her eyes like a scandalized schoolmarm. "A *Negro*."

Tightness clenches my lungs.

"Now, why is that?" Sandy muses. "And isn't Mitchell supposed to be your date?"

"Leave it alone," I say. "It's none of your business."

A ghost of a smile tickles her lips. "I guess that depends on who you ask. I think it *is* my business—and if you don't come on, I'll make it everyone else's business too. You see?"

"So . . . you're threatening me? That's the incentive?" I'm stalling, but it backfires, because she gets a look in her eyes—in her *eye*—that makes my fear plunge deeper. For just an instant, she stops looking cunning and instead looks uncertain, and somehow that's worse.

"Bliss, I don't want to force you," she says. "It'll hurt far less if . . ."

If *what*? I'm scared. I'm scared to the very core of me.

She pulls herself back from the void and straightens her spine. Her mocking manner returns. "She's a Snow Princess, after all. Surely her loyal subjects deserve to know the truth."

"Sandy . . . that would destroy her," I say unsteadily.

From behind me, someone touches my shoulders, and I whip around as if I've received an electric shock.

"Whoa," Mitchell says, grinning. Now he shows up, great. He leans close and pecks my cheek. "Destroy who?"

"No one!" I say.

"Girls, play nice," he says, mock-scolding. "We're at a dance, after all, not a catfight." He loops his arm around me. "Let's go, Bliss."

"I'm not done talking to you, Bliss," Sandy says, ignoring Mitchell altogether. "We need to go . . . somewhere private."

"Sorry, but it'll have to wait," Mitchell says. "I need some time with my girl." He takes in Sandy's eye and winces. "Ouch. Crap, Sandy, what happened to your eye?"

"Meet me in our special place," she tells me coldly. "I'll give you five minutes." She turns on her heel and strides for the bleachers, ridiculous in her yellow dress.

"I think someone's eaten a few too many Froot Loops," Mitchell says when she's out of hearing range. He chuckles and squeezes my arm. "Come on, let's grab some punch and go sit down."

I twist away and step backward. "I can't."

"What do you mean, you can't?"

"I'll hurry—it'll only take a sec."

"Wait a minute. You're ditching me for her?"

"I thought you liked it that I was nice to her!" I say nonsensically. I try to find her in the crowd.

"Yeah, but this is our night." He notices the front of my gown. "Hey, baby, did you spill something?"

I rise to my tiptoes and spot her exiting the gym.

"I'm sorry," I tell him, "but I've got to go. I'll be really quick and I'll come right back, okay?"

"No, it's not okay," he says, annoyed. "You're acting weird, Bliss—even for you."

Tears blur my vision. That Mitchell would say that . . . Mitchell, of all people . . .

I look at him to let him know he's hurt me, and then I take off after Sandy.

"Most of the people at the ranch
that you call the Family were just people
that you did not want, people that were
alongside the road, that their parents had
kicked out, that did not want to go to
Juvenile Hall. So I did the best I could
and I took them up on my garbage dump
and I told them this: that in love there is
no wrong . . ."

—Charles Manson

I hurry up the bleachers out of the gym, and to the trail. I wobble in my high heels, so I kick them off and hike up my gown. My heart pumps blood through my body, making me warmer than a girl should be on a cold winter evening.

The door to Hamilton Hall opens easily, and I'm greeted with dark air. I slow my pace, because now that I'm here, I don't want to be. My panting breath is the only thing I can hear, and that's not good, as it makes me too aware of who else might be breathing, or not, in this desolate building. Then the door sighs shut, and I clasp my hand to my mouth to stifle my cry.

I can't, I think. *I can't, I can't.*

You have to, responds a deeper part of me.

I gather myself together and enter the stairwell. One flight, two flights, three flights. My muscles burn.

"Sandy?" I say when I emerge on the third floor. My voice echoes. "I'm here, okay?"

Nothing.

I walk down the hall, all the way to the heavy door that

leads to the unrenovated wing. I push on the metal bar, and the door opens unto utter black and tomblike silence.

"Sandy?"

From farther in I hear what sounds like a match being struck, and my muscles seize.

She's here.

I edge deeper into the hall, releasing the metal door only when I can no longer cling to it and still step forward. When it shuts behind me, I'm in a darkness that's darker than anything I've experienced, darker even than the pigeon coop on a moonless night.

My eyes slowly begin to adjust, and I can begin to make out the numbers on the doors. Three-oh-seven, three-oh-nine, three-eleven. I don't know how my legs manage to keep moving, because I'm woozy and my skin is covered in sweat. My heart is a trapped bird flapping at my rib cage.

Three-thirteen. Here it is. The room that called to me the first time I was here, the room that hummed with sorrows and secrets and *please, won't you please come inside?*

And when I didn't, a blast of rage sucked my breath away.

This time, the way has been made easy. The dove carved into the door is gone, as is the key that lay behind it. Sandy has the key; the dove is at home in my satchel. I wish I'd brought it with me. If only I'd brought it with me.

Only, what protection could it offer me here?

None. I am on my own.

The door to Liliana's room is cracked open, and through

the narrow gap, I see the flickering light of a candle. I enter a sort of altered consciousness in which I'm still insanely scared, but there's nothing I can do about it, so I step out of myself, almost, as I step into the room.

Sandy looks up. She's kneeling by a large white candle, which rests on a cinder-block table. Arranged in a circle around the candle are—what *are* they?! Unblinking eyes in mummified corpses? Exactly what dark art is Sandy dabbling in?

Oh. Not mummies, but Sandy's cat figurines. Amongst the cats is a multitude of other odds and ends: barrettes, ribbons, a necklace boasting a shiny gold teddy bear.

On the floor, resting on a folded cloth, is a kitchen knife with a gleaming blade.

Oh, God.

Sandy smiles. "So, what do you think?"

"I think . . ." I pause, aware that I need to choose my words carefully. "I think it's . . . very symmetrical. Um, good job, Sandy."

"Not 'Sandy,'" she says sharply. "Lurl." She rotates her head to relieve her stress, then brings back her smile. "And thank you. I agree."

She pushes herself up with a grunt, then brushes past me and shuts the door. It happens before I can react. I've never liked enclosed spaces. I especially don't like enclosed spaces right now.

"Well, I'm so glad you're here," Sandy says, as if we're at a dinner party. "Now we can begin."

I try to think what to do. *Why does she have a knife?* The shine of its blade makes it hard to do anything but breathe in shallow pants.

"Shall we proceed, then?" Sandy walks to the back of the room and squats by a cat carrier, obscured until now by the murky gloom. As Sandy unlatches the wire door, Regular growls.

"Now, now, you should get to be part of it too," Sandy says. She has to reach in and pull Regular out, and in doing so she exposes Regular's underbelly. Peeking through Regular's sparse fur are two rows of rosy nipples, protruding so noticeably they look grotesque.

"I don't think this is a good idea," I say foolishly.

Sandy giggles, and the little hairs on my arms stand up. "Bliss, you're so adorable. I just love you."

She stands and kicks shut the door of Regular's carrier so that Regular can't retreat. Regular, who has a swollen abdomen and yet still manages to appear half-starved, crouches and flicks her tail.

I press one finger to my forehead, pushing hard at the spot between my eyebrows. "Sandy . . ."

"Lurl."

Fine, whatever.

"Lurl," I say. "The only reason I'm here is because of . . . you know. Sarah Lynn and Lawrence. You said you wouldn't tell if I came here, and here I am. So you're not going to tell, right?"

She blinks and smiles.

"I mean . . . why do you even care who she goes out with?"

"I don't," she says.

"Then why . . . ?"

She rolls her eyes in a horrible imitation of embarrassed modesty, as if I'm teasing her on purpose. "You're the one I care about, silly."

She unclasps her purse and draws out a jeweled box. Like a happy hostess, she says, "We need this and the knife, and then we're all set. All the crucial elements. Have you decided where you want to do it?"

My blood pressure drops. "Where I want to do what?"

"Make the cut."

"The . . . cut?"

"For the offering, you noodle. Or would you rather I do it? I'll be gentle like I promised. We won't want to overuse any one spot, of course, but for tonight—since it's special . . ." She swallows, almost as if she's nervous. "The inner thigh, do you think?"

My legs clamp involuntarily.

Sandy, raising her eyebrows to confirm, lifts the knife.

"Um . . . y-yes," I stutter. *Breathe,* I tell myself. *Don't faint.* "But first . . . can I . . ." I gesture at her hands. She's got the knife in one, the box holding the relic in the other. The "other" is the one I want.

"May I please . . . ?"

Sandy is delighted. "Of course!" She readily hands me

the box, and though I reel from the fury of Liliana's outrage, Sandy doesn't seem to feel it. She switches from one foot to another as if she's got to pee.

"Go on, open it," she says.

I sway from the tumult of vying impulses: flee, stay, faint, throw up.

worship! obey! feel my power! FEED MY POWER!

My hand shakes. I haven't heard Liliana's voice in so long, and it's strong, so strong!

feed cut lick obey feed cut lick obeyfeedcut lickobeyfeedcutlickobeyfeedcutlickobey

Her words are a frenzied torrent. I open the box. The relic is dark and shriveled, and when I tip it into my palm, the attached hairs seem to caress me. Bile rises in my throat.

"Now put it back," Sandy says, her good eye twitching. Liliana is getting through to her at last. "I just wanted you to see it. Put it back now."

I close my fingers around the relic and shake my head.

"Give it to me, Bliss." She comes closer, and her face is enormous. Is it growing? Her arm whips out and she grips my wrist. "Don't be naughty."

"Sandy, you're hurting me," I say. I try to twist free, and her grip tightens.

"Give it to me!" she commands.

I splay my fingers, and the relic skitters across the floor. "Get it, Regular!" I shriek. "Yum-yum! Treat!"

Regular pounces, and Sandy flings me away.

"Noooo!" she cries, lunging for her cat. But it's too late. Regular gulps down the relic in a graceless, jerking swallow, and a disjointed part of my brain thinks, *Should have fed her more often, you silly noodle.*

Sandy kneels and pounds Regular's back. She thrusts her fingers into Regular's jaws.

"Spit it out, spit it out!" she repeats. Her voice is high and thin. "Spit it out, you bad cat!"

Regular's ears press back, and a butterscotch paw snakes out and rakes Sandy's forearm, right across her scabbed-over scratch. Blood bubbles up, and Regular squirms free and attacks. She gnaws at Sandy's flesh as if she hasn't eaten for days.

Outraged, Sandy flings Regular off of her. Regular hits the wall and slides to the floor, and Sandy turns to me. She rises to her feet.

"Oh, shit," I say. I dart to the door, but Sandy is as quick as a quarterback and as strong as an ox. She grabs the back of my gown as I struggle with the old-fashioned latch. "Sandy, let go!"

"*I said call me Lurl the Pearl!*" she bellows.

At last I manage the latch. The door flies open, and we both tumble backward. I hear the sound of ripping fabric. When we land, I sink into Sandy's soft stomach. I smell her rank sweat. Regular darts for the corridor, and Sandy rolls out from under me and grabs Regular beneath the ribs.

"Oh, no you don't," she snarls, and this is all the distraction I need to be up and out the door and away, so far away, from Sandy's demented rage.

As my feet slap the floor, a howl of defeat shakes the ancient walls.

FROM AN AFRICAN AMERICAN SPIRITUAL

"This little light of mine, I'm going to let it shine! This little light of mine, I'm going to let it shine. This little light of mine, I'm going to let it shine! Let it shine, let it shine, let it shine!"

The relic is gone, and I am out of that cursed room. Only I can't fall to pieces, not yet. Can't fall to pieces until after I find Sarah Lynn. *First Sarah Lynn, then breakdown,* I chant silently. *First Sarah Lynn. Then breakdown.*

I can't find my high heels, but I register little pain as I hurry barefoot toward the gym.

When I reach the entrance, I rush inside and trot down the bleacher stairs. It is surreal to be stepping back into this world of swooping lights and tinsel snowflakes. As I scan the dance floor, Thelma spots me and comes over. Relief washes over me, because Thelma is so *Thelma,* and always will be.

"Where have you been?" she asks. She doesn't wait for me to respond, but goes barreling on. "It's almost nine—they're going to announce the Snow Queen. Come on!"

"I need to talk to Sarah Lynn," I say as she pulls me toward the freshman float.

"Nope, sorry. She's too busy doing her final preparations."

"Her final preparations? Doing what?"

"Stuff," Thelma says impatiently. She points behind the giant toilet, where Sarah Lynn is being fussed over by Heather and Melissa. "She needs her hair to look good, obviously. Do you not want her hair to look good?"

She takes in my own hair, and her eyebrows shoot up. At the sight of my dress, they go up even further.

"I'll be back," I say. I shrug her off and make a beeline for Sarah Lynn.

She makes a sound of indignation. "Mitchell's P.O.'ed, by the way!" she calls. "You really shouldn't abandon your boyfriend at the Winter Dance!!!"

I keep going. *Sarah Lynn, then breakdown. Sarah Lynn, then breakdown.*

"Bliss!" Sarah Lynn says when she sees me. She takes in my appearance, and her eyes widen. "Omigosh, are you okay?"

"Can I talk to you?" I say. I glance at Melissa and Heather. "Alone?"

"Um . . . sure," she says. She dismisses Melissa and Heather with a nod that says, *It's all right.* They regard me suspiciously, but do as she asks.

"What happened?" Sarah Lynn asks worriedly.

"That's what I need to tell you," I say. "But it's going to sound really weird. Really, really weird."

So weird I don't know if I can voice it, I think. *But I have to.*

I take a breath. "It has to do with Sandy."

"Sandy?" she repeats, bewildered.

"Oh, gosh, where to start," I say. I close my eyes and push my fingers to my eyelids, and spots of light pop in my brain. I let my hands fall free. "I can't tell you everything. It's such a mess—there's no way. But you know she hates you, right?"

Her expression stays confused. The band is winding down, and I know I don't have much time.

"Because of what you did to her in fifth grade," I say. "I'm not blaming you. It was years ago. Only, Sandy . . . well, she never really forgave you."

Sarah Lynn isn't reacting the way I thought she would. "I'm sorry . . . what are you talking about?"

I don't want to go on. It feels dirty, and she's so pure. Especially tonight, in her white dress.

"In fifth grade," I say. "When you made everyone in the class stop talking to her."

She draws her eyebrows together. "When I . . . what?"

"And then her birthday party, how you didn't go and how you told everyone else not to either, because you said she was—" I break off, trying to block the thought of fingers and nightgowns and inner thighs.

"Unnatural?" Sarah Lynn says in a strange tone. She *does* remember.

I nod.

"Bliss," she says, "Sandy made everyone stop talking to *me*. At least, she tried to."

Now I'm confused.

"I was new, and she . . . I don't know, *claimed* me," she goes on. "Which was fine for a while. But then other people started wanting to be my friends, and she didn't like it."

She draws her knuckles to her mouth. "She wanted me to dump them, the other girls. And when I didn't, she pitched a fit. She said she wouldn't come to my party unless she was the only guest."

"Oh," I say faintly.

"And yes, I used . . . that word," she says. Her cheeks color. "I shouldn't have. It was cruel. I just didn't want to spend the night at her house anymore, that's all."

On the dance floor, people are clapping. The song has come to an end. Sarah Lynn rises on her toes and peeks around the float, then looks back at me. She furrows her brow.

"But, Bliss, I don't understand what that has to do with . . . why you're such a mess," she says.

The emcee's voice booms from the mike. "Let's hear it for the Handsome Devils!" he says, and the clapping builds in intensity.

Sarah Lynn's eyes dart in the direction of the stage. "Oh, dear. Can we finish this later?" she asks. "It's just . . . I'm supposed to be out there. I really do have to go." She touches my arm in apology, then starts for the dance floor.

I shake myself out of my stupor. "No, Sarah Lynn, wait!"

She turns.

"I got it all wrong," I say. "Or a lot of it, anyway. But Sandy is sick. Like, crazy sick." I speak the next part fast. "And now she's mad at me—really, really mad—and I'm afraid she's going to take it out on you." I swallow. "She knows about you and Lawrence. She's threatening to tell people."

"Is *that* what you're worried about?" Sarah Lynn says, astonished. To my surprise, her features soften. "Oh, Bliss."

Over the mike, the emcee jovially asks everyone to settle down. "And now, ladies and gents, it's time to crown our Snow Queen. Snow Princesses, please take your seats on your thrones."

Heather is fast-walking around the back of the float. "Sarah Lynn, get out here," she whispers urgently.

"This has been the most perfect night of my life," Sarah Lynn tells me earnestly. "What Lawrence and I have . . . it's love, Bliss. And once people see that, maybe they'll understand. There's a chance, don't you think?"

"Sarah Lynn," Heather hisses. She beckons insistently from several yards away.

"After all, you accept us, and so does Mitchell," Sarah Lynn goes on. "And I told Heather and Melissa, because I just couldn't keep it a secret anymore."

"You did?"

"They weren't thrilled, but they'll come around." To Heather, she calls, "I'm coming, I'm coming!"

I'm still not fully caught up, but the heaviness within me is lifting. "So . . . you don't care if Sandy tells?"

"Let her!" she says, laughing. "I'm in love with Lawrence, and he's in love with me. The till-death-do-us-part kind of love—and I know that sounds starry-eyed and naïve, but I mean every word of it."

She gives me an impulsive embrace, then runs on light feet to Heather.

"You're a good friend, Bliss," she calls, looking over her shoulder as Heather propels her toward the front of the float. She laughs again, perhaps at the way she's being hurried along, or perhaps at my expression. "Don't worry!"

FROM *THE ANDY GRIFFITH SHOW*

"You know, Andy, I never thought our town would come to this. Mayberry— gateway to danger."

—Deputy Sheriff Barney Fife

azed, I walk out from behind the float and merge into the crowd. Everyone's arranged according to class year, so I find a spot at the back of the freshman contingent. Sarah Lynn is perched on the tank of our giant toilet rather than on the seat, because although it *is* a throne, Thelma decided it was too crass for Sarah Lynn to appear to be actually, well, pooping. She holds the plunger-slash-scepter in one hand and a roll of toilet paper in the other. She glows.

From way up front, Thelma cups her hands around her mouth and yells, "Go, Sarah Lynn! Go, freshmen!"

Sarah Lynn smiles and flings the toilet paper toward the crowd, and the crowd laughs and claps.

The emcee starts in on a corny speech about the royal Crestview tradition, and I search for Mitchell, knowing he's got to be up there somewhere. But I can't find him.

"Did you know that witches were once thought to have a third teat?" comes a whisper that stirs my hair.

My body goes rigid. *No. No, no, no.* I don't even turn around for fear of what I'll see: Sandy, in her ripped dress, with skin hanging in shreds from her cat scratch and her one good eyeball swimming in the socket.

"The witch would allow her familiar to suckle from this teat," she goes on, "and in this way, a sacred bond was formed between the two."

My mind is in revolt, because why is she back again? She's like the zombie in a horror movie that refuses to die.

"I don't have a third teat," she confesses. "But after you left, and I was so"—she pauses theatrically—"*disappointed* . . ."

"Go away," I say.

She chuckles softly, and her breath smells of lemons. "It got me thinking. Regular has teats—why shouldn't the transfer work both ways?"

I'm dizzy, and the antics of the emcee aren't helping. He's drawing out the ceremony as the minute hand on the clock edges toward the twelve, and in response, the crowd is heckling him good-naturedly. Everything's too bright. People's mouths, stretched in laughter, look distorted.

It's one minute before nine.

"As the relic nourished Regular, so Regular nourished me," Sandy says. "And through this hallowed transfer, Liliana and I have joined."

"Please," I whimper. I try to edge away, but bodies crush against me.

Sandy leans in. Her lips are so close I can hear the slickness of her saliva. "All We need is the offering, and the assimilation will be complete."

The tip of her tongue flicks my earlobe, and that small muscular wetness jars me from my paralysis. I turn, and she's as gruesome as I imagined. Her bad eye oozes yellow goop. From her good eye, hunger gleams.

"I won't do it," I say. "Go away. Go away!"

"I called Sarah Lynn's daddy," she says, her voice like silk. "I didn't want to, but you were so naughty. So very, very naughty."

My blood pressure plummets. "What did you tell him?"

She watches me with half-lidded pleasure. I shake her, and her smile slips and slides over her face.

"What did you tell him?!"

"Nothing that everyone on the dance floor didn't already see for themselves. Lawrence's black hands on Sarah Lynn's white dress. His leg between her thighs as he held her close—"

I shove her away from me and force my way through the crowd. "Sarah Lynn!" I call out.

My voice is lost in the drumroll of hands slapping knees that the emcee has requested. His voice projects throughout the gym.

"So it is with great pleasure—"

"Sarah Lynn!" I cry.

"—that I now announce this year's Queen." He makes an upward gesture with his hand. "Ladies, if you please?"

The four Snow Princesses rise. Sarah Lynn teeters—that's the one thing Thelma didn't think of, that a toilet seat, even one that's oversize, is hardly a sturdy place to stand—but she finds her balance and smiles. It's an intimate smile. I track her gaze and see Lawrence right up front, regarding her with loving pride.

Then several things happen in rapid succession, and my heightened senses register them almost simultaneously: the clomp of footsteps on the metal bleachers—people in the crowd twisting to look—a medley of reactions. *Who is that? Nice muttonchops, man. Holy shit, is that a rifle?*

People's faces turn in a ripple effect as I push forward, but I don't look behind me. The people at the front of the gym have yet to figure out what's happening. I've got to get to Sarah Lynn before her daddy does.

Lawrence winks at Sarah Lynn, who lifts her fingertips to her lips and blows him a kiss for all the world to see.

"Sarah Lynn, you get away from that nigger!" her father thunders. He cocks the rifle and fires at the ceiling, and the mirrored ball shatters into a million glittering fragments. People scream. There is a rush for exit, and the floorboards shake.

The giant toilet shudders, and Sarah Lynn's arms fly up as she loses her footing. Her blue eyes go wide with surprise.

"Sarah Lynn!" I scream.

Her body is graceless as she falls. Her limbs flail, and one leg points straight up as she goes down. Her skull strikes the floor with a sickening smack.

There's a rushing in my veins like the flapping of thousands of wings. Lawrence gets to her first, and his mouth shapes words, but the words don't matter. I drop to my knees on her other side, and she turns her head toward me. Her blue eyes are bewildered. A pool of blood spreads on the floor beneath her head, and then, as I hear myself pleading *no, no, no*, the light inside of her goes out. My sobs come in great, hot gasps.

Mr. Lancaster shouts his daughter's name. He's almost to her when a teacher tackles him and brings him down. His rifle slides past me across the floor.

Now others trickle back, gathering around Sarah Lynn's sprawled body. There's Heather—and Thelma—and Ms. Phillips, who begs someone to call an ambulance, though she must, like the rest of us, know it's too late.

One of the onlookers is a girl in a ripped yellow dress, and she makes a show of being as devastated as everyone else. When she kneels beside me, I recoil, and I want to call out that there is a monster among us. But I can't, because I can't stop crying.

My tears make everything waver, but I'm perfectly capable of seeing what Sandy does. She dips her finger in Sarah Lynn's blood and, looking straight at me, puts it in her mouth. When she pulls it out, she smiles.

"You expect to break me?
Impossible! You broke me years ago.
You killed me years ago . . ."

—Charles Manson

n Monday, Dr. Evans delivers a eulogy for Sarah Lynn. The service is held in the simple chapel in Wesley Hall, since to herd us into the gym, which is no doubt still strewn with silver confetti, would be heartless.

Dr. Evans praises Sarah Lynn's beauty, intelligence, and school spirit, in that order. He acknowledges the great loss we must all feel and lets us know that the school counselor is there for us if we need her. He also assures us that Crestview does not tolerate "rogue outbursts from disgruntled parents," and that appropriate measures will be taken to ensure our safety at future school events.

"As for the student's father," he states solemnly, "I leave that matter to the appropriate authorities."

A boy in the pew in front of me leans toward his friend. "My dad's on the force, and he was at the station when the call came in," he says. "The chief said it was a damn shame, and that Buel Lancaster's a fine man. Said no nigger's worth going to jail for."

"The judge'll slap his wrist and send him on his way," his friend says. "Least, that's what I'd do."

I'm so numb that the words just roll over me. I do think to look for Lawrence, and my neck muscles make the appropriate movements to swivel my head from side to side. No Lawrence. Also, no one will meet my gaze except Jolene, but her sad brown eyes do nothing but make things worse. So I look away.

Dr. Evans closes by informing us that the parents of the deceased have chosen to hold a private funeral, for family only. He knows, however, that our prayers would be appreciated.

Afterward, we're sent to our homerooms, where everyone speaks in hushed tones. Several girls are absent, and I wish I could count myself among their number. I don't want to be here, but Grandmother made me.

Grandmother is being very kind. I sense she doesn't know what to do to help me, so she falls back on routine and worried glances. She brought warm vanilla milk to me last night, up in my room. I do love her, my prim and worried grandmother, and I believe she's grown to love me in return.

It's not enough.

I sit at my desk and lay my head on my folded arms, staring off at nothing. I get up and move when the bell tells me I'm supposed to, and then I sit and stare again.

I do this for days.

Thelma and DeeDee each try to talk to me, but I reject their overtures. Perhaps I'm being ungenerous, but I can predict how DeeDee's eyes will widen, how Thelma will say it's such a tragedy. Which it is. Talking to them will take none of that away.

Jolene is more timid in her approach, but also more authentic. No matter. I tell her to leave me alone, and she does, though not without one last attempt at reaching out.

"But, Bliss," she says. "If you ever . . ."

"I won't," I say.

Mitchell gives up less easily than Thelma and DeeDee, more easily than Jolene. Perhaps because he's a boy. Perhaps my cold shoulder wounds his pride. Or perhaps I disgust him. Perhaps he blames me, as he should, for Sarah Lynn's death.

I certainly don't deserve his comfort, and as for him, I have no comfort to offer. I feel always on the verge of crying, but I refuse myself that solace. I keep my tears inside. Often I push my hand deep into my satchel and wrap my fingers around the wooden dove, squeezing so tightly that it digs into my flesh.

A week after the dance, I see Sandy sitting in the cafeteria at my old table, and I wonder if the world has turned upside-down. She's in my old spot, eating with Thelma and Jolene and DeeDee. Thelma nudges Sandy, who turns her large head and pins her eye on me. The other eye is still swollen. Instead of a headband, she's clipped her hair back with a sparkly barrette.

Thelma says something to Sandy, and Sandy shakes her head. She pats Thelma's arm and rises from the table. I want to turn and leave, but I don't. My palms grow clammy as she approaches.

"So how does it feel?" Sandy says, planting herself before me with an arrogance that makes me sick.

I'm not answering that. Instead, because I fear for Thelma and the others, I say, "Why are you sitting with my friends?"

"I'm not."

"I saw you," I say, gesturing at the table. DeeDee, Thelma, and Jolene quickly avert their gazes.

"And?" Sandy says.

"Fine, I'll repeat the question." I try to be strong. I try to be fearless. "Why are you sitting with my friends? And this time, don't lie and say you're not."

Sandy laughs. "They're dull and stupid, and Thelma smells like dog. But I'm sitting with them anyway, because from now on I'll sit with whoever I want. And when you say, 'Why are you sitting with my friends?' my reply will always be, 'I'm not.'" She appraises me. "Do you understand?"

I search the face of this monster in front of me, this monster who smells of lemons. Is Sandy even in there anymore? The old Sandy, the Sandy before the . . . assimilation?

Something flickers in Sandy's good eye, something just barely human. She blinks and says, "It's not too late, you know." Her voice is suddenly unsure. "They're drawn to my power, but you can have it too. You're special. You're my best friend."

"Did you mean to do it, Sandy?" I ask.

She can't hold my gaze.

"Did you mean for her to *die*?"

"For one to rise, another must fall," she says desperately.

"That's not true, and you know it."

"It is true." She hiccups. "It *is*, and I'm glad it happened. I'm glad!"

I look at her, and I'm sickened. She must have a shred of humanity left within her, because she blushes.

"Stop being mean to me," she pleads. "Stop being mean, or I won't share my power!"

"I don't want your power," I say. I turn to go.

"Good, because you'll never have it!" she says to my back. "The others appreciate me, but you don't know perfection when you see it! *You're* the one who's unnatural!"

I leave the cafeteria and vomit in the girls' bathroom.

FROM *THE ANDY GRIFFITH SHOW*

"Daylight's precious when you're
a young'un."

—Sheriff Andy Taylor

nother week passes, and people stop talking about Sarah Lynn quite as much. By the time we return from Christmas break, they rarely speak of her at all, and if her name does come up, it's followed by confusion and immediate retraction.

"I have no idea why I said that," I hear one girl muse, after wondering out loud whatever happened to Sarah Lynn. "Maybe it's my cousin I'm thinking of. Or, wait—that's just another of those ghost stories, isn't it? The Crestview girl who died?"

Sandy, however, is alive and well. In January, she joins the Pep Club, the Booster Club, and the Branching Out Club, which she herself founds. "Strangers Are Just Friends Waiting to Happen" is the club's motto.

I hear through the grapevine that she's started volunteering at Good Mews, and that she plays her harp for the stray cats. She brings a litter of kittens to the quad, and they all look like Regular. Dr. Evans commends Sandy's humanitarianism and allows the kittens to prowl the campus at liberty.

For a long time I torture myself with *why*'s: why did I believe Sandy about Sarah Lynn; why did I give Sandy the key; and for heaven's sake, going way back to the beginning, why did I befriend Sandy in the first place?

Because she helped Gayla, I remember. The day Gayla tumbled down the staircase, and everyone laughed. Or is it possible I was wrong about that too?

I hunt down Gayla and follow her into the girls' bathroom. We're the only two in there, which makes it hard for her to ignore me, though she tries.

"What did she say to you?" I press, after jogging her memory of the day she fell and her skirt flew up. "What did she say to make you get up?"

"I . . . I don't know," Gayla says.

"Yes, you do. Tell me." I step closer, and she cringes.

"She said . . . she said . . ."

"Go on."

Gayla's cheeks turn bright red. She gulps and whispers, "She said I was showing my bits and pieces, that they were on display for everyone to see." She raises her chin. "But the girl who was mean to me, it wasn't . . . who you said it was!"

"Yes, it was," I say, reeling at Sandy's malice, which I interpreted as charity.

Gayla shakes her head. "No. Lurl would never say something like that. It was someone else."

After that, I give up trying to make sense of anything or anyone. I walk the halls alone.

Mitchell, when I spot him, is usually alone as well. He

devotes himself to his studies, and as soon as school lets out, he roars away on his motorcycle.

One day I see him sitting by himself on a stone bench, wearing the leather jacket he lent me so long ago. His expression is lost, and I almost approach him. Then I think about Sarah Lynn and Lawrence, and how we tried to help them, and how horribly we failed.

I don't know where Lawrence is. He's certainly not at Crestview. I hope that wherever he is, he's safe—and that he's far away from Mr. Lancaster.

Next fall, I hope to convince Grandmother to let me join my parents in Canada. Until then, I move through the world like a ghost. Sometimes I visit Agnes's grave at the Salem Hills Cemetery, and since I can't talk about school, I catch her up on the events of the world. I tell her about Janis Joplin and how it sounds like she's crying while she's singing, and I tell her about a new plane called the Boeing 747, which can seat 374 passengers.

On the day the verdict is announced in the Tate-LaBianca trial, I lay a bouquet of blue pansies on Agnes's grave. Charles Manson is convicted on multiple counts of murder, as are his supplicants Sadie Atkins and Patricia Krenwinkel. I tell Agnes how they giggled when their sentence was handed down.

One bleak Thursday in March, I feel especially lonely. In homeroom, Thelma and the others are already planning next year's Winter Dance, and it numbs my soul.

"Only we'll call it the Winter Carnival, to mix it up a little," I hear Thelma say to a girl named Midge. "Because to call it the Winter Dance"—disorientation dims her features—"it's sad, isn't it? There's something about that name that just feels sad."

"Maybe because 'dance' rhymes with 'chance,'" Midge suggests. "And 'chance' means, like, leaving it up to chance, which can go either way: good or bad."

"Maybe," Thelma says uncertainly.

"Or maybe because it rhymes with 'pants'!" She giggles. "Who wants to go to a dance called Winter Pants?"

Thelma doesn't giggle, but she smiles.

"Let's mix it all up, a whole fresh beginning," Midge goes on. "Not a snowflake theme but icicles. And instead of Snow Princesses, maybe Ice Maidens?"

Thelma's enthusiasm returns. "I think that's a marvelous idea. And Lurl's a shoo-in, of course. She'll be the perfect Ice Maiden! It's so exciting!"

I can't be part of this. I can't even be around this. So I ask for a pass, and I go and sit in Wesley Chapel. Instead of Winter Dances or Winter Carnivals, I think about death and black holes and endless stretches of darkness. I think about how the universe cracked open and Sarah Lynn fell in.

And when the air in my lungs gets tight, I close my eyes and pray for this cursed school.

When I open my eyes, my gaze is drawn to the stained-glass window at the highest point of the chapel. I've never noticed it before, this particular pane. It shows a white bird, wings lifted in flight.

I rise from the pew and walk to the altar. I keep my eyes on the stained-glass dove, because I don't want to blink and risk it flying away.

"Sarah Lynn?" I say, kneeling on the hardwood floor. It's the first time I've said her name since the night she died. A lump rises in my throat.

Shhh, whispers a draft in the chapel. I smell the pure scent of lilac, the scent of Sarah Lynn's perfume. Shhh.

My vision blurs, and I give myself over to sobbing. My head aches, my throat aches, my heart aches. But I keep crying. My tears wash me clean.

When I'm finished—when the sounds I'm making are shuddery gasps, but I'm no longer weeping—I'm not surprised to see that the stained-glass dove is gone. I wipe my eyes. I take a deep breath.

I walk the few steps back to my pew and draw the wooden dove out of my satchel. I hold it in my cupped hands. It's warm. It warms me, too.

I return to the altar and place the dove upon it. Behind the dove is a collection of candles, varying in size and color. A container of matches rests discreetly nearby.

I choose a simple white candle, and I light it for Sarah Lynn.

I close my eyes and say *good-bye*.

About That Creepy Charles Manson . . .

(A NOTE FROM THE AUTHOR)

"Facts and truth really don't have much to do with each other," claimed William Faulkner. I find this observation both funny and smart, especially when it comes to storytelling. As I wrote *Bliss*, I wanted the real-life Tate-LaBianca murder cases to be a backdrop for the drama playing out in Bliss's own life. Since the actual trial stretched over several years, however, I condensed the timeline of facts in order to better serve the truth of Bliss's story.

Bliss moves to Atlanta in the summer of 1969, and the novel follows her through the spring of 1970. Throughout the novel, she refers to the gruesome murders committed by Charles Manson and his "Family," and she and her friends discuss various aspects of the trial. At the end of the novel, Bliss reports to Agnes that Charles Manson and two members of his cult are found guilty of murder and sentenced to death.

Here's the factual timeline: The Tate-LaBianca slayings occurred on August 9 and 10, 1969, but no arrests were made until two months later, in October. The murder trial itself began in July of 1970 and ended in January of 1971. And, while Manson and his followers were indeed sentenced to death, these sentences were later commuted. Charles Manson is still alive, still in jail, and still one of the few humans I can think of who, by every indication, has no soul.

While I accelerated the judicial process, all quotes, trial excerpts, and details about the slayings are—to the best of my knowledge—both factual and true.

Acknowledgments

Woo-boy, here we go:

Thanks to my mom, Ruth White, for planting the dread seed of this novel in my brain in the first place. Also, thanks to everyone in my big ol' family—as always—just for being cool, supportive, and encouraging.

Thanks to Dee Wanger and Candy Gilliland for sharing your stories of growing up in the sixties, and thanks to Tim White for educating me about "old Atlanta."

Thanks to Jim Shuler, doctor fabuloso, for filling my head with the flutterings of Pigeon Carrier's Disease. Jim, you da man.

Thanks to Holly Black for talking to me about suckling and teats, and to Libba Bray for continuing the conversation with—ahem—details of her own experience with such. Thanks to my agent, Barry Goldblatt, who takes great care of all his clients, two of whom are Holly and Libba. Without Camp Barry, the "suckling" discussion would never have occurred.

Thanks to my Starbucks darlings, who kept me hopped up on caffeine and chocolate whipped cream.

Thanks to my sweetie-pie Abrams family: Michael, Howard, Amalia, Maria, Scott, Chad, Tamar, Maggie, Vivian, Mac, and Laura. I am insanely lucky to have y'all. A special thanks to Jason Wells, who is secretly the Energizer Bunny, only cuter. (Which is saying a lot, because that bunny is pretty darn cute . . .)

Thanks to Bob, who offered congratulatory high-fives, groans of commiseration, and sage advice on a near-daily basis. You rock, Bob!

Huge thanks to Sarah Mlynowski, queen of plotting, who read an early draft of Bliss and said, "Someone must die."

Warm and hug-filled thanks to my brilliant and goofy husband, who channeled Marlon Brando in order to read my Agnes sections aloud to me. Jack, you always give me wonderful ideas. I love you.

And finally, there is no frickin' way on earth, in heaven, or in the depths of hell (and we journeyed through all three realms, I think) that this book would exist if not for my beloved editor, Susan Van Metre. Bliss started off as a lumpy blob of clay, and Susan rolled up her sleeves, dug in, and got messy. Sheesh, we both got messy. But I'm so proud of the end result, and Susan, I owe it all to you. You are the ghost behind my blood voice.

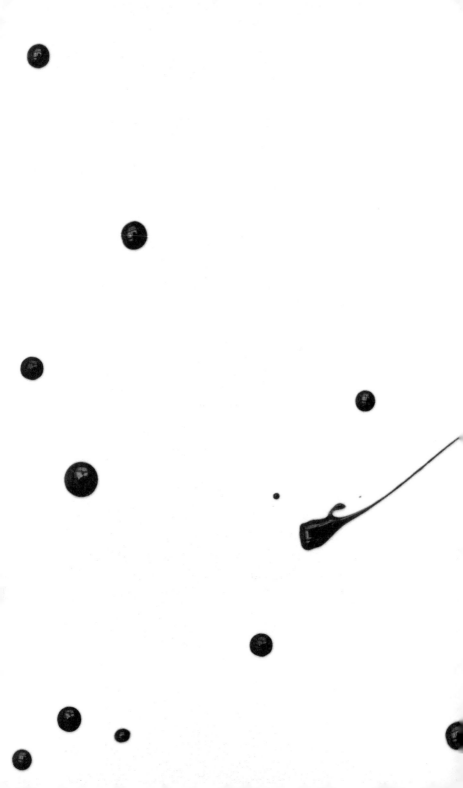

About the Author

LAUREN MYRACLE is a graduate of the Vermont College MFA program in writing for children and young adults. She is the author of the *New York Times* bestselling *Internet Girls* trilogy—*ttyl*, *ttfn*, and *l8r, g8r*—and *Rhymes with Witches*, as well as many other books for tweens and teens. She's fascinated by magic, supernatural forces, and the "world unseen," yet nonetheless finds it freaky to have written a book dripping with blood. Visit her Web site at www.laurenmyracle.com.

This book was designed by Maria T. Middleton and art directed by Chad W. Beckerman. The text is set in 12 point Joanna, a typeface drawn by Eric Gill in the early 1930s and later digitized by the Monotype Foundry.

The display type was created by painting with Hershey's syrup—a technique inspired by Alfred Hitchcock, who first used Hershey's syrup to simulate blood in his 1960 black-and-white thriller, Psycho.

A sneak peek at the stunning new novel from
LAUREN MYRACLE

shine

Bloody Sunday
Teen Brutally Attacked

On a sweltering June Sunday, stunned residents of Black Creek, North Carolina pray for one of their own after seventeen-year-old Patrick Truman was beaten and left for dead outside the convenience store where he works.

"There was blood in his hair, blood on his face . . . blood everywhere," says retired realtor Dave Tuttle, the motorist who discovered the unconscious teen. Tuttle was driving from Atlanta to his well-appointed mountain house in Tuckaway, North Carolina when he pulled off the single-lane highway to refuel and stretch his legs.

"Stopping at the Come 'n' Go has become a tradition," a visibly shaken Tuttle told *The Pulse*. "They sell boiled peanuts and homemade jams. Sometimes fresh cobblers. It's a reminder of simpler times."

Simpler times which, apparently, aren't so simple after all.

Truman, who worked the closing shift the previous night, was scheduled to open the store at seven A.M. on Sunday morning. But when Tuttle pulled up to the store's single pump at seven-thirty, he found Truman slumped on the pavement, bound to the guardrail of the fuel dispenser. The gasoline nozzle protruded from his mouth, held in place with duct tape. Across the teen's bare chest were the words, "Suck this, faggot," scrawled in the victim's blood.

Truman's battered body reeked of gasoline, which Tuttle assumed came from the fuel dispenser. Law enforcers, however, suspect otherwise.

"The pump would'a been turned off at closing," Transylvania County Sheriff Bubba Doyle explained. "Course a can of gas ain't hard to find in these parts—though why you'd pour it on a person is beyond me."

FIGHT FOR LIFE

Since the tiny town of Black Creek boasts neither a hospital nor an urgent care facility, the teen was transported thirty miles by the local EMS unit to the Transylvania Regional Hospital in Toomsboro, where he was treated by Dr. James Granville.

According to Granville's report, Truman suffers from a fractured skull, multiple injuries to the face, and four cracked ribs. The depression in Truman's skull indicates a violent blow from behind, possibly inflicted by a pipe or a baseball bat. While epidural bleeding is the most likely cause of Truman's comatose state, the inhalation of gas fumes might also play a role.

As for how soon—or if—the teen will recover, it's simply too early to predict. "I'll tell you one thing," Dr. Granville told *The Pulse*. "He's durn lucky that driver came along when he did."

ANOTHER MATTHEW SHEPARD?

The discriminatory slur written on Truman's chest, coupled with the insertion of the gasoline nozzle into the victim's mouth, posits a troubling question: Was Truman's attack motivated by anti-gay sentiments? The manner in which Truman was roped to the fuel pump lends support to this assessment, as it is eerily reminiscent of the 1998 murder of twenty-one-year-old Matthew Shepard. Shepard, an openly gay young man residing in Laramie, Wyoming, was beaten, bound to a remote fence, and left to die.

"They just wanted to beat him bad enough to teach him a lesson, not to come on to straight people," stated the girlfriend of Aaron James McKinney, one of Shepard's killers. Anti-gay groups went so far as to picket Shepard's funeral, holding up signs that said, "God Hates Fags" and "Matt Shepard Rots in Hell."

Was North Carolina teen Patrick Truman assaulted because he is gay? Tommy Lawson, who attended high school with the victim, doesn't discount the possibility. "He never did hide what he was, if that's what you're asking," says Lawson, son of Ronald Lawson, who owns the Come 'n' Go as well as several other businesses in Black Creek. "He doesn't swish around or nothing, but it's no secret what team he plays for."

Verleen Cox, organist at the Holiness Church of God, holds a different opinion. "Patrick's a good Christian boy who knows right from wrong," she avows. While she acknowledges that the teen struggled in the past with "sexual brokenness," she informed *The Pulse* that ". . . he faced his demons and escaped their bondage with the help of the Lord Jesus Christ." Blinking back tears, she added, "When Patrick didn't show up for the nine o'clock service, I got a real bad feeling. The church is his family. We're all he's got."

That much certainly seems true. Orphaned at age three after his parents were killed in a car accident, Truman was raised by his grandmother, a woman described as "a saint if there ever was one." Be that as it may, church deacon Steven Raab laments the teen's lack of a male role model during his formative years. "The male's role in a young boy's life is critical," the deacon asserts. "A boy needs his daddy."

Last winter, Truman faced further hardship when his grandmother passed away. At this point, information regarding involvement of North Carolina's Department of Social Services is unknown. What is known is that Truman maintained residence at his grandmother's small but tidy house, fending for himself as best he could.

A TOWN FORGOTTEN

For upper and middle-class Americans, the story of Truman's hardscrabble life might read as fiction. But for those who endure it, the gritty truth of poverty is far too real. Almost three million children in rural America are poor, and the majority of these children live deep in the heart of the Bible Belt. Truman's hometown of Black Creek, North Carolina, for example, has a median household income of eighteen thousand dollars a year, less than a third of the nation's median income.

As in many poor rural towns, the residents of Black Creek—population, 343—struggle to survive in an environment where all odds are stacked against them. "What with the new Wal-Mart in Asheville, all the stores in town done up and closed, pretty much," says Misty Treanor, who worked at a nearby paper mill until it went out of operation last August. "Do I wish things were different? Heck yeah. But they ain't."

And yet young Patrick Truman tried to keep his spirits up. "He's one of the special ones," says Verleen Cox. "Hasn't dropped outta school, doesn't do drugs, got hisself a good job. He was gonna make something of hisself."

Motorist Dave Tuttle's assessment is equally positive, saying that from what he could tell from previous visits to the Come 'n' Go, the victim ". . . is a good kid, always polite. Always ready with a smile."

For now, Patrick Truman has nothing to smile about—and neither do Transylvania County law enforcers, who have no leads in their search for Truman's assailant(s). Yet Sheriff Doyle assures *The Pulse* that he and his colleagues "will do everything in our power to make sure justice is served."

The question is: Will it be enough?

Sunday, One Week After

ONE

Patrick's house was a ghost: its windows blind, the front door locked. The petunias in the flower box were brown and shriveled. The front porch needed to be hosed down. Spiderwebs clung to the eaves, wispy and ephemeral, and I suppose I would have found them beautiful once. Today I saw them for what they were: strands of silk slowly squeezing the life out of the sawflies and katydids too dim to see the truth right in front of them.

Movement drew my attention to the upper corner of the porch, where a bulging sack of a web, bigger and denser than the others, swayed as if it were alive. I squinted and stepped closer, and a sour taste rose in my throat. A mourning cloak was caught in the web's sticky threads. One wing was pinned to its body; the other fluttered feebly, brown and dull except for its border of shimmering gold, just exactly like the gilt-edged pages of Mama Sweetie's Bible.

If I tried to free the butterfly, it would die. If I didn't, it would die. By evening, the mourning cloak would be a corpse and the web its shroud, and it would happen like that regardless of what I did. My existence meant nothing to the butterfly or the spider. My existence was something separate and alone, and knowing that made me feel invisible. Or maybe I *was* invisible. Maybe God was a giant eyeball in the hazy June sky, only there was a burn mark on His pupil in the exact spot of Black Creek, North Carolina, and that was why He didn't see me.

If He didn't see me, that meant He didn't see Patrick. But not seeing us was better than seeing and not caring.

I backed away from the porch, trying to remember why I'd come. Church started in half an hour, and it would take almost that long to bike there. What had I hoped to accomplish?

My heart said I was here for Patrick. But Patrick wasn't here.

The last time I was here was three years ago, about this same time of year. It was warm, but not too warm, so it must have been the end of May, the sweet spot between the caress of spring and the heavy June heat pressed down on me now. Sweat pasted my hair to my skin, and if Patrick were here—if we were kids again, that is, and if Patrick's grandma wasn't around to shoo us out for fear of snakes and rats—we'd probably worm into the coolness of the crawl space beneath the house and tell secrets, with no one to hear but the bugs. *Ugly* bugs, blind and sluggish and moist. The sort of bugs that would eat us one day, we used to say for the shiver of it. Coffin bugs.

The entrance to the crawl space was a small access door made from a scrap of plywood painted the same shade of yellow as the siding. You wouldn't know it was there if you didn't know where to look. The only thing giving it away was the rusty hook-and-eye latch that kept it shut.

Patrick didn't much like the dark, so we brought down candles and a box of matches, which would have given Mama Sweetie a fit if she'd found out. Mama Sweetie was Patrick's grandma. He lived with her since his parents were dead. Patrick and I spread out a tarp to sit on, and we set up a milk crate for a table, and as soon as we were settled in with our snacks, we'd gab about anything and everything. That was the wonderfulness of it, that Patrick and I could just talk and talk.

I walked around the house now and found the access door. I dropped onto the overgrown lawn and leaned against the house, right next to the small plywood door. I knew Aunt

Tildy would kill me if I got grass stains on my church clothes, but I didn't have the energy to care. I drew up my legs, tucked my skirt between my thighs, and hugged my shins. Tiny no-see-ums nipped at my ankles. Sweat rolled down my spine . . .

I pictured Patrick alone at the Come 'n' Go. It would have been dark because of how late it was. No one would have been around for miles. Patrick would have known that. He would have known just how helpless he was when his assailants—maybe a group, maybe one or two—roared into the dirt pull-off outside the store.

Except I was projecting. Hindsight permitted such a thing. Patrick probably hadn't felt helpless, not at first. He wouldn't have seen the wolf in redneck's clothing.

I wasn't there that night, but I could imagine how things played out. The shadowed woods surrounding the store. The dim and flickering light by the single gas pump. The too bright lighting within the store, illuminating Patrick as he went about his closing duties.

Then what? A truck engine abruptly cut off. The slamming of doors layered over boisterous, drunk laughter. A male voice—one Patrick knew, if my suspicions were right—calling, "Patrick. Bro. Get your butt out here!"

And Patrick would have. Why not? He'd have shaken his head and grinned as he pushed through the store's door, and he wouldn't have realized how wrong things were until he spotted the baseball bat bouncing against someone's palm.

Then the fear would have kicked in. Then, too late, he would have grasped what he was up against: A predator, or a pack of predators, there to do what predators did.

I hated whoever it was who hurt Patrick, and I hated myself as well. Fury boiled inside me, pushing to get out, and I made a fist and slammed it backwards against Patrick's house. It made my hand hurt, but it wasn't enough. I leaned over, flipped the hook-and-eye latch on the door to the crawl space, and jerked it open. With grim determination, I rolled onto my stomach and squinted into the gaping hole. It took my eyes a moment to adjust, but then I saw the milk crates, the candles, the tufts of pink insulation drooping from the floor joists.

It was a postcard from our childhood, except Patrick was no longer a child. He also wasn't yet a man. He was seventeen years old and stuck between, trapped in the deep sleep of a coma.

Mama Sweetie, who would have watched over him day and night, was gone.

I should have been there in her place. I should have protected him; I should have been strong. I *used* to be strong, but my strength was ripped away. I used to talk up a storm and laugh at the silliest thing. Now I silently watched the world. Worst of all, I turned my back on Patrick. He lost his best friend, and he didn't know why.

Losing Patrick was like losing myself, even though I was the one who broke things off.

The full measure of what I'd lost seeped into me and made me dizzy, as if I were swaying on the edge of a cliff. Then I got mad, and not just mad, but crazy mad, because it was all so awful, and because none of it should have happened, not in a fair and just world. What happened to Patrick was wrong. What happened to me was wrong. Every single thing was wrong, and when that great mass of accumulated wrongness reached my heart, my heart swelled and roared and cast it back out, leaving in its place a white-hot clarity like nothing I'd ever experienced.

Three years ago, everything changed.

And now, things had to change again.

Do you hear me, God? I asked inside my head. *Are you listening?*

Then came the next revelation, and with it, my anger grew. It didn't matter if God was listening or not. Someone needed to track down whoever went after Patrick, and that someone was me, with or without God's help.

It had been a week since Patrick was attacked, and as far

as I could tell, Sheriff Doyle hadn't done squat. He claimed he was looking into every lead, but I bet he'd buried those leads instead. Slogging around in the muck of our godforsaken town would only bring Sheriff Doyle trouble, especially if my suspicions about what happened that night were right. Sheriff Doyle wasn't interested in trouble.

He'd draw out the investigation a little longer for show, but eventually he'd pin the crime on a truck full of college boys from out of town. That was my guess. "None of our local boys did this," he'd say with a great show of conviction. "We might never find out who done it, but I can tell you this: Nobody from Black Creek would'a stooped so low."

Yeah, right.

I'd seen things since Patrick was attacked that weren't quite right. Like my brother talking urgently to Beef, then shutting up quick when Tommy Lawson approached. Like Bailee-Ann sitting by herself at the sandwich shop, her expression troubled as she chewed on a strand of her hair. Like Tommy straddling his ugly yellow motorcycle at the intersection of Main Street and Shields, so lost in his thoughts that he didn't notice when the light turned green. Normally he'd have accelerated hard and fast, showing off the power of his BMW's expensive engine, but on that day, an old lady had to tap the horn of her Buick to rouse him from his trance.

Something was up. Something bad.

I closed the crawl space door. I got to my feet and brushed myself off. My chest was tight, but I looked at the blue sky, clear and pale above the tree line, and said out loud, "Fine, I'll do it." *I* would speak for Patrick. I'd find out who hurt him, and when I did, I'd yell it from the mountaintop.

"I said I'll do it," I repeated, raising my voice. "Did you at least hear that?"

A moment passed. Sweat trickled down the base of my spine. Then, out of nowhere, a breeze lifted my hair and jangled Mama Sweetie's wind chimes, which she'd made by stringing up mismatched forks and spoons so that they dangled from the lid of a tin can.

It scared me, to tell the truth. But I lifted my chin and said, "Good."

I was done being silent.

Check out these other books by *Lauren Myracle*

RHYMES WITH WITCHES

Hardcover $16.95

Paperback $6.95

ttyl

Hardcover $15.95

Paperback $6.95

ttfn

Hardcover $15.95

Paperback $6.95

l8r, g8r

Hardcover $15.95

Paperback $6.95

Amulet Books
An imprint of ABRAMS
WWW.AMULETBOOKS.COM

SEND AUTHOR FAN MAIL TO:
Amulet Books, Attn: Marketing, 115 West 18th Street, New York, NY 1001
Or e-mail marketing@abramsbooks.com. All mail will be forwarded.